To Thine Own Self Be True

Also by Judy Clemens

Till the Cows Come Home

Three Can Keep a Secret

To Thine Own Self Be True

Judy Clemens

Poisoned Pen Press

First Edition 2006

10 9 8 7 6 5 4 3 2 1

Library of Congress Catalog Card Number: 2006900730

ISBN: 1-59058-298-5 Hardcover

Poisoned Pen Press
6962 E. First Ave., Ste. 103
Scottsdale, AZ 85251
www.poisonedpenpress.com
info@poisonedpenpress.com

Printed in the United States of America

For Tristan and Sophia
May you always be true to yourselves

In memory of
Thomas D. Halteman
1969–2006
Farmer & Friend

Acknowledgments

This book would not have been possible without the help of some very important people.

Ron Krauss and Emma Bowman of Bad Ronald's Custom Tattooing & Exotic Body Piercing in Lansdale, Pennsylvania, put many hours into this book. They allowed me to observe at their shop, where Ron tattooed a guy's ankle while Emma regaled me with stories, many of which appear in this book. Emma read the manuscript to make sure I had the facts and lingo right, and that my descriptions of the tattoo culture rang true. Ron drew the beautiful steer head which appears on the cover of this book. Stella would be proud if it were hers. Check out Bad Ronald's at www.badronaldstattooing.com.

The dairy farmers once again gave without asking for anything in return. Tom Halteman showed me around his farm in winter, while Marilyn Halteman offered stories and answered questions. Don and Louella Chapman shared anecdotes from their winter farming days (thanks to Louella for Stella's hair dryer incident). Randy Meabon answered a multitude of questions, and Paula Meabon was kind enough to read the manuscript to make sure I got the dairy details right.

Detective Randall Floyd of the Telford Borough Police Department, as always, generously answered my questions about PA law enforcement.

Dr. Lorin Beidler shared information about how ERs work and how paramedics and physicians would respond to certain crises.

Mary Detlor is a part of this book as a surprise from her sister. Mary, I hope you enjoy the chance to get to know your alter ego!

Thanks again to all the folks at Poisoned Pen Press for believing in me and being so great to work with.

My parents, Philip and Nancy Clemens, read the first draft to make sure it made sense, and, as always, their comments and support were most helpful.

Finally, thanks to Steve and the kids for putting up with my writing stints and book trips, and for being the loves of my life.

This above all: to thine own self be true,
And it must follow, as the night the day,
Thou canst not then be false to any man.
—William Shakespeare, *Hamlet*

Chapter One

"So I said to him, 'You know what could happen if I pierced you there?' The stooge went white so fast I thought he was gonna do a face plant right there on the Linoleum. Never seen anybody change his mind so fast."

I laughed at Mandy's detailed storytelling, and Wolf clamped an iron hand on my arm. "Quit shaking, Stella."

"Then tell your wife to stop telling funny stories."

"You want this tattoo all over crooked, you keep on laughing. You want it straight, you control yourself."

"Yessir." I would've saluted, but for the grip he had on my forearm. "You just know too many crazy people."

Mandy Moore plopped down in the dentist's chair across from me, the chair where she poked holes through people's body parts. "Talk about crazy. Remember that lady, Wolf? The huge-ass Nordic woman with the scrunchy 'round her forehead?" She looked at me. "Comes in here one day, says she was in an airplane over the Bermuda Triangle and her tattoo disappeared. Fell off right there and evaporated into the sky. So she's demanding her money back. I tell her she can take a flying leap right back into the Triangle, and she vanishes into our bathroom. Stays there for a *half hour.* We finally pound on the door enough she opens up. Turns out she's cleaned our bathroom *and* washed our lunch dishes in the back of the toilet!"

"No laughing," Wolf muttered.

"Still as stone," I said.

The phone rang and Mandy pushed a button on the cordless in her hand. "Wolf Ink. Yes, ma'am, I'm in here all day piercing. She's how old? Twelve? Can't do it. Sorry. State law. That's right, you do that." She punched the button again. "Idiot woman. You know she's going to take her daughter to some hack down an alley. Land her in the hospital. Shit. All for a ring in her belly button." She lurched out of the chair and stomped to the front desk.

"Weren't you having trouble with one of those guys?" I asked. "What's his name?"

"Asshole," Mandy said.

Wolf grunted. "Which one? There's too many to count. But you're probably thinking of Gentleman John—John Greene. He's one of the worst."

"Asshole," Mandy said again.

I twisted my head around so I could see Mandy. "I thought he got sued last year."

She snorted. "Three times. And there's more this year. Jerk-off. Makes the rest of us look like scum, too."

I laid my head back down. "You can't look bad. I mean, who could come in here and complain?"

The place was spotless. Detergents everywhere. In fact, that's the first smell that hit me when I walked in the door. The green soap surgeons use, antiseptic, alcohol. You name a cleaning solution, they probably used it.

"That's the problem," Mandy said. She came back and leaned against her chair, arms crossed. "The people who think badly of us don't come in. They think all tattoo artists are drug-addicted dirtbags."

"I guess they don't see the commendation from the Chamber of Commerce on your front window."

The plaque declaring the business a "non-smoking establishment" enjoyed a place of pride next to the door.

She snorted again, and leaned over to look at the tattoo Wolf was inking into my skin, her mane of brown hair brushing my face. "Looking good. It's your old farmhand's name, you said?"

I nodded and glanced down at my wrist. The image of a leather-banded ID bracelet was taking shape, with just Howie's name left to go. A little something to honor his memory.

"You going to have Wolf fix this sometime?" Mandy pulled up my sleeve to see my arm. The skin grafts had healed nicely over the past five months since my motorcycle accident, but it still left my "To thine own self be true" tattoo illegible and ugly.

"Sometime," I said. "When the scars heal a bit more."

Scars. Physical and emotional. The wreck had happened the same week I'd lost Howie, and it was still hard to face. Getting the tattoo on my wrist was a small step in the healing process.

"So where's Billy?" I asked Mandy.

She smiled, knowing I'd changed the subject on purpose. "My mom's house. Wolf and I have a meeting tonight that'll probably go late, assuming it's still on with this weather, so we thought it'd be better if he crashed with her. If school's not canceled, the bus will pick him up there in the morning."

"Handy," I said.

The door swung open, blasting in a frigid draft tinged with sleet.

"Shut the goddamn door," Wolf said. "I'm gettin' frostbite back here."

"Sorry." The man shut the door firmly, clicking it into place.

"So what's up, Tank?" Mandy said.

He looked like his name. Huge and solid.

"Wanted to see when I could get this guy filled in."

His arm was covered with a black and greywash dragon, the red flames shooting out its mouth the only spark of color.

Wolf paused in his work and looked up. "Uh, Tank—"

"You pay up from last time, we'll talk," Mandy said. "We aren't running a permanent tab for you."

Tank's face darkened. "I paid you."

"With what? A word of thanks?"

Wolf watched calmly while his wife stepped up belly to belly—more like chest to belly—with the would-be customer. "You were supposed to put some time in on our truck, Tank.

Remember? Work out those dents Billy put in with his bike? Seems to me when I got in the driver's side this morning the door still looked like it had been attacked."

"I haven't had time," Tank said.

"Oh, I'm sorry. What is this, December? I would've thought you might've had half a day since July."

He shifted his weight awkwardly. "I've been busy."

"As have we. Come back when you're ready to do some body work. And I mean on our truck, not your arm."

Tank huffed and jutted out his chin. "Wolf?"

Wolf picked up the needle and got a fresh hold on my wrist. "You heard her, man. I ain't no charity. Gotta feed my family."

Tank clenched his hands into huge fists, made an animal-like snarl, and spun on his heel. He left the door flung wide open.

Mandy stalked to the door and slammed it shut. "Cheapskate. I heard through the grapevine he's been out of work. If he would've come in and told us he had money problems, we could've worked with him. But to act like he wasn't stiffing us…"

"So we turn him away," Wolf said. "No biggie."

Mandy tapped her finger on her teeth and peered out the front window. "Yeah. I guess."

The phone rang and Mandy plucked it off the counter, where she'd left it when Tank had come in. "Wolf Ink. Yeah, we're here. You want to reschedule? Not a problem. Can't blame you for not wanting to come from way out there. It's not supposed to let up by tomorrow, either. How 'bout the next day? We can get you in if you don't mind late evening. Say eight? You're in the book. Okay. Thanks for calling."

She hung up and turned to Wolf. "Angel's not coming. His wife said she wouldn't be pulling him from some ditch if he came out in this weather to get his body inked."

Wolf smiled. "Sounds a lot like our family, don't it, honey?"

She cheerfully gave him the finger while looking at their appointment book. "Stella's it, then. You get her done, we're closing up. No reason to hang out here if we can go home. Want to be sure we make it there."

I laughed. "You have a hard time walking upstairs to your apartment?"

"Hey, those steps can get icy." She started tossing Wolf's ink tubes into an ultrasonic tray. "I'm gonna load the autoclave. You got anything else to sterilize?"

Wolf shook his head. "Not yet. Can you put on some Stray Cats or something?"

"Sure, hon." She searched through a stack of CDs and slid one into the player, turning the volume up before heading toward the back. "Could just stick this dirty stuff outside and it would freeze off all the germs."

Wolf grunted a laugh, and Mandy disappeared into the back room. Wolf hummed under his breath, keeping time with the tattooed lead singer of the band, and I sneaked a peek at my wrist, where Wolf was finishing up the "w" of Howie's name. I also sneaked a peek at Wolf himself. Living up to his nickname, Wolf kept his beard full and his hair long. Dark chest hair curled out from the open V of his shirt, his wolf tattoo almost obscured by his hide. A wild man, in an attractive, alternative kind of way.

A crash from the back startled us both, and I bit my lip when Wolf poked me with the needle. "Sorry, Stella."

I shook it off.

"Hey, Wolf!" Mandy called from the back room. "Can you come here, please?"

He sighed deeply and sat back, putting aside the machine and pulling off his gloves. "Gimme a minute."

"No problem."

He left and I turned to see what it was looking like out the front window. Crap. I hoped he really would be back in a minute, or next thing I knew I'd be getting snowed in there. I didn't want to spend the night on Wolf and Mandy's floor. I laid my head back down to wait.

Twenty minutes later I jerked myself out of a catnap, groggy and cold. Late afternoon was a bad time to be reclining in a comfortable dentist's chair, and I was amazed the phone hadn't interrupted my doze. Must've been the weather. Folks weren't thinking about getting a tattoo when they were worried about blizzard conditions. But where the hell was Wolf? And why was I freezing?

"Wolf?" I struggled out of the seat, rubbing my eyes. "Mandy?"

I stuck my head through the doorway to the back room, and immediately saw why I'd been feeling a draft. The exit door at the far end of the room was wide open, snow and sleet pelting against it.

I stepped around the tray Mandy had been carrying. It was now on the floor, the equipment scattered across the vinyl. That must've been the crash we'd heard, right before Mandy had called Wolf to come back.

I looked outside briefly to make sure Wolf and Mandy weren't standing there, and saw no sign of them. The blowing snow had obliterated any footprints they may have made on the sidewalk or the steps up to their apartment.

"Wolf? Mandy?" My voice evaporated in the wind. I shut the door and stomped my feet off on the snowy mat.

A glance at the clock on the wall told me I had to be heading home if I had any thoughts of doing the evening milking.

I went back into the store and called Wolf and Mandy's apartment. No answer, except their machine. Well, crud. I looked down at my new tattoo—"How"—and tried to push down my irritation. There must be a good reason Wolf had deserted me mid-sitting. I guessed I needed to take care of myself and go home.

The A & D ointment lay on Wolf's counter, and I smeared some over the tattoo. I found the non-stick pads and unwrapped a sterile piece large enough to surround my wrist, taped it on, and pulled my sleeve gently over it.

A cube of Post-its sat on the desk, and I peeled one off, scribbling a message for Wolf to call me. I stuck it on the computer monitor, where he and Mandy would be sure to see it when they got back. I didn't leave any money. There would be plenty of time for that once Wolf finished the job.

Chapter Two

It took me forty-five minutes to get home, a trip usually done in twenty. My truck plowed through the snow okay, but visibility wasn't worth crap. I finally pulled into a cleared-out space in my tractor barn and sat for a moment to close my eyes and rub my temples. I'd be seeing snowflakes that night in my sleep.

I hunched my head down toward my chest to make the trek to the house. Icy shards spat into my face, and I jogged through the snow drifting across the driveway. I flung the door open and scooted inside, slamming the door behind me.

"Glad to see you home." My farmhand's eyes were shadowed with concern, but she was smiling.

I shook the snow from my hat and slid my jacket off, pounding the snow off my boots. "Glad to be here."

A flannel shirt hung warm and cozy over Lucy's jeans, and she held out her foot to show me her wool socks, an early Christmas gift I'd given her to ward against the cold wooden floors of my house.

"Let me see! Let me see!" Tess flew out of the kitchen, her nose, chin, and shirt dusted with flour.

"Cookies?" I said.

Lucy made a face. "Just don't look in the kitchen. Eight-year-olds aren't exactly the neatest chefs."

"As long as I get to eat whatever you made, I don't care how messy she is."

"Where is it?" Tess asked, hopping on one foot.

"Well, it didn't exactly get finished. Give me a second and I'll take the bandage off. Then you can see it better."

"What happened?" Lucy asked.

"Not sure. Wolf and Mandy disappeared right in the middle of the sitting. Couldn't find 'em anywhere."

"That's strange." Lucy frowned.

"I know. But then, they're not exactly your run-of the-mill folks."

"But to take off in the middle of your tattoo..."

I slipped off my boots and walked to the bathroom, Tess hopping along behind. At the sink, I gently pulled off the tape and tossed it and the gauze into the trash can. I held out my wrist so Tess could see it.

"*How*?" she said. "What's that supposed to mean?"

"It's going to say 'Howie,' for the man who was my farmhand before your mom."

"I didn't know him," Tess said.

I regarded her sadly. "No. You didn't know him."

We rejoined Lucy in the living room just as the timer on the stove hummed. Lucy padded back into the kitchen. "Oh," she hollered out. "Abe called."

"What did he want?"

"Said he's coming home for Christmas. Wants to know if you'll be around this week."

"Where would I go?"

"That's what I told him. Anyway, he said you can call him or let Ma know. Either way."

I thought about my once-upon-a-time-could-be-boyfriend, Abe Granger, now back in the regular-best-of-friends category, and realized how much I'd missed him since he'd returned to New York in August. I'd for sure make time for him this Christmas.

"Take a load off," Lucy said from the kitchen. "I'll bring you some milk and cookies."

"Sounds great." I dropped onto the sofa and set my feet on the coffee table. I had a few minutes till I needed to get out to the cows and freeze my ass off again. I was running a bit late, but it wouldn't take long to set up the cows in the milking parlor since they'd been there all day. Icy barnyards make for broken legs, so we weren't chancing it with the herd.

"Did the tattoo hurt?" Tess sat beside me, stretching her legs like mine; but she could only reach the coffee table with her toes.

"A little. When he's got the needle against my skin it stings, but as soon as he lets up the pain goes away."

She wrinkled her nose. "Was there lots of blood?"

"None at all. The needle doesn't actually poke through to my insides. It just goes through the top two layers of skin, so I don't bleed, just kinda ooze a little, like if I get cut."

Tess glanced over her shoulder toward the kitchen, then leaned toward me. "Can I get one for my birthday?"

I hid a smile, not wanting to dash her hopes too harshly.

"You know, that would be great, but you have to wait a few more birthdays."

She pouted. "How come?"

"It's the law. You have to be sixteen before the artist is allowed to give you a tattoo. And then only if your mom says yes."

"Says yes to what?" Lucy set a plate of candy cane cookies on the table between Tess' and my feet, along with three mugs of milk, her fingers hooked through the handles.

"For me to get a tattoo," Tess said.

I laughed at Lucy's expression. "When she turns sixteen. No sooner."

Lucy raised her eyebrows. "And even then we'll see."

"Oh, Mom."

I grabbed a cookie and licked buttery crumbs off my fingers. "Wow, these smell great."

Lucy sat across from us, a cookie in her hand. "I don't know. Tattoos aren't the safest thing."

"If you go to the guy breaking the laws," I said. "Come with me to Wolf Ink sometime, and you'll see another side. He's a pro all the way. And Mandy could pierce you anywhere you like."

"Oh, gross," Tess said.

I laughed again and picked up a couple more cookies. "I'm heading out."

Lucy stood. "I'll be there in a minute. I have to put a few more things in the crockpot."

"No problem."

We usually took turns with the milking—me in the morning, Lucy in the evening—but during this frigid weather neither of us wanted to be outside any longer than we had to, so we made it a joint effort. I went out to the foyer, where I pulled on my warm coveralls, dry boots, and a different stocking cap. I shoved another cookie in my mouth before pulling on my gloves. My remaining cookie I stuck in my pocket wrapped in a napkin for a mid-milking snack.

The barn was warmer than outside, but a pervasive chill leaked through the old timbers. Queenie, my collie, wriggled out of her nest of straw in the corner, and stuck her nose in my hand.

"Hi, sweetums," I said, rubbing her head. "Can't blame you for not meeting my truck today."

The cows were lethargic, half of them lying in stalls, half of them standing, and only a few of them bothered to glance my way. I turned the radio on to Temple University's classical music station and started down the row, clipping the cows' collars to the chains on the pipes. I didn't bother to make the cows stand yet. I was just about done when Lucy came out, her face ruddy and wet from the short trot to the barn.

"Gee whiz," she said, then stopped suddenly. "Is it just me, or is it too warm in here?"

I thought about it. "I think it's just you, but go ahead and check the temp and the airways."

She headed toward the thermometer. It wouldn't do for the air in the barn to get too warm or confined. That was asking for trouble. Pneumonia, diarrhea, any kind of airborne illness—those bacteria love the damp warmth of the big animals.

"Looks okay here," Lucy called. "I'll check the vents."

I finished clipping the cows into their stalls and ran warm water and soap into a bucket to start cleaning their udders. I'd sponged off the first two when Lucy came back.

"Vents are working fine. I guess I was just sweating from all my layers."

I nodded. "Good."

She stayed there, and I glanced up at her. "What?"

"Aren't you curious where your tattoo guy went? I mean, what if he and his wife had an accident or something?"

"It *was* bizarre." I thought about the tray and the bags of tubes on the back room's floor. "All I could imagine was that some emergency came up, like with Billy or something, but that doesn't make any sense. The phone didn't ring, and Mandy didn't come back in for her purse." I rested my elbows on my knees. "I'll try calling them after milking. Maybe they'll be back by then."

Lucy moved away, her coveralls swishing like corduroys. "I'll start on the feed."

We went through the motions, and about an hour and a half later I was switching the milker to the last cow. Lucy came and leaned on the cow's hip as I stood up and stretched my back. She sucked her lips to her teeth, avoiding my eyes.

"What's wrong?" I asked.

She sighed and looked down at her boots, kicking a clump of dirty newspaper back into the stall. "You know I'd talked about visiting my folks over Christmas?"

"In Lancaster."

"Yes."

I nodded. "Sure. When are you going? I'll be fine here."

She crossed her arms. "I've decided not to go."

"Oh. Okay."

"Is that all right?"

I laughed. "What do you mean? Of course it's all right."

"We won't be spoiling Christmas plans of yours?"

"What plans? I only have plans by default. I figured on heading over to the Grangers, and I guess I'll see Abe sometime." The Grangers had been my adopted family since I was eleven and saved Abe from drowning. My throat tightened. "There wouldn't be anyone else here, since Howie's gone."

"So we can stay?"

I blinked, hoping the tears in my eyes wouldn't show. "I'd love it if you'd stay."

Lucy smiled, and the lump in my throat lessened.

"Well, good," Lucy said. "Because this has become home, and it just seems right to spend our first Christmas here with you."

She glanced up and her mouth dropped open, her eyes widening as she stared toward the door. I whipped around, wondering what on earth had happened, and saw the man standing in the doorway.

"Hello, Stella," Nick Hathaway said.

Chapter Three

My throat went dry, and I stared at Nick dumbly, like an idiot. My hormones, however, did anything but shrivel, and heat rushed through my body just as it had in July, when he'd first driven up my lane. I could see Lucy out of the corner of my eye, and I didn't have any trouble interpreting her expression. I had mentioned Nick maybe once since hiring her, but I knew she'd remembered. Not too many men like Nick would pass through my dairy barn.

Queenie charged out of her corner, her feet dancing on the concrete. Nick squatted down to ruffle her fur, and laughed while she covered his face with kisses. After this rush of frantic welcoming, Queenie settled down, panting happily.

Nick stood up, his hand entwined in her fur. "Hope I'm not barging in at a bad time."

His smile, although tentative, was as milky white as I remembered, and his body looked just as delicious, at least what I could see of it under his ski jacket. I still couldn't find my voice. The last time I'd seen Nick was after a hellishly emotional kiss during the same week as my motorcycle accident and Howie's death. Hellish in that I wasn't sure at that point if I should be hating Nick or loving him. I still wasn't sure. But it was absolutely amazing to see him standing in my barn.

"Um," Lucy said. "I think I'd better go check on dinner." When neither Nick nor I answered, she scooted down the row and left through the far door.

Nick and I looked at each other for about a minute before I took a step around the cow beside me. A step closer to Nick.

He tried out another smile. "I'm on my way back home for Christmas. Was up in New York state visiting a college buddy who owns a nature preserve. I'd played around with the idea of stopping here, but hadn't made up my mind till this storm hit. Seemed as good an excuse as any to drop in and see how you were doing."

Still nothing from me.

"Okay," he said. "You have a couple of options. You could say 'hi.' You could say, 'Get the hell out of my barn.' Or you could come up with something on your own."

I looked at him and swallowed. "You never called me. Never wrote."

His eyebrows rose. "What? The phones and mail don't work from your end?"

He was right, of course. It was as much my fault as his. But that didn't mean I had to admit it.

"It's good to see you," he said.

I breathed through my mouth, then closed it, nodding, not sure what to say. I was facing my most recurring and secret daydream, and realized I had never gotten to the point in my fantasies where I actually had to respond. I was no help to myself, whatsoever.

"You want to help me finish up milking?" I finally asked. "Supper's waiting."

He smiled. "Why not? Last time I was here was in the role of employee."

My eyes shot to his, wondering if he was teasing or complaining, but his gaze was pleasant. I handed him a pitchfork, and together we cleaned out the stalls. It was more of a job than summer cleaning, since the cows had been holed up in the barn all day and now we had to move around their huge bodies, so we had our work cut out for us. Forty-five minutes later we took a last look at the clean barn, made sure Queenie was comfortable in her warm straw nest, and carefully orchestrated our exit so we didn't touch at the doorway.

Holding our hands at our faces, we fought our way toward the house as quickly as we could through the blizzard. Nick's Ranger, a familiar sight, already cowered under a couple inches of snow. I had a disconcerting feeling Nick wouldn't be going anywhere else that night.

Tess met us at the door, her eyes wide and bright. "Are you Stella's boyfriend?"

Nick opened his mouth, but I said, "No, Tess. He's just a friend stopping by to say hello."

Tess' brow furrowed. "But Mom said—"

"Ah! There you two are!" Lucy sailed in from the kitchen. "Come on, Tess, let's give them room to take off their coats and boots." She threw me an apologetic glance.

I pointed the closet out to Nick. "Plenty of room for your coat in there. And you can leave your boots on that mat."

He was done first, since I had to struggle out of my coveralls. I was glad when he took a step into the living room, so I wouldn't accidentally lose my balance and brush against him.

He smiled at Lucy and Tess, holding out his hand. "Nick Hathaway."

Lucy shook his hand, smiling back, her cheeks pink. "Lucy Lapp. Stella's farmhand. And this is Tess."

Nick leaned over, his hands on his thighs. "Hi, Tess. Very nice to meet you."

Tess giggled and held a hand to her mouth.

I closed my eyes, sighing. Even eight-year-olds were at risk when around Nick. I shut the closet door louder than necessary. "I'm starved. Anybody else?"

"Me!" Tess squealed. She grabbed Lucy's hand and pulled her toward the kitchen.

I snuck by Nick, averting my face. The way my damn hormones were acting you'd think I was a teenager. Especially seeing how I was still mad at him—and myself—for how things had ended last summer.

"Stella," he called after me.

I turned.

"Lucy took over for Howie?"

I swallowed. "Yes."

"And she cooks for you?"

I glanced toward the kitchen. "Actually, she lives with me."

He was startled at that.

"You can't see it tonight," I said, "but the garage, along with their apartment, is gone. Tornado took it in August."

His mouth dropped open.

"So," I continued, "the best option was for Lucy and Tess to move in here."

"With you." He sounded doubtful.

"What? You don't think they could tolerate me?"

"I was thinking more the other way around."

I shrugged. "We plan to build a new garage this spring. So it's temporary. Until then, I enjoy the meals." I turned toward the kitchen, and Nick followed.

Lucy and Tess waited for us at the table, where a fourth setting lay, looking awfully normal. It actually *was* normal, since Lenny Spruce, Lucy's boyfriend and my biker buddy, often joined us. But tonight the fourth person was there for my benefit. Or detriment. I wasn't sure.

I focused my eyes on my plate while Lucy gave the blessing. Once she said 'Amen' I did my best to act like usual. I filled my plate and ate while Tess kept up a running monologue about snow, school, and Christmas. Her voice faded in and out of my thoughts until I heard the word, "tattoo."

I looked up.

"So she only has half of it," Tess was saying. "The guy left right in the middle of giving it to her. It says, 'How.'"

Nick looked at me, a question in his eyes.

"It's true." I held out my wrist, displaying the aborted design. He leaned over my arm, and his breath made my hair stand up.

"Where did he go?" Nick asked.

I put my hand back on my lap. "I have no idea. One minute he and his wife were there, and the next… Well, twenty minutes later, actually, since I fell asleep—"

Lucy blinked. "Fell asleep?"

"Those chairs are comfortable. Anyway, Wolf and Mandy were just...gone." I glanced at the clock. "I'll call them after supper, see if they're around."

"That's awfully strange," Nick said.

"Tell me about it." I chewed my final bite of beef stew and swished it down with milk. "Actually, I'll call now, since I'm thinking about it."

All I got for my effort was Wolf and Mandy's answering machine. I hung up on it.

"Not there?" Lucy asked.

I sat back down at the table and took one of the candy cane cookies she held out. "Huh-uh. But then, they did tell me they were going to a meeting tonight and wouldn't be back till late."

Lucy glanced toward the window, where frost had obliterated any view. "Hope not too late, or they won't be getting home at all."

"Will I have school tomorrow?" Tess asked. "We're supposed to have our Christmas party."

"Holiday party," Lucy corrected. "And we can check the news, see if they've called it off yet. I kind of doubt you'll be going."

"But I didn't give Mrs. Albrecht her present." Tess' lower lip stuck out.

Lucy patted her hand. "She'll still like it after Christmas. Maybe even better then. Come on. Let's watch the news."

Lucy walked to the living room, the rest of us following. I stopped behind the sofa, and while I couldn't see Nick, I could feel that he stood a few feet behind me to my left. I willed myself not to move.

The TV channels were snowy, but clear enough we could see that the blue band declaring school closings was already sliding across the bottom of the screen. We watched as the listings worked their way through the alphabet to the P's.

"Well, there you are, honey," Lucy said. "Pennridge schools are closed tomorrow. Guess you'll be home with us. It'll be fun."

But I stopped listening to her then, because the newscaster was saying something new. Our county's roads had been designated a Level Three emergency. Anyone caught driving a non-emergency vehicle would be arrested. Or at the least, left to freeze. I snuck a glance at Nick. It looked like he would be staying, whether I was comfortable with that, or not.

"I gotta go make sure everything's okay outside," I said.

Lucy raised her eyebrows. "But you just came in."

"The heifers. I need to check the heifers."

She looked ready to say something else, but the glare I gave her was enough to silence her.

I went to the front closet and yanked out my coveralls. Nick followed me over. "Okay if I come? I'd kind of like to see your new heifer barn."

I groaned inwardly. I'd thought for sure he'd opt to stay warm in the house, but I'd forgotten how much time he'd put into fixing up the old heifer barn before someone had burned it to the ground.

"Fine. There's an extra pair of coveralls, if you want them."

He pulled them off their hanger and put them on. By the time we were all bundled up, it would've been hard to recognize either of us.

"Kind of reminds me of another outfit of yours," I said.

He laid a hand over his eyes. "Oh no. Not the painting stuff."

Remembering the multiple layers of clothes and eye protection he'd worn when powerwashing, I had to grin. But that memory quickly merged into the one where Nick had discovered me holding a near-lifeless Howie in the milking parlor's feed room. Nick had raced to call the ambulance, and had sat with me through the next horrible hours. He'd been a rock. I'd almost fallen apart.

Swallowing the pain of my memories, I opened the door and stepped into the night. The task of protecting our faces from the sleet and snow kept any conversation at bay until we made it to the heifer barn, where we keep the female cows who are still too young to be milked. Inside, I flipped on a light, and Nick stared at the beautiful new building. The heifers blinked sleepily at us, cozy and safe in their cocoon of straw and insulated steel.

"It's something, huh?" I said.

"Amazing. And it's practically warm."

"Never gets below fifty or fifty-five. Thermostat controlled."

"Wow."

"The best thing is the tunnel ventilation." I led him to the six-foot fan at the end of the barn. "No way air will get stale with this baby working."

Nick shook his head, his face still registering his shock. "Can't say the fire was a good thing for you, but this is quite a step up from what you had."

"It is."

We stood for a few moments watching the cows, and Nick turned to me, his eyes searching mine. "Stella, can we—"

"Uh-uh, Nick. I can't. You have to at least give me until tomorrow." It would take me that long just to believe the man was back, let alone talk about it intelligently—if at all.

He watched my face, probably looking for signs of weakening, but he smiled gently. "I at least had a few days to think about stopping in. I guess I blindsided you."

A heifer stepped close to the gate in front of us and mooed loudly.

"Okay, girl," I said, rubbing her nose. "We'll turn the lights out and let you get some sleep."

I tromped back toward the front of the barn, flipped the switch, and put my hand on the door.

"Ready for this?" I said over my shoulder.

"I'm ready for anything," Nick said.

Lord help me, I wasn't even close.

Chapter Four

Bolting across the driveway, I almost ran into a Chevy Blazer parked at the end of the sidewalk. I stopped abruptly and Nick bumped into me, knocking me sideways. The Blazer bore the insignia of the Lansdale police. Lansdale. Wolf and Mandy's shop was in Lansdale. I darted around the four-wheel drive and ran into the house, spraying snow into the foyer. Lucy looked up from the loveseat, where she sat across from two people—one in uniform, one in plain clothes. Her face had paled almost to the color of the snow outside, and her eyes were dark holes of sadness.

"Oh, no," I said.

The woman, the cop in the gray suit, stood and stepped forward. "Detective Shisler, Lansdale police. This is Officer Beane."

"You're here about Wolf and Mandy," I said.

Her lips formed a straight line. "Would you please sit down?"

Nick closed the door behind me, nudging me into action, and I stripped out of my coveralls. My boots banged onto the mat, and I threw my hat to join them.

The officer and detective sat only when I had found my way to the loveseat and perched beside Lucy. My voice stuck in my throat and I could only stare at the cops, their faces blurs.

"Scott and Mandy Moore," Detective Shisler said. "You know them?"

I nodded. "Sure. Except everybody calls him Wolf, not Scott. Have you found them?"

She smiled grimly, but didn't answer. "You saw them today? You had an appointment?"

"About four o'clock. Got a tattoo. Or part of one." I held up my wrist. "It's supposed to say 'Howie.' You can see it doesn't."

She and Officer Beane inspected the design without touching it.

"It didn't get finished?" Shisler asked.

"Wolf disappeared in the middle of it. Mandy, too."

Shisler's eyes flicked to the officer, and the two colleagues seemed to share a thought.

I sat forward, my hands clenched on my knees, and spoke very slowly. "Tell me what happened."

Shisler's head jerked to one side. "I'm sorry. I need to ask you some things first. Can you please describe their disappearance? What exactly occurred?"

I explained how Mandy had gone to the back room and soon called Wolf, who excused himself and joined her. "Twenty minutes later I realized I was alone."

"It took you that long?"

"I fell asleep."

Shisler and Beane stared at me, incredulous.

"I was tired," I said. "The chair was comfortable." The same defense I'd used at supper. "Anyway," I said, "when I woke up they were gone."

The detective stared down at her notebook, which she hadn't yet used.

"Are they all right?" I asked.

She sighed, fingered a page of her notebook, and met my eyes. "How well do you know Mr. and Mrs. Moore?"

I lifted a shoulder. "Not real well. He did my arm tattoo several years ago—"

"Not that one?" She pointed toward the cow skull on the back of my neck.

"No. Another artist, down in Philly. Anyway, I see Wolf and Mandy occasionally at a biker event or something. Nothing regular."

She nodded. "Can you please tell me what you remember of your time there this afternoon? Did anything seem strange? Did they mention troubles they're having with anybody?"

Afraid of where this conversation was heading, I rested my elbows on my knees and hung my head, rubbing the back of my neck. "Mandy was in a great mood. Told lots of funny stories, like the one about the lady whose tattoo fell off in the Bermuda Triangle..." I stopped and cleared my throat. "They mentioned that Billy, their son—I think he's in junior high—was staying overnight with his grandma because of a meeting they had that might go late."

"They mention who the meeting was with?"

"Didn't say."

I considered the rest of our conversation. "There's another tattoo artist they talked about who they don't like, who'll give underage kids tattoos and piercings. What was his name?" *Asshole*, Mandy had said. "Gentleman John. John something. A color. Greene. And there was a guy who came into the shop and wanted Wolf to fill in his tattoo."

"Did he?"

"Said he wouldn't till the guy paid what he owed from last time. Guy got mad and stormed out of the place. Huge man Mandy called Tank. I didn't know him."

Detective Shisler wrote something on her pad. "Any problems that you noticed between the two of them?"

"Wolf and Mandy? You kidding? They got along like always. Comfortable, happy with each other." I pictured Mandy flipping off Wolf, a smile on her face.

Shisler nodded, not meeting my eyes. "Anything else you can think of? Anything out of the ordinary?"

"Yeah. There was a crash. Mandy had taken some instruments back to the autoclave, for sterilizing." I could picture them clearly—bags of shiny, silver tools scattered across the snowy mats. "She dropped them right before she yelled for Wolf. I figured she was calling him because she broke something."

"Yes, we saw those items on the floor."

My breath caught. "You've been to their place. Something *has* happened."

The detective's eyes closed briefly before they fixed on me. "Mandy's mother, Mrs. Eve Freed, was concerned about Mr. and Mrs. Moore going out to their meeting tonight, in this weather. She tried calling them long before they were supposed to leave to ask if their plans had changed, but there was no answer, even on their cell phone. So Mrs. Freed called one of the Moores' neighbors, who could see that their truck was still in the driveway. He went over to check on them, and when he couldn't find them in their shop or apartment, he looked around back." Her eyes clouded. "Their Dumpster was open. He thought he'd close it so it wouldn't get filled with snow. When he reached for the lid, he saw her."

I breathed through my mouth. "Mandy?"

She nodded. "She was lying behind the Dumpster, where she couldn't be seen from the road or any neighboring building."

My throat tightened. "Is she…?"

"I'm very sorry, Ms. Crown. Mrs. Moore is dead."

I closed my eyes and hung my head, fighting for breath. "How?" I asked. *How*, like my tattoo.

Shisler bit her lips. "We don't know officially. But it looks like she was concussed—hit very hard on her head—then left there. She most likely died of hypothermia."

My breath came quick and shallow. "She froze to death?"

"I'm afraid so."

I tried to make sense of the patterns on the rug beneath my feet, but they were moving, shifting under my gaze.

"That means," I said, "that she was lying there for a while."

"Yes."

"Perhaps even while I was still there. When I was sleeping. When I looked outside."

She looked at me sadly. "It's possible."

The patterns on the floor stopped moving.

I ran to the bathroom. And threw up.

Chapter Five

The wind whistled through my windows most of the night, finally dying down around four. I know this because I spent those hours intensely aware of a piercing pain behind my temple, and a deep ache in my chest. A bucket sat by my bed in case whatever was left in my stomach decided to come out. Mandy was dead. That lively, obnoxious, funny woman was left to die thirty feet from where I lay, taking a nap.

I didn't ever want to sleep again.

After my quick exit to the bathroom, the detective and Officer Beane hadn't stayed very long. Shisler had told Lucy—for I was beyond being able to absorb anything she told me—that she would be in touch to see if I could help with anything more. Wolf was still out there somewhere, and they had to consider whether or not he was the one who killed his wife, no matter how much I protested the idea. Shisler had said she'd appreciate a call if something additional came to mind about the afternoon, or if I thought of some other source that could help. Her card lay on the kitchen table.

I rolled out of bed, head pounding, and stood by the window, watching as clouds of snow blew by, obscuring the night sky. During one of the still moments I got a view of Nick's Ranger, blanketed under almost a foot of snow. My head pounded even harder. With the horror of the evening I'd basically forgotten the man sleeping downstairs on my sofa. Lucy had taken over as hostess, offering to sleep in Tess' room so Nick could have a real bed, but Nick wouldn't hear of it. Said if he couldn't handle a sofa, what kind of man was he?

I leaned my forehead against the window, wondering what the hell I was going to do if Nick stuck around very long the next day, wanting to talk about things. About us. It wasn't like I could just forget that his family lived on money made from developing land in Virginia. I mean, developers were my arch-enemy, and had been since I was a kid. Nick was now the CEO of the family business, after his dad had died earlier in the year, and I had no idea what he'd done with Hathaway Development since taking it over.

I went back to bed, but turned off my alarm just before five, not sure exactly how much sleep I'd gotten in those semi-conscious hours. It would have to do.

Coming out of the bathroom I almost ran over Lucy, who was heading toward the stairs.

"Hey," she said. "How're you doing?"

I shook my head and stumbled after her.

"Maybe you should go back to bed," she said. "I'm sure the storm was generous in the amount of problems it brought, and you need energy to deal with it. I can do the morning milking."

"I need to work," I said.

She understood.

In the living room I turned on the TV with the volume down low. The five-o'clock news was just starting, and of course one of the headlines was Mandy's murder. I waited through some commercials and world news before they finally got to the story. I watched, numb, before clicking the remote and entering the kitchen.

"What are they saying?" Lucy asked. She stood at the counter, buttering a piece of toast. "I couldn't make myself watch."

"No suspects they're admitting to, and no leads on where Wolf might be."

"So nothing we didn't already know." She hesitated. "I called Lenny last night and told him. Shook him up, too. Said he's not close to them, but Bart knows them pretty well."

Bart Watts, Lenny's business partner, was another friend of mine with more tattoos than your average citizen.

I turned toward the cupboard and glimpsed Nick standing at the kitchen door, rumpled and sleepy. I took a deep breath and concentrated on finding a cereal bowl.

"Should I make the coffee?" he asked.

My stomach clenched. "Only if you want it."

Lucy opened another cupboard, revealing a coffeemaker. "Here. It's just a two-cupper, but it makes good java."

Nick stood silently for a moment, watching me pour cereal. Not that I had any appetite for it.

"I'm really sorry about your friend," he said.

I nodded, knowing if I talked any more about Mandy I might as well dump my Wheaties down the drain. "Lucy and I will be out most of the day fixing up whatever the storm damaged. I'm not sure what time you're taking off, but at least come find me before you go."

Lucy became very interested in whatever the refrigerator held, her head ducking down behind the door. Nick looked at me steadily.

"I thought I'd stick around, help out where I could. I mean, you do have those extra coveralls." He smiled, and I wondered how on earth he could be so pleasant that early in the morning. "Besides, the roads aren't open for us regular travelers yet."

"Oh," I said. "Okay."

Lucy emerged from the fridge and set a gallon of milk on the table. "We've got a line-up of cereal in the cupboard, or if you're not ready for that we have orange juice and bananas."

"Those Lucky Charms are looking good," he said. "Tess' choice?"

Lucy laughed. "How'd you guess?"

I turned and leaned against the counter. "Will she be okay in here by herself today?"

Lucy sat at the table and poured some of the Wheaties into her bowl. "She'll sleep for a couple more hours, I would think.

I left her a note telling her I'll be outside. I'll check on her when we're done milking."

I took a deep breath, remembering that Billy Moore's mother wouldn't be checking on him that morning. Or ever again.

Nick took a seat, prompting me to eat my cereal standing up. Lucy gave me a look I couldn't quite read, but I was pretty sure she thought I was being ridiculous. I soon set my empty bowl in the sink and reached for the Bag Balm on the window sill. My hands, never in great shape, dried out and cracked like mad during the winter. It's impossible to wear gloves during milking, and the constant cold and wetness wreaked havoc on my skin. I took special care to rub ointment over my new tattoo, which had become slightly red and sore. A normal reaction to a new tattoo, and nothing to worry about. I looked at the inscription, wondering for the hundredth time where Wolf had gone, and if he was okay. Or even alive.

"All right," I said. "I'm headed out."

Lucy waved her spoon at her bowl. "I'll be there soon."

I smothered myself in outerwear and waded through the drifts toward the barn. Queenie greeted me in the parlor, straw clinging to her fur, and I rubbed her head and ears, trying to transfer some of her positive energy to myself. She was warm and content, feeling virtuous, I was sure, for guarding the herd through the night. I was almost done clipping the cows into their stalls when Lucy appeared.

"You okay?" she asked.

I snapped another cow's collar in place. "I'll be better when I know what's happened to Wolf."

"Right." She hesitated. "You know, about Nick, at least he's making the effort to—"

"Don't, Lucy."

She shrugged. "All right."

Temple Radio was playing Mozart, and I was glad for the upbeat music. I was a little surprised the DJ had made it to the station, until I remembered he probably lived on campus and could walk to work. On snowshoes.

I had just finished a sneeze brought on by hay dust when Nick came through the door.

"Bless you," he said.

"Thanks."

We looked at each other. Or what we could see of each other, underneath the layers. Queenie jumped out of her corner to say hello to Nick, licking his face and receiving a good rubbing in return.

"What do you want me to do?" Nick asked.

I gestured him over. "Here. The cows all need hay." I pulled a clump of it apart and scattered it on the floor. "Just spread it out like this in front of them."

He grabbed some hay from the bale and yanked at it, sending more dust into the air.

I sneezed again.

Nick smiled. "Sorry."

The three of us worked companionably, distributing grain, feeding the calves, checking on the soon-to-be mothers, and doing the milking itself. We didn't talk much for the next couple of hours, except for giving instructions to Nick, and I began to breathe easier.

We were almost done milking when Lucy took a break to check on the heifers. Nick and I worked in silence, only once bumping into each other as we reached for a towel.

Lucy was soon back. "The heifers say 'good morning.'"

I put my towel in her hand. "Thanks. Can you finish up my last one? I'm going to call the milk hauler."

Lucy took the towel. "When we're done I need to check on Tess. I'll be back."

I gave her a backhand wave as I headed to my office, where I pulled off my stocking cap and sank into my chair. The hauling company answered on the first ring.

"Royalcrest Farm here," I said. "Wanted to see if you'll make it out this morning."

I heard a computer keyboard clicking. "Yep," the gal said. "We're planning to be there. But the truck'll probably be a little late, seeing how the roads are so bad."

"Still Level Three, from what I hear?"

"Yup. So at least our trucks won't have to deal with stupid drivers."

"Okay. Thanks." I hit the flash button and called Bart's house.

He growled a hello.

"Hey," I said.

"Damn, Stella, what news about Mandy and Wolf. I hear you were the last one to see them."

I swallowed the lump in my throat. "Pretty much."

"Christ Almighty." I could picture Bart crossing himself, saying a short prayer for Mandy's soul. "You hear anything new this morning?"

I rubbed my forehead. "No. That's why I'm calling."

"Nothing on this end, either."

"But you knew them well, right?"

"I ought to. Wolf did my serpent."

Bart's snake travels from one wrist, around his shoulder blades, and back down the other arm, the creating of which used up a considerable chunk of time at Wolf Ink.

"So what do you think?" I asked. "Who would do this?"

"Can't imagine."

"The cops suspect Wolf, especially since they can't find him."

"Huh-uh. No way. He'd never hurt Mandy. Or anybody."

"I agree. So where do you think he is?"

I heard the flick of a lighter, and Bart sucking on a cigarette. "If I knew, woman, I'd be telling the cops."

"I know. I just feel so…"

"Responsible?"

"Geez, don't hold any punches, pal."

Another inhale. "I'm not saying you *are* responsible, just that knowing you, you'd feel that way since you saw them last."

Mandy, lying in the snow while I napped.

"There is one thing," Bart said.

"Yeah? What?"

"Maybe you heard about it. A month ago Wolf and Mandy's son—"

"Billy."

"Right. Billy. Anyway, he got messed up at school. Some kids grabbed him at a junior high basketball game, took him to the bathroom, and beat the crap out of him."

I blinked. "They know who did it?"

"Some high school boys."

"Why?"

"Not sure. Don't know any more than that. Wolf and Mandy weren't talking about it, and the grapevine just had vague details. Nothing in the papers, since they were juvies."

I let that sink in. "And you haven't heard from Wolf and Mandy in the past few days? Before they…before yesterday?"

"Not a word."

I was silent.

"You still there?" Bart asked.

"Yeah. Sorry. If you hear anything else, will you tell me?"

"I'll tell you. And I'll do some calling around. See what I can come up with. We gotta find Wolf in one piece. For Billy."

"For Billy. Talk to you soon."

I pulled out the phone book to look up the Lansdale police. Shisler's card was in the house, and I didn't feel like trudging back there. An officer answered on the first ring.

"Detective Shisler, please," I said.

"Sorry, she's not in. You want to leave a message?"

"It's about the Moores, and she asked me to call if I remembered anything. This is Stella Crown."

He breathed in sharply. "I'll relay the information to her and have her call you. Can I have your number, please?"

I gave it to him, and he promised to get a hold of the detective right away. I hung up and stood at my office window, pondering the drifts. Time to get to work if Doug, our milk hauler, would be able to do his job.

The office door opened, and I turned to find Nick staring at some photos I'd hung.

"You've done some decorating," he said. "Your folks?"

"The first one. My mom and dad."

"And you. Look how cute you were. Two years old?"

"Three."

He nodded. "So it wasn't long after that, then, that your father died."

"Right."

"How old were you in this one?"

The second picture showed my mom, Howie, and me, leaning against a fence.

"About ten."

We didn't say anything as we looked at the last picture. My birthday party, the same day I met Nick. Howie and I sat at a picnic table, happy and comfortable with each other. I turned away, glancing at my wrist, where Howie's name at least partly commemorated him. I tugged my sleeve over it, hiding it from view.

"So what now?" Nick asked.

"Time to clear out the snow."

I pulled my stocking cap back on and we went out to the tractor barn, where I had readied the tractor when I'd heard the storm was coming. I pointed Nick toward the snowblower.

"See if you can clear paths to the house and barn so we're not fighting through it all day. I'll start with the drive."

"You got it."

I found Lucy checking water pipes on the far side of the barn.

"Luce, I'm going on the tractor. If you hear the phone, give me a holler. I'm expecting to hear from the detective."

She eyed me, pursing her lips, but didn't ask anything. "No problem."

For the next hour or so Nick and I worked, creating huge piles of snow, clearing enough space so our milk could be taken. Since milk can only remain in the tank forty-eight hours and Doug hadn't been to our place since the day before last, he had to have access today, or we'd be screwed. I was thankful the snow hadn't had a chance to melt and freeze, or the tractor would've had a terrible time pushing it out of the way. I'd just hopped down from the tractor to give Nick more instructions when Lucy found us.

"What?" I said. "Phone?"

"Nope. Auger's frozen."

"Oh, shit. All right."

"What?" Nick asked.

I pointed toward the back of the barn. "It's how we move grain from one place to another. We gotta thaw it out or we'll be shoveling feed ourselves."

"We might end up doing that, too," Lucy said. "The silage is starting to freeze to the walls and the unloader."

I sighed. "Why don't you start hacking away at that. Nick and I will work on the auger."

"I'm on it."

Nick followed me into the barn and I handed him a hair dryer.

He laughed. "What's this?"

"Our un-freezer. Come on."

An extra-long extension cord later, Nick was standing with the blow-dryer in his hand, pointing it toward the frozen mechanism on the auger. I got to work trekking in and out of the barn with hot water, attempting to hurry along the melting process where ice had locked up the gears. When the auger finally began to move, Nick cheered.

"Nice work," I said.

He smiled, and I couldn't help but smile back. "Ready for some more?"

"Lead on, oh fearless leader."

I didn't know about fearless. But at least working was better than thinking.

Chapter Six

We were loading newspaper into the shredder when a car pulled into the lane. Queenie bounded out to check on it, and I straightened up.

"Friend?" Nick asked.

I shook my head. "Don't know the car."

A woman stepped out of the white Caprice Classic, bundled in a knee-length coat, her head and face covered with a scarf.

I went to the doorway of the barn. "Help you?" I called.

She looked up and I saw it was Detective Shisler. My breath caught.

"You find Wolf?" I asked when she reached me.

She met my eyes. "No. I'm sorry. But I got your message. Can we talk?"

"Sure," I said. "We can go to my office." I turned to Nick. "Why don't you go inside and warm up? I'll get you when I'm done. Or Lucy can give you something to do, if you want."

"Don't worry about me. I'll finish this." He held up a fistful of *Souderton Independent*s and *Philadelphia Inquirer*s.

I nodded and led the detective through the parlor and into my office, where heat from the electric baseboards greeted us.

"Oh, that feels good," she said.

"Go ahead and have a seat." I pulled off my stocking cap and unzipped the top part of my coveralls, circling around to my chair. My stomach was suddenly back to the cramps that had afflicted it up until I'd begun work that morning. I made sure the wastebasket was in easy reach, and waited.

Detective Shisler sat down, unwinding the scarf and revealing a short cap of brown curls that stuck out at all angles from her head. Her mascara was smudged, and the eyebrow pencil a bit much, but her smile was genuine, if sad, revealing slightly crooked teeth. I'd noticed none of these things the night before.

"You never did tell me how you knew I'd been at Wolf Ink yesterday," I said.

She took off her gloves and laid them on my desk. "That was the easy part. I saw your note on their computer, and matched you up with the appointment book."

I nodded.

She crossed her legs. "We kind of shook you up last night—"

"Kind of? I was a wreck."

"Sure. I'm sorry." She pulled her tablet out of her pocket. "You called me this morning?"

"Yeah." I relayed the information to her about Billy's thrashing at the school.

She nodded. "We know all about that. In fact, we investigated it."

"So you know who was involved."

"We do."

I waited, but she said nothing more.

"Any chance they're involved?" I asked.

She lifted a shoulder. "Sure, there's a chance. We're checking it out."

"Okay. Good."

She shifted in the chair. "That's why you called?"

"Yup. Sorry it doesn't help more."

She smiled. "I'm just glad you're willing to share information. Speaking of that, could you please tell me some names of people who know Mr. and Mrs. Moore?"

"Don't know many. But my friend Bart Watts knows the Moores pretty well."

Knew Mandy. Hopefully still *knows* Wolf.

I gave Shisler Bart's number at home and at the Biker Barn. Not that he'd be getting to work that day. "He'll tell you whatever he can."

"Thank you. And thanks again for calling. I was going to stop by today, anyway, to make sure I got all the details from you about yesterday, and to ask a few more questions."

I sighed, but waved my hand over my desk. "Ask away."

She sat back. "The man who came into the parlor—Tank, I believe you said? Do you remember anything more about him? Who he might be?"

"I have no idea. Bart might. I didn't think about asking him."

"I'll follow up." She scribbled on her pad. "And the meeting the Moores had planned? Any chance you remember what it was about? We can't find anyone or anything that tells us. Mrs. Moore's mother doesn't even know where they were headed. Lots of ideas, but nothing concrete."

I shook my head. "They never said. Just mentioned it would go late, so Billy was staying at his grandma's."

She sighed and put away her tablet. "Thanks again for calling. I appreciate any help you can give me."

"Whatever I can do."

She took a card out of her coat and wrote something on it. "My cell phone. Feel free to call anytime."

I took the card and stuck it in the front pocket of my coveralls. "I'll try to think of anything else I've forgotten. Can't imagine what it would be, though."

"Thanks." She stood and re-wrapped the scarf around her head. "You able to keep ahead of the snow here?"

I stood, too, and moved to the window, where I could see flurries beginning outside. "We do our best."

She walked toward the door and opened it. "At least we won't have people complaining about not having a white Christmas."

Just not having a merry one.

She left, shutting the door behind her, and I watched until she made it out to her car, backed around in the space we'd cleared, and headed out the drive. I jammed my hat back on my head, zipped up my coveralls, and went to find Nick.

We finished shredding the newspaper and broke for lunch, a short affair punctuated with Tess' comments about Christmas and computer games. Lucy had sent her upstairs when the cops had arrived the night before, and we'd told her nothing about their visit. So Tess was still in the Christmas spirit, even if the rest of us were finding it difficult to cooperate.

The remainder of our day was filled with transporting hay, filling feed bins, moving more snow, helping Doug with the milk truck—which arrived almost two hours late—thawing a couple of frozen water bowls, setting up space heaters at problem areas, and cleaning out the heifer barn and the soon-to-be-mother pens. All of which, of course, led us right up to the evening milking.

Nick worked smoothly with me in the parlor, helping to feed the cows and taking his side of the aisle during the milking. By the time we'd cleaned out the stalls and re-filled them with new straw and shredded newspaper, he was yawning.

"Come on," I said. "Let's see what Lucy's cooked up for supper."

The fragrance hit us as soon as we walked in. Garlic, ginger, and steamed rice.

"Oh, wow," Nick said. "Will it taste as good as it smells?"

"Better," I said. Even my touchy stomach responded with a positive rumble.

We hung up our coveralls, washed our hands, and greeted Tess, who held a kitten in her arms. She held her out to Nick. "This is Smoky."

Nick stroked the kitten's head. "How old is she?"

"Six months."

"Very sweet." He looked at me. "The litter from this summer?"

"Yup. You can tell how long it's been by how big she is."

His chest rose and fell as he pondered this. I hadn't meant it to be a dig at him, but he apparently took it as one.

"Come on," I said. "Let's see if Lucy's ready for us."

She was, and we almost did justice to her stir-fry chicken, followed by an incredible German chocolate cake.

"Geez, Lucy, what is this?" I asked. "Gourmet dining?"

She grinned. "Just thought I'd make a little something special. It's not every day we have out-of-town guests."

Nick sat back in his chair. "Guess you wish I'd come around more often, huh, Stella?"

I looked at him. "For the desserts?"

He lifted a shoulder, his expression turning pensive.

"Can-I-be-excused-Mom-thank-you-for-supper," Tess said. "Nick, come look at my computer game. I just got to a new place."

"Tess—" Lucy said.

Nick smiled. "It's okay. I'll be glad to see it. Thank you very much for supper."

He followed Tess into the living room, and I got up to help clear the table.

"He's nice, Stella," Lucy said, watching him go. "Really nice."

I didn't answer, concentrating on stacking plates in the dishwasher after rinsing off the most offensive food hangers-on.

"Pretty darn cute, too," Lucy said.

I spun around. "He's a *developer*, Lucy. He lied to me, working here under false pretences, and left. He hasn't called or written in six months, and now he stops in here without warning? It's *not* nice."

Lucy scraped rice into a Tupperware container. "So he stays until the roads are open, and goes home. You never have to talk to him again. Is that what you want?"

I sank against the counter. "I don't know what I want."

She opened the fridge and stacked the containers of leftovers inside. "Well, you have at least until tomorrow to decide. The roads will probably open, and he can go. Until then, I guess you'll survive."

I gave a small laugh. "I guess."

She flicked me with a towel. "Now come on. Stop being a chicken and talk to the man."

We were headed toward the living room when the phone rang. I answered.

"Stella?"

"That's me."

"Rusty Oldham."

"Rusty? Geez. It's been forever."

"Longer. How's that steer head treating you?"

I reached up to touch the tattoo on the back of my neck. The tattoo Rusty had inked as soon as I'd turned eighteen and Howie couldn't stop me. "Never looked better."

"Listen," he said, "I'm calling about Wolf and Mandy. I got a call from Bart Watts, said you were asking questions."

Thank God for friends who did what they promised.

"Yeah. It's a mess. Wolf was doing a tattoo for me and left right in the middle of it. And, well, you know what happened to Mandy." I breathed carefully, then said, "Wolf's still missing."

"I know." His voice broke, and he paused. "I don't like that one bit. And I don't care what they say, it's not 'cause he did anything to Mandy."

"I'm with you. That's why I've been checking around. You have some news?"

"Just some info for you to pass on to your detective, if you've got his number."

"Her number. And yes, I'll pass it on, unless you want to call her yourself."

"I'll let you do it. Can't say I'm too comfortable with cops. Never have been, since they raided my place back in the nineties."

"I'll relay your info. Although she'll probably want your name."

He sighed. "If it will help Wolf."

"She's a good cop. At least she's treated me well, tattoos and all. So what you got?"

"Last spring at the Forged in Ink convention in Wyomissing, an artist named Lance Thunderbolt—"

"No way. Lance Thunderbolt?"

"'Fraid so. Claims he's part Perkasie Indian. Anyway, Lance about went apeshit 'cause he said Wolf stole some of his flash. Went around telling everybody Wolf was a thief."

"It wasn't true."

"Course not. Wolf's a far superior artist."

My mind went to the flash, Wolf's art, displayed on the walls at Wolf Ink. Detailed, colorful, beautiful designs, begging to be etched into someone's skin.

"But?" I said.

Rusty grunted. "Lance spent a lot of time and effort, not to mention money, trying to prove Wolf plagiarized his work. Never did amount to anything but a pain in the ass, and he finally slunk away with his tail between his legs."

"Did he threaten Wolf and Mandy?"

"Lots of times. But only with money stuff. Never violence."

"But you're still calling to tell me this."

Rusty sighed again. "Thunderbolt was humiliated. Basically told by the entire community that Wolf's art made his look like little kid scribbles. Or worse. Who knows where that could lead a man?"

I leaned against the wall, thinking. "So when exactly did this happen?"

"Started in...well, Forged in Ink was in April. So it was from then until, I'd say, about October till he finally gave it up."

"So pretty recent."

"And who knows? Maybe something happened to remind him."

I picked up a pen. "You got information where my detective could reach him?"

He rattled off the business name—Ink Warrior—and where he was located in Pennsburg.

"I already been by his place, and it's locked up tight. Thought if he had anything to do with Wolf's kidnapping, with Mandy's... Anyway, I wanted first crack at him. But he ain't there. So you can tell your detective, but I don't know what good it'll do her."

"Thanks, Rusty. Where are you these days, anyway? Still in Philly?"

"Actually, no. Moved up to North Wales. Wanted to be more in the country."

"The country? Up here in development heaven?"

"Compared to Philly it's the country. No skyscrapers."

"Okay. I hear what you're saying. Thanks."

I hung up and walked out of the kitchen to the foyer, where I pulled the detective's card from my coveralls. I could feel eyes on me—wasn't sure whose, exactly—but didn't look back.

Back in the kitchen I dialed Shisler's cell phone, and she answered before I'd heard a complete ring.

"Stella Crown," I said. "Got something for you."

"Shoot."

I relayed Rusty's story, as well as his and Thunderbolt's contact information. I cringed as I gave out his name, but knew he'd okayed it. For Wolf and Mandy.

"Thanks, Ms. Crown," Shisler said. "I'll get on this right away."

I hung up, wondering what else I could do, but couldn't come up with anything. I reluctantly joined the others in the living room, where Tess was taking Nick through the newest Spy Fox game on the computer we'd gotten as a hand-me-down from Zach Granger, my summertime fourteen-year-old farm helper. Nick and Lucy both looked up at my entrance.

"News?" Lucy asked.

"Just info to pass on to the detective." I stood behind the couch.

"Okay," Lucy said. "How about doing something all of us can play, now that Stella's off the phone?"

I groaned.

"Come on," Lucy said. "It'll get your mind off things. How about a round of good old Uno, or Dutch Blitz?"

"Dutch Blitz?" Nick said.

"It's a Pennsylvania Dutch game," Lucy said. "I'll show you." She grabbed a small box from the cupboard and tossed it to him.

"'A Vonderful Goot Game!'?" he said, reading from the cover, which displayed drawings of an Amish boy and girl.

"Told you. P.A. Dutch. I've got aunts and uncles who speak like that. Anyway, there are four decks of cards. You want to be the pumps, buggies, barrels, or hand plows?"

"If I have to play," I said, "I'm the pumps. I'm always the pumps."

Lucy threw them to me and distributed the others. "Now we shuffle, deal them out, and try to be the first to get rid of our ten-pile and make the most points."

Nick was lost. But Lucy was a good teacher and it gave me an opportunity to watch Nick as he listened. He really was nice, as Lucy had said. And darn it, he was more than cute.

Before we knew it, Nick and Tess were going head-to-head at the speedy game, and Lucy and I wound up throwing in the towel and letting them go at it.

"Losers have to put the game away!" Tess announced. Lucy and I rounded up all the cards and rubber-banded them into stacks.

"And the winners," Lucy said, "or the youngest winner, anyway, has to go to bed."

"Aw, Mom..."

My heart started pounding. If they went to bed, that meant it was getting close to my bedtime, too, and I didn't want to sleep, not after yesterday. But if I didn't go up, I'd be all alone with Nick. Two uncomfortable choices.

Lucy herded Tess toward the stairs before I'd made any kind of decision. "Goodnight, you two."

"'Night," Nick said.

I waved.

The door at the bottom of the stairs shut.

I clasped my hands together and placed them on my ankles, since I was sitting crossed-legged on the floor. Nick looked up from where he lay on his stomach across from me, leaning on his elbows. I avoided his eyes.

"You want to talk about your friends?" Nick asked.

"No."

He was silent. "Okay, then. How about this? I've been here about…" He looked at the clock. "Twenty-eight hours. If you don't want to talk about your friends, do you think maybe we could talk about something other than the weather or the farm?"

I ran a finger over my new tattoo, buying whatever time I could. "Like what?"

Nick was sitting up now, his back against the TV stand. He draped his hands over his bended knees and studied them.

"Lucy and Tess are nice," he said, unconsciously echoing Lucy's thoughts about him.

"They are," I said. "They're the best."

He looked up. "But you miss Howie."

"Of course I do. He was… Yes. I miss him."

The wall clock ticked, filling the silence.

"I'm sorry about what happened this summer. I mean, besides Howie. Your farm problems, and all." He gestured toward my arm. "Your accident."

I glanced down to where my mutilated tattoo was hidden under my flannel shirt. "How'd you know about that?"

He lifted a shoulder. "Just because I left doesn't mean I didn't check up on you."

My chin jerked up. "What? How?" *How*, again.

"Combination of things. The Internet. A few phone calls."

"Phone calls? To who?"

He grimaced. "Don't want to get anyone in trouble."

"Nick, who did you call?"

He looked away, then back at me. "Your vet."

"Carla?"

"Yeah. Her."

Carla Beaumont, my veterinarian, a close friend who had admired Nick's looks along with me. She'd been in touch with him and hadn't told me? I knew who I'd be calling the next day.

"I haven't talked to her recently," Nick said. "Just a week or so after I left. I wanted to make sure you were all right."

I swallowed. "I assumed when you didn't call here that you wanted to forget it all. Forget me."

"What? You don't think I figured the same about you? That you were glad to be rid of me? After all, I'm a *developer.*" His voice caught, and I cleared my throat uncomfortably, touching my new tattoo.

"I was in shock. You *had* lied to me, saying you were a barn painter."

"So it's all my fault. You blame me."

I balled up my hands and pushed on my thighs. "I wasn't the one pretending to be something I wasn't."

"Oh, no. You're so sure of who you are. What's important." He pushed himself off the floor and looked down at me. "It's too bad your priorities tend to lean toward bovines and buildings instead of people."

I stood up, seeing him eye-to-eye across the room. "What's that supposed to mean?"

"I think you know. Now, I'm going to bed."

"Fine. The roads should be good for driving tomorrow, so you want to get plenty of sleep for your trip home."

His jaw bunched, but he didn't reply. Instead, he turned on his heel and disappeared into the next room, where the sofa sat, waiting for him.

I stayed for a moment, hands on my hips, breathing deeply and trying to relax my neck. Nick should know I had to keep my farm and protect it if I wanted to stay connected to my history, my life.

Shit.

I flipped on the TV and saw nothing but cop shows with autopsied murder victims. Not exactly what I needed.

I turned out the lights and went to bed.

Chapter Seven

I was the first up in the morning, having slept like a rock, despite my fears. I awoke with a start and jumped out of bed, heart pounding. What if something had happened while I was asleep? I flung open my door and dove into the hallway, where all was quiet, of course. I forced myself to take a deep breath. Everything was fine. Just fine.

I used the bathroom, then tiptoed downstairs. I turned on the kitchen light and worked as quietly as I could to get my breakfast. I was standing at the kitchen sink, eating a piece of peanut butter toast, when I heard a noise behind me.

"Morning, Lucy," I said.

When she didn't answer, I turned and saw Nick in the doorway.

"Oh," I said.

He stuck his hands in the pockets of his jeans. "Okay if I watch the news, check on weather?"

"Be my guest."

He went back into the living room, and I heard the TV click on, voices droning about the day. I stood in the doorway just long enough to see there were no new developments about Wolf and Mandy. Wolf was still missing. Mandy was still dead.

I was back at the sink, choking down my toast, when I heard the stairway door close, and Lucy talking to Nick. I braced myself.

"So things didn't go well last night?" she asked quietly when she came into the kitchen.

I shrugged. "I slept good."

Lucy sighed, crossing her arms. "He looks bad."

I leaned forward on the sink, bracing my hands on the edge of the counter.

She clucked her tongue. "You don't look so good, either."

"Thanks, Mom."

She sucked in her breath.

"Sorry," I said. "Sorry."

She walked up beside me and gazed out the window at the yard and barn, lit in the glow of the dusk-to-dawn light. "Anything I can help with?"

I turned away, grabbing a glass from the cupboard. I filled it with milk and drank the whole thing. "Not unless you want to find Wolf."

Not fair, and I knew it.

"Okay," she said kindly. "I'll leave you alone."

I set my glass on the counter and walked into the living room, where Nick stood in front of the TV.

"What are they saying?" I asked.

His shoulders tightened. "Another storm's on its way. Already hitting Virginia. All the Harrisonburg area schools are closed." He paused. "You'll just get a few snow showers here."

"Will you be able to get home?"

"As long as they don't declare it a snow emergency in Virginia. But that seems likely to happen soon."

I rubbed my forehead and sighed. "You can stay today yet, if you want."

He turned and looked at me.

I avoided his eyes.

"Really?"

I lifted a shoulder. "Sounds like you shouldn't be on the road down there."

"I'll help work again."

"Whatever."

I went over to the entryway and started pulling on my cover-alls. I could feel him watching me as I clothed myself in layers, until I walked out the door. Twenty minutes later he joined me in the barn, where he was greeted effusively by Queenie, who hadn't been nearly so enthusiastic when I'd arrived. Once he'd given her a good rub-down, Nick started on the jobs he'd done the last two times in milking. At least he was a quick learner.

Lucy checked on us partway through, then went about other business, visiting the heifers and calves and making sure nothing more had frozen. Our luck held, and we didn't have to drag out the hair dryer again.

When we finished, I turned to Nick. "I'm going to make some calls."

He nodded, his hands in his pockets. "Okay. I guess I'll go find Lucy. See if she needs any help."

"Fine."

He left with Queenie—the traitor—trotting behind him. I went to my office and shucked my hat, pulling out my phone book. Once again, the number I needed was in the house, but I didn't want to go get it. No need. Rusty Oldham's new number in North Wales was listed. He answered after three rings, his voice crusty from sleep.

"Sorry to wake you," I said.

"No problem. What's up? News about Wolf?"

"Unfortunately, no. I was calling to see if I could come by, have you look at a tattoo, talk about Wolf and Mandy a bit. You open today?"

"Wasn't gonna be, but I'm not doing nothing. Becky and the girls are off doing some last-minute Christmas shopping. They let me beg off. So come on over."

He gave me directions to his shop, and I was pulling my hat back on when I glanced at the wall and saw the calendar from Carla's veterinarian practice. The little sneak, talking to Nick and never telling me. I picked up the phone and called her house. No answer, except for her machine, which suggested I try the clinic. I called there and the receptionist answered.

"Dr. Beaumont? Sorry. She's out of the office until after Christmas. If you have an emergency, I can put you through to one of the other doctors."

"That's okay," I said. "I'm a friend of hers. Stella Crown. Just trying to find her."

"Oh, Ms. Crown! Sure. Dr. Beaumont went up to State College, visiting her folks. She'll be back in a few days. Want me to leave her a message?"

Duh. Christmas-time. Of course she'd be with her family.

"No message. I'll get in touch with her when she's back. Thanks."

I hung up, pulled on my hat, and went to find Lucy. She was in the house, starting a load of laundry.

"I'm going out for a while," I said.

"Where to?"

"Tattoo place. Rusty Oldham's."

Her eyes flicked toward the living room. "And Nick?"

"What about him?"

"You taking him with you?"

I blinked. "Wasn't planning on it."

Her eyes flashed. "Stella, the man is here to see you, not us."

"Well, I didn't ask him to come."

She stared at me. "He can't go home, although I wouldn't blame him if he tried. The roads in Harrisonburg and the surrounding counties were just declared off-limits to non-emergency drivers."

I sighed, rubbing my eyes. "Fine. *Fine.* I'll take him with me."

Chapter Eight

I slid a Kenny Wayne Shepherd tape into my truck's stereo for the ride to Rusty's, thinking it would ease the silence, or at least keep us from having to talk. But "Deja Voodoo" soon came on, and I realized that a song about nighttime desires featuring someone of the opposite gender—tossing and turning—wasn't exactly what we needed. I punched the off button and we suffered through the last ten minutes with more tension that we would've had, had I just left the stereo alone to begin with.

Eventually we reached Rusty's shop. I knocked on the door, but didn't get an answer, so I studied the decals displayed on the window. Several proclaimed Rusty a member of APT—the Alliance of Professional Tattoo artists. Another advertised Amnesty International, and the last said Rusty was a member of WXPN, the local public radio station. I turned the doorknob, and the door swung open. Rusty wasn't in the front room.

"Hello?" I called.

His voice came from the back. "Be out in a minute."

"So," Nick said. "Tell me what I'm looking at."

"Huh?"

"I've never been in a tattoo parlor before. It's not what I expected."

"Nicer, right?"

"And cleaner."

I looked around the room, wondering where to start with an explanation. The Harley paraphernalia? The flags? The magazines? The old license plates or "Easy Rider" poster?

"Well," I finally said. "See all the art on the walls? That's called flash. It's mostly Rusty's work, with some old generic favorites thrown in, that he'll customize for you."

"Don't see yours. Your cow skull."

"Nope. One-of-a-kind. I'm probably in one of those." I pointed to a shelf unit, packed full of thick photo albums. "He takes a photo of every tattoo he does, so he has a record and people can check out his style. And look here." I grabbed an album off the shelf labeled "Cover ups," and flipped it open. "Rusty specializes in tattoos that fix something—a scar, birthmark, or even another tattoo."

Nick glanced at my arm. "He could fix the one you messed up in the accident?"

"Sure. Could make it look pretty good, too."

"Could Wolf?"

I nodded. "Yup. In fact, Mandy even mentioned that the other day." My throat tightened, and I closed the album, sliding it back onto the shelf.

"What are those?" He pointed to a section of flash on the wall.

"Some of the old standards. Memorials." Crosses. Angels. Doves.

"You didn't get a standard for Howie."

"It's not that unusual. An ID band just fit me better than those others. Now if Bart got a memorial, he'd probably go with the religious theme. Depends who you are."

"Explaining my business?" Rusty came out from the back, wiping his hands on a paper towel. He dropped the towel in a trash can and came forward, holding his hand out in a fist. I thumped it with my own, smiling. He hadn't changed much, except for his head. He now had no hair, and his scalp was covered with a tattoo of the world, the continents a deep green surrounded by various blues, blacks, and mythical figures. A steel loop adorned his nose, making him resemble a bull more than I remembered, and each of his fingers was encircled by a ring. His arms looked mostly the same. An eagle, a dove, and a swallow on one arm, the other arm showcasing a broken heart and the face and flowing hair of a woman he'd once loved who'd been killed in a motorcycle accident. I assumed the extremely detailed oriental city still graced his chest and stomach. Compared to him, I felt positively naked.

"Good to see you, man," I said.

"And you."

I thrust a thumb toward Nick, whose mouth had yet to shut at the vision Rusty presented.

"My friend, Nick. Never seen your kind of place before." Or Rusty's kind of person, at least up close.

Rusty nodded. "Come for a Christmas present?" he asked Nick. "Could do you up a nice little tattoo."

Nick found a smile. "No. Thank you. Just came along for the ride."

"Sure. But you're missing out. Without a tattoo, you're just a hairless ape." Rusty turned back to me. "So what's up? You here about Wolf and Mandy?"

"Yeah. I want to pick your brain about people they know. I also want you to take a look at this. Maybe finish it up." I held out my wrist, showing him the aborted design Wolf had begun.

Rusty took a hold of my arm and turned it from side to side, checking out Wolf's work. "Nice stuff, like always." He let go. "I can't, Stella. Not till we know. Finishing it up would feel almost like… Wolf will be back. He'll finish it."

I let my wrist drop. "Sorry. You're right. I shouldn't have asked."

"No, no, it's fine."

"How about the one on your arm?" Nick asked me.

Rusty's forehead puckered. "What's that?"

I slid off my coat and pulled up my shirt sleeve, exposing my mutilated quote.

"Yikes," Rusty said. "What happened?"

"Bike accident this summer."

"Skin grafts?"

"A couple."

He studied it a bit longer. "I could fix that up. Take a little while, though. Have to think about it."

I let my sleeve back down. "Don't know if I'm up for that today. Rain check?"

"I need time, anyway. Hang on a sec." He grabbed a digital camera from the shelf and I pulled my sleeve back up so he could get a couple of shots. He then took out a tape measure, held it to my arm, and jotted some notes on a yellow notepad. "I'll make a drawing," he said. "Get back to you when it's ready. Now let me see my baby." He set down the tape measure, put his hands on my shoulders, and swiveled me around, pushing my head forward. "Ah. I've always been proud of this one. Never done another like it."

"It's been a conversation starter," I said. "Or ender, depending on the person."

He let me turn back around. "You know," he said, "I've been thinking about Wolf."

I swallowed.

"And I wonder if we can't help out the cops a little. Talk to some folks, see what we can find out."

I was relieved. I'd been afraid he'd balk at helping the police. "Like who?"

"Got some people in mind. I could take you around."

I thought of Billy. Wolf. Mandy lying in the snow. "Let's do it."

"All right."

I hesitated.

"What?" he said.

I grimaced. "I'm thinking I should call the detective. See if she wants to tag along."

Rusty frowned. "You do that, no one will talk. We might as well not go."

I knew he was right.

"You can fill her in at the end of the day," Rusty said. "Let her know if we found out anything."

"What about me?" Nick said. "Will I be a problem?"

Rusty looked him over. "Nah. You're obviously not a cop. We'll vouch for you."

Nick grinned at this. Being vouched for by me and a man who had more colors on him than Nick's painting clothes.

"Let me call home first," I said. "Make sure everything's okay."

Rusty pointed at the phone. "All yours. And while you're talking, I'll show your boyfriend here the tools of the trade."

I opened my mouth to protest the boyfriend notion, but stopped when I saw Nick's face. He thought it was funny, damn him.

I grabbed the phone off the cradle. Lucy and Tess were fine, and Lucy encouraged me to do what needed to be done. She'd take care of the farm. Man, I was lucky to have her.

I hung up and found Nick receiving a lecture from Rusty. One he'd probably given hundreds of times. He had Nick over at the work station, pointing out instruments.

"You want to insist on several things," he said. "Single-use items—things the artist uses only on you then throws them away or sterilizes them. You watch him open the sterile packaging, so you know for sure. Needles, ink, tubes, gloves. You watch your artist pour a new ink supply into a new disposable container. A righteous artist will do all these things, and if yours doesn't, go find a professional who will."

He gestured around the room. "You make sure the surroundings are clean, as well as your tattoo artist, and you feel free to ask anything you want about his sterilization procedures and isolation techniques. And you watch him work. Observe someone else getting a tattoo and make sure you like what you see. None of this hiding in the back room stuff. If he's not doing his work out in the open, you don't want to know what goes on where you can't see. If he's a qualified professional, he'll have no problem with you doing these things. In fact, he'll be glad you're taking so much responsibility. The artist himself is actually in more danger than the customer, with all the people he sees and the bodies he works on. The gloves are as much protection for him as for you."

Nick took a breath to ask a question, but Rusty barreled on.

"This is, of course, after you've found someone who does the quality of art you're looking for. After all, you're gonna have this thing forever. Oh, and you'll have to sign this waiver before a qualified artist will even touch you." He held out a sheet of paper I recognized, a release that waived Rusty's responsibility for things from infections following the work, to allergic reactions to the ink, to variations in color pigments. It even said that you realize a tattoo will be a permanent change to your appearance and you're not under the influence of any mind-altering drugs.

"Change your mind, Nick?" I asked. "You ready to take the plunge?"

He smiled. "I was thinking of something small. Like a hammer."

A hammer. For a developer. I forced a smile. "Would fit."

Rusty, oblivious to the sudden tension, clapped his hands once, a sharp, jarring slap. "So, we ready to go?"

We went.

Chapter Nine

Our first stop was a house not far from Rusty's shop, an attractive, older home on Washington Street. We'd driven in two vehicles, since we weren't sure where we'd wind up at the end of the day, and Nick and I parked behind Rusty's Explorer, inventing a space in the semi-plowed street.

We stepped out, gawking at the Christmas scene. Two ten-foot blow-up snowmen waved from the front lawn, while an equally large Grinch swayed where the front walk met the sidewalk. Strewn about the yard were carolers, candy canes, moving reindeer, multiple strings of blinking colored lights, and a nativity scene with an all too life-like cow as part of the livestock. I almost felt like I should check her teats for frostbite, it was so cold. A glance upward revealed a full porch roof, with eight reindeer pulling a sleigh holding Santa himself. A fully lit star and wreath, bright enough to compete with the day's light, ornamented the eaves.

"Wow," Nick said.

Rusty grinned. "Come on. You'll love these guys."

We were greeted at the door by two large rottweilers with heads as big as Queenie's entire body. Fortunately, a person came close behind them to welcome us. Her eyes loomed dully above dark semi-circles, and she moved slowly, clutching her arms across her middle.

"Rusty. It's good to see you." She turned back into the house, shrugged, and gave Rusty a half smile over her shoulder. "Mickey will be out in a minute, I'm sure." She shooed the dogs away and gestured us inside. "Come on in."

She was a small woman, in her early forties, I'd say, about Wolf and Mandy's age, with an orange and red butterfly tattooed on her pale cheekbone. Creeping up her neck from under her shirt collar were the tops of several varieties of flowers.

"Oh, Rusty," she said softly. "I can hardly bear it about Mandy." Her painted nails clutched Rusty's arm, then fell away.

Rusty studied her face. "Would it be okay if we asked you some questions about her? About Wolf?"

She glanced at me, and at the tattoo on my neck.

"Stella Crown," I said.

She gasped. "But you were the last one to see them!"

I tried not to show my dismay. "Yes, ma'am. Yes, I was."

"And this is Nick," Rusty said, jutting his chin toward him. "Stella's friend."

"Nice to meet you," she said.

Rusty put his hand on her frail-looking shoulder. "This is Jewel Spurgeon."

"Hi, Jewel," Nick said, smiling.

"You touching my woman?" A bellowing man hurtled toward us down the hallway, his hair flowing behind him. A Fu Manchu mustache drooped over his mouth, and his face sparkled with numerous piercings. I was about to step protectively in front of Rusty when the man lunged forward and hugged my friend so hard I thought his ribs might crack.

"Where you been, man?" the guy said.

"Around," Rusty gasped.

"And you brought friends!"

I was next to receive the hug, and Nick accepted his with grace. In fact, I could see a smile niggling at the corners of his mouth.

"Mickey, honey," Jewel said. "They're here about Wolf and Mandy."

"Oh, no," Mickey said, his voice lowering several decibels. "I just can't believe it."

"They want to ask us some about them," Jewel said.

"Well, what are we standing here for, then?" Mickey said. "Who wants to stand up all day?"

He herded us into their living room, a space decorated with an eclectic collection of furs, velvet paintings, and Harley knick-knacks. I took a seat on a leather and chrome chair beside a lava lamp, while Rusty dropped onto a harvest gold recliner. Nick chose to stand. Jewel perched primly on the edge of a flowered couch, but Mickey hovered over us.

"Something to drink? Soda? Beer?"

"No, thanks, man," Rusty said.

Mickey spun toward me and I shook my head. Nick thanked him, too, but refused anything.

"Relax," Rusty said. "We're not here to put you out, just to ask some questions."

Mickey sat close enough to Jewel she had to wiggle a bit to get out from under the side of his leg, and he put his arm around her. "How come you're asking?"

Rusty jerked his chin toward me. "You already know Stella's involved. She was there when Wolf disappeared and Mandy…" He took a breath. "So now she wants to help the cops find Wolf, before it's too late."

Mickey peered at me through narrowed eyes. "The cops? I don't want no cops."

I held up my hands. "I'm not a cop. I just want to do whatever I can to get Wolf home."

"You don't see any cops here, do you, Mick?" Rusty said, an edge to his voice. "I wouldn't bring the Man to your house. You know that."

And I'd suggested it earlier. Talk about dumb.

Mickey looked at me again for a long moment, and his face finally relaxed. "Sorry, Rusty. I'm just…it's been rough. We've been trying not to think too hard about Mandy and Wolf." His voice broke, and he cleared his throat. "We called Mandy's mom and offered to keep Billy, us being his godparents and all, but he's best staying put with her for now, poor little tyke."

Jewel sniffed and wiped an eye with a carefully manicured finger, a gem of some sort shining on her middle nail.

"You're good friends with the family?" I asked.

Mickey pointed at some wedding photos displayed on top of a glass and stone coffee table. "Wolf was best man at our wedding. He and I grew up together, on the same block in Lansdale. Never lost touch except a couple years when I was in the army."

I leaned over and searched the faces in the biggest picture, a wedding party. It wasn't hard to pick out Wolf in the bunch, his hair and beard long and unruly even for the formal occasion.

"You have any idea where Wolf might be now? Who might've hurt Mandy?" Rusty asked.

Hurt, not murdered. Even now he couldn't handle the reality.

Mickey and Jewel looked at each other for a long moment. Jewel put a hand on Mickey's thigh. "Tell them what we've been thinking, honey."

Mickey shifted uneasily, glancing at Rusty, me, even Nick. "Okay. You guys hear about the new bill they're trying to pass through the state senate? The one about tattoo artists?"

"Sure," Rusty said. "Pain in the ass if it passes."

"I don't know it," I said. "Fill me in?"

Mickey stood, walked over to a roll-top desk in the corner, flung open the cover, and grabbed a stack of papers. He brought them over and dropped them in my lap.

"PA House Bill No. 752," he said. "The Tattoo, Body Piercing, and Corrective Cosmetic Artist Act. Should be called the Bunch of Bullshit Act. The State wants to regulate tattooing, all because of those damn scratchers who get people sick."

I thumbed through the pages, but couldn't make sense of the legalese at first glance. "So what exactly are they proposing?"

"Bunch of crap," Mickey said.

"It's a hypocritical, ill-written, open-ended bill, made for people who don't like seeing tattoos or people with body modifications," Rusty said.

Mickey raised his hands. "Preach it, brother."

I scanned the pages again, hoping something would jump out at me. "Like what?"

"Okay, first thing," Mickey said, "they say all piercing would be regulated by the government, but that's bullshit. It's the people who do it right who would get in trouble. The ones who don't know what they're doing have no problems at all."

"Why?"

"Because there's a powerful piercing gun industry, that's why. They're calling the shots. I mean, we now have a law that says if you're under eighteen you need parental consent to get pierced, but do you see police cracking down on those jewelry stores in the mall, where you get 'free piercing with the purchase of studs'? I don't think so. They'll do pre-teens, even babies, if the parents—hell, if the kids themselves—shell out their money. People like Mandy, who know what it's about, they don't use piercing guns at all." He was rolling now. "Another thing. The bill talks about safety regulations, but says the Department of Health still has to define them. So they want to pass a bill that basically states it's 'to be announced'?"

Rusty sat up. "What really gets me is they want to make tattoo artists get a notarized statement from a doctor saying they don't have any infectious diseases. They gonna make customers get statements, too? The artists are more at risk than the folks getting the tattoos."

"And how about that part that says you can't tattoo anybody's face?" Mickey said. "You want to tell me Jewel's butterfly isn't gorgeous?"

We all looked at Jewel, who slanted her cheek away, embarrassed.

"Sounds pretty biased," I said. "Who came up with this stuff?"

"His Righteousness," Mickey said. "Trevor Farley."

"The state senator?"

"Himself. The bastard."

"Why does he care about tattoos?"

Mickey shrugged. "All I know is he's trying to make life hell for those of us in the community."

I looked from him to Rusty. "So how does this involve Wolf and Mandy? I mean, obviously it does because of their professions. But is it more?"

Rusty shrugged. "I don't know. Mickey?"

Again Mickey looked at his wife. She nodded.

"Wolf and Mandy have gotten real involved in the cause," Mickey said. "You heard of Dennis Bergman?"

I shook my head.

"Tattoo artist in Harrisburg. Also a lawyer, believe it or not. He's heading up the lobby, which is made up of tattoo artists and piercers from all parts of the state. Call themselves Artists for Freedom. Wolf and Mandy found out about Bergman a few months ago, and, well, you know Mandy. Not about to let the government tie her hands, or Wolf's. Jumped in with both feet."

I spread my fingers on top of the papers on my lap. "And you think it could lead to this? To Wolf disappearing? To Mandy…dying?"

Jewel whimpered, and Mickey returned his arm to her shoulders.

"Just last week Mandy was on a rampage," he said. "Said Farley was trying to sabotage their lobby. Said he sent a spy to infiltrate the meetings and get dirt on whoever was there."

I sat up. "You think Farley had to do with Billy getting beat up last month?"

Jewel's face hardened. "Asshole boys, whoever they were. I could just kill them."

Mickey patted her arm. "Wolf and Mandy wouldn't talk about that. Never told us who was behind it. But they kept on with the lobby. In fact, they were going to meet with Artists for Freedom the night Mandy died. Mandy had gotten hold of something she said would stop Farley in his goddamned tracks."

I whipped my head toward him. "They were meeting that night? In Harrisburg?"

"Well, sure. That was the plan."

A plan no one else knew about. I wondered if a certain state senator had been informed.

Chapter Ten

"You don't happen to have your cell phone on you, do you?" I asked Nick. We were back in the truck, while Rusty made tearful good-byes with the Spurgeons.

"Sure." He reached into his coat and pulled out the smallest phone I'd ever seen.

"This thing actually works?"

He smiled. "Has every time I've tried it."

I took it from his outstretched hand, at the same time pulling Detective Shisler's card from my pocket. She answered almost immediately.

"Stella Crown here. You haven't found Wolf, have you?"

"I'm sorry, no."

"I know where Wolf and Mandy were going the night Mandy was killed."

"What? Where?"

"They've been active in a political lobby called Artists for Freedom. They're pushing against a bill that's working its way through the Pennsylvania senate, restricting tattoo artists and body piercers."

"I think I've heard about that. Isn't Senator Farley heading that up that bill?"

"Yup. And he apparently has no love lost for these folks. No one's quite sure why he's so gung ho about coming down on these artists, but he's going after them with everything he's got."

"Interesting, but I can't see him killing Mandy over body art."

"Perhaps if you could find out what she had on him, it might be clearer. She told her friends she'd discovered something big that would make him think seriously about continuing with the bill. She was going to tell the group that night at the meeting so they could formulate a plan."

"And you think Farley found out about this?"

"Mandy told the Spurgeons Farley had a spy in the group. He could've easily known about the meeting."

She was silent for a moment. "You have someone I could talk to about this?"

I sighed. "Not sure. I hate to say it, but these people aren't real up on cops. Been raided and discriminated against too many times. But they've promised to call me or Rusty if they think of anything else."

"Rusty Oldham, the artist I talked with?"

"That's him."

"I guess it'll have to do." She paused. "I finally ran down Lance Thunderbolt, the tattoo artist who'd been trying to sue Wolf for plagiarism. He's in New Jersey, visiting family. I've been able to verify that he's been there since Saturday."

"I guess that's good."

"Sure. One less suspect. Wish I could say the same for that other guy. Tank. I still haven't found him. Any ideas?"

"Nope. Never set eyes on the guy before that day. I'll see what I can find out."

"I'd appreciate it. I don't know where else to look. I have calls in to other police districts, but with Christmas and all, it's hard to find the right people." She sighed. "So where are you now?"

I glanced toward the house. "Going to talk to some more people in the community. In fact, here comes Rusty now."

He walked down the sidewalk toward us, and Nick lowered his window.

"Gotta go," I said to Shisler.

"I guess from what you said before I shouldn't tag along?"

"Not if we want these folks to say anything worthwhile."

"You'll keep me informed?"

"I am right now."

"Yes, I know. Thank you. Talk to you soon."

I hung up and handed the phone back to Nick just as Rusty got to the window.

"Where to now?" I asked.

He leaned his elbows on the door, his eyes rimmed with red. He swiped at them with his thumb and forefinger, not even trying to hide that he'd been crying. "I was thinking Giovanni's deli, but I can't say I'm real hungry."

I glanced at the clock on my dashboard. Just about noon. "There something there other than hoagies that you want?"

He nodded. "Gio's good friends with lots in the tattoo community. Could know things I don't."

"We don't have to eat, right?"

"Guess not. But maybe once we're in the place I'll find my appetite."

"Then why don't we head there?"

He slapped Nick's open window. "Let's go."

We followed him through the salty streets toward Hatfield, where Giovanni's took up one corner of an intersection. We parked in the well-plowed lot and found a place in line in the noisy restaurant. Giovanni himself, his olive skin flushed from heat, was busy behind the counter, taking orders and sliding pizzas into the two-tiered oven. His well-muscled arms displayed several tattoo artists' work, and I had a feeling Wolf and Rusty had each done their part. His right arm was criss-crossed with an unusual barbed-wire design—not just the kind that circles the biceps—and his left held a panorama of eyes. I imagined it would be rather spooky under the right circumstances.

When we reached the front of the line and Giovanni saw Rusty, his eyes sparked with sadness. He obviously knew about Mandy. "Hey, my man."

"Gio," Rusty said.

"Can I get you something?" Gio asked.

Rusty sighed, checking out the menu board above the owner's head. "Just a plain turkey hoagie. No onions or nothing."

"Oil?"

"Better not."

Gio nodded and turned to me. "You look familiar. At least that tat on your neck does."

"Stella Crown. And the skull's some of Rusty's work."

"Thought so."

"Can I get a pizza steak hoagie? Extra sauce? Sweet peppers?"

He cocked his finger at me and looked at Nick. "You with them?"

Nick smiled. "I am. Italian hoagie, please. Oil, vinegar, oregano."

"Fries for anybody? Chips? Drinks?"

We declined the fried stuff, but agreed to the drinks, and Gio barked our orders to two men working at the food spread behind him. His brothers, probably. Or sons. Nephews.

"Any chance we could get a little of your time?" Rusty asked Gio.

He nodded shortly. "Rush will soon be over. You sit and eat, and I'll be out."

We took our number and found an empty table toward the back of the room where we sat, Nick taking the chair beside me. I made sure our legs didn't touch.

It was a busy scene. Guys in working-class uniforms, women with bickering children, some of each gender in suits and business casuals. Working right up to Christmas.

Just about everybody, no matter their dress, sent surreptitious glances toward Rusty and his colorful head. Probably his nose ring, too. I guessed I couldn't blame them, but it made me feel like we were in the zoo, and I wanted to snap at them all to mind their own goddamn business.

"Harrisonburg's beginning to look just like this," Nick said. "Barely space to eat lunch."

I grunted. "That's what happens when every square inch of land gets developed."

He didn't say anything, focusing on the tabletop. Rusty looked at me, eyebrows raised, but I shook my head. Gio caught my eye across the room and pointed at a loaded tray. I went up and got the food, stopping off at the drink machine to fill my cup with birch beer. I'd let the guys get their own drinks.

Twenty minutes later we were piling our trash on the tray when Giovanni sat in the empty seat next to Rusty. The line up front had dwindled to just a few business people, and one of Gio's relatives had taken over behind the counter.

"You aren't just here for lunch, I take it?" he said to us.

Rusty jerked his head no. "Wondered if you could shed any light on Wolf and Mandy."

Giovanni slouched in his seat and ran a hand over a face shadowed with dark whiskers. "Wish I could."

"You don't think Wolf had anything to do with Mandy?" I asked.

He glared at me like I'd cursed in church. "No way. Stupidest thing I've ever heard."

"Chill," Rusty said. "We feel the same. Just wanted to make sure you were with us."

The big Italian's face relaxed again, and he pulled on his thick mustache. "Been wracking my brain, trying to imagine who would do it. Where Wolf could be."

"Think of anybody who had troubles with them?" I asked.

Giovanni barked a laugh. "Lots of folks. But none who would…do what they did."

"Like who?"

He shrugged and rested his elbows on the table. "Don't know his name or his boys, but some gangbanger stopped by their place a week ago or so. Wanted Wolf to do him up a tattoo in a half hour. He was headed to jail the next day, and wanted to use up his remaining time scoring dope down in Philly."

"Wolf do him?" I asked.

Rusty was shaking his head. "Couldn't have in that amount of time. Wouldn't have, anyway."

"Nope," Gio said. "Mandy basically told the kid to go to hell. Wolf tried to calm her down, but she wasn't having any of it. Told the guy where to go, and that's the truth."

I almost smiled at the image it presented. "What happened?"

He did smile. "Guys left. Even apologized. Guess they like strong women. But who knows? Maybe they thought about it later and decided it wasn't cool. Be back in a minute." He went up to the counter, grabbed a cup, and filled it with water. "Sorry." He sat down again. "All dried up from working back there."

"Any other ideas?" I asked.

"Sure. Could be somebody we don't even know about. Like, a little while ago some guy, completely high on crack, burst into the shop, started screaming that the Warlocks had just broken him out of Norristown Hospital. Accused Wolf of stealing his money, said if Wolf would just give back the cash, he'd forget everything. Wolf and Mandy couldn't remember ever seeing the guy before, but they were afraid what he might have under his clothes. You never know what these crackheads are concealing. They held him off long enough for Mandy to call the cops, who didn't find weapons, but discovered a good stash of bills in the guy's sock. Once he saw it he remembered putting it there. Had somehow fixated on Wolf and was sure he'd been robbed."

I shook my head. It was hard to imagine folks like that on the streets of Lansdale, but I guessed crazies could pop up anywhere.

"What about Lance Thunderbolt?"

Gio raised an eyebrow. "What about him?"

"Rusty told me about the problems he caused Wolf. The detective says he was out of town the night of…the night I went to get my tattoo, but what if he came back and his family's covering for him?"

Gio sneered. "That wuss? He wouldn't know to go to sleep at night if somebody didn't tell him first."

Rusty laughed. "That's about right."

"So you think his alibi's for real?" I looked from Gio to Rusty, watching their eyes.

Gio shrugged. "More believable than him actually having the balls to confront someone in person. Lawyers, sure. Rumors, trash talking, gossip. That's his style."

So maybe Thunderbolt really was in the clear.

"What about Wolf and Mandy's activities?" I asked. "Politics?"

"Sure. You heard about Artists for Freedom?"

Rusty nodded. "We were just at Jewel and Mick's."

"Then you know all about that."

"Any idea why that senator's got it in for tattoos?" I asked. "Trevor Farley?"

He bunched his mouth, shaking his head. "No idea. His own family's famous for their unadorned white skin. Always look like they're ready for mass. Although there's no telling what's under their shirts, I guess. Could be his kids defied him and got some art nobody's telling about. Or maybe he's got a moneybags who's offended by walking art and asked him—or forced him—to take a stand. Who knows?"

"Anybody else?" I asked.

He puffed out his cheeks. "Could be any number of people Mandy's pissed off along the way, but nobody who comes right to mind. Nobody who'd hate her enough to kill her."

I closed my eyes and breathed through my nose. Giovanni was the first person to actually admit what had happened. Bluntness didn't feel any better. Nick touched my leg under the table, a gesture most likely made to comfort me, but my knee jerked involuntarily and he pulled his hand back.

"There is Gentleman John, of course," Gio said.

"Who?"

"John Greene. A hack. Wolf and Mandy got him in trouble different times."

Ah. The asshole Mandy had mentioned.

"Right," I said. "What's the deal with him?"

"A slimy piece of work," Gio said. "But I don't know. If Mandy saw him at her door she certainly wouldn't let him in. And if he got in anyway, she'd just kick the crap out of him."

Rusty snorted. "That's about right."

"But it sounds like he might want payback?"

Gio shrugged. "It's not like Wolf and Mandy are the only ones who ever ratted him out. He had plenty of people wanting him out of business, including parents of kids he'd worked on. I can't see him going after Wolf and Mandy but leaving the other folks alone."

I looked at Rusty, and he shook his head, shrugging. "It would seem strange if he'd single them out. We all hate him. And anyone like him."

"Hey," I said. "What about a guy named Tank? You know him?"

Rusty looked at me. "I do. What about him?"

"I forgot to tell you. He came by Wolf Ink when I was getting my tattoo."

"And wanted Wolf to work on him?" Rusty's face clouded.

"Yeah."

"Figures," Gio said. "I wonder..."

I glanced back and forth between Rusty and Gio. "What? Who is he?"

Rusty shifted in his seat, his lips tight. "I didn't know he'd been there. If I'd'a known that—"

"He's a dude who harasses tattoo artists," Gio said. "Gets work done, doesn't pay, then expects them to run a tab. When they won't do him anymore, he threatens them."

"Does more than threaten," Rusty said. "When I refused him he came by, cut down two trees in my shop's front yard. Only trees I had. Then he doused the branches with gas and set them on fire on my front step. Lucky the whole place didn't burn down."

Gio nodded. "Lucky, too, he didn't know where you lived."

"He's a menace," Nick said.

Rusty looked at him. "He is."

We were quiet, wondering how far his anger had gone at Wolf Ink.

"He ever do anything violent that you know of?" I asked. "To living things other than trees?"

"Beat up my friend Cash's dog a while ago," Rusty said. "Left the poor mutt for dead. Cash spent a fortune at the vet's."

I flashed on an image of Queenie, and my stomach tightened. "The dog okay?"

Rusty shook his head. "Lost an eye and partial use of his hind legs."

Gio's face went red. "Asshole who does that, wouldn't be too much of a stretch to do people, too."

"And he's huge," I said. "He wouldn't have had trouble subduing Wolf or Mandy. One swipe could've done the damage."

Mandy lying in the snow, her head bashed in.

"What's his real name?" I asked.

Rusty's face went blank. "Don't know. Don't know where he lives, either. When he cut down my trees I called the cops, but couldn't tell them where to find him. That was a while ago, before he'd scammed too many folks. I haven't seen him since, but I'm sure somebody knows him, especially if he's still running this shit." He glanced at Gio. "You think I'd'a heard."

Gio shook his head slowly. "Maybe he's just now getting back into it. Maybe he was away for a while or something."

I wondered if Detective Shisler had gotten a name yet.

"I'll ask around," Gio said, his face hard. "It comes out he had anything to do with this, I can't promise the police will have anything left to bring in."

I nodded, knowing he was probably right. I'd better get the info to Shisler before Gio got too far with his inquiries.

"Well," Rusty said to Giovanni, "we might've found our answer, if Tank's anywhere close by. But if you think of anybody else connected to Wolf and Mandy, can you give me a call?"

Gio raised an eyebrow. "What you up to?"

Rusty jerked his chin toward me. "Stella was the last to see them."

He pointed at my wrist, which I slanted toward Gio.

"How'?" he said.

I pulled my sleeve over my wrist. "Supposed to say Howie."

Understanding gradually lit his eyes, and he nodded. "I heard about you."

I wasn't sure if that was good or bad, from the glint in his eye.

Mandy dying by the Dumpster while I slept.

A group of high schoolers swung in the door, and the guy behind the counter shot Gio a desperate glance. Gio stood and pushed his chair under the table. "I'll be in touch if I think of anything else."

"Thanks, buddy," Rusty said.

Gio placed a hand briefly on Rusty's shoulder, and left. Rusty grimaced at the trash piled on our tray. "Well, I can't say my sandwich is sitting too well. Let's get out of here."

I grabbed our tray and dumped it on the way out.

Chapter Eleven

"Where to now?" I asked. "If you're feeling up to it. Tank might be our answer, but we can't be sure."

Rusty winced and pressed a hand on his stomach. "Give me a minute."

We stood and watched traffic, the cars and trucks clogging up the convoluted intersection beside the parking lot. You'd never know from the amount of vehicles that we'd had a blizzard just days before. The snow was now in the form of small mountains at the back of the parking lot, and shoved to the sides of the roads.

Rusty grimaced again.

"It's okay," I said. "If you're not up to any more, we'll just go home."

"It's not that. It's just... Talking in there made me realize there's somebody we probably ought to see, but it's never pleasant."

"Nothing about this situation is pleasant."

"That's true. It's just, this guy's not the greatest to see ever, let alone right after lunch."

I glanced at Nick, who lifted a shoulder.

"We'll try it," I said to Rusty. "You lead."

He eased himself into his Explorer while Nick and I turned to my truck. I tossed Nick the keys. "You want to drive while I call the detective?"

He stared at me, a smile tickling his lips.

"What?" I said.

"You trust me to drive your truck?"

"Oh, shut up. And hand me your phone, will you?"

He smiled some more, and we climbed into the truck. We followed Rusty out of the parking lot and headed out Cowpath Road toward Souderton. Nick negotiated the busy street while I dialed the detective's number.

"Shisler," she said.

"Stella Crown. Got some information on Tank."

"Great. I ran down some facts this morning, but I can always use more. What do you have?"

I told her Rusty's story about the trees, and about his friend's dog.

"Nasty character," Shisler said.

"You know his real name?"

"I finally got it, but you'll never believe it. Matthew Snyder."

I gave a bark of laughter. "Sounds like a Mennonite."

"Mennonite family, anyway. Got a rap sheet longer than my night stick. Spent some time visiting our lovely prison facilities from the late nineties up until last year."

So it was no wonder the tattoo artists had forgotten about him. He hadn't been around to scam or threaten.

"Have you talked to him about Wolf and Mandy?"

"Haven't found him yet. We're looking. Probably visiting his family for the holidays."

"Now there's a scary thought."

"Thanks for the information. If you find him, I'll be really grateful. You got anything else?"

"Nothing that helps much. Some gangbangers that visited Wolf and Mandy, and some crazy guy on drugs. No names or anything."

"Folks that threatened them?"

"Sort of. They called the cops on the one guy, but I don't know when it was or anything."

Shisler sighed. "All right. Well, thanks for this."

"Sure."

"Where are you now?"

"Off to visit somebody. Rusty didn't say who."

"Keep me informed?"

"Like always." I disconnected and placed the phone on the seat.

"I like Rusty," Nick said.

I glanced at him. "Even with how he looks?"

He grinned. "Because of it. Who's ever met anyone else like him? Besides, if you were blind you'd never know it, he's such a nice guy."

"You looking for a marketing job? These folks could use it."

His smile grew.

"What?"

"You say 'these folks,' as if you're not one of them."

I thought about that. "Okay. Us folks. I just don't have a globe on my head."

Nick laughed. "I guess I'd have to say I'm glad about that."

We passed through Souderton, within shouting distance of my place, and kept on toward the Ridge and Sellersville. Rusty soon pulled off the main road into a wooded section, and wound around some curving back roads until we ended up at a little cottage built like a log cabin. Smoke drifted out of the chimney, and the sun that made it through the bare trees sparkled on the new snow. I didn't see any vehicles, or even tire tracks, but there was a closed garage door on an unattached building to the left. The house wasn't new—some shingles were missing, and a shutter hung crooked by a window—but overall it looked tidy.

"Not what I expected, from how Rusty was talking," I said.

Nick raised his eyebrows. "I guess it's the guy himself he can't stand."

We stepped down from the truck, the smell of wood smoke sharp in the air, and met Rusty on the front porch, a covered platform with timber railings. The high strains of opera leaked out from inside the cabin, and a faded sign by the door made it clear where we were.

"Gentleman John's Tattoos?" I said. "Is this the guy we were talking about with Gio? John Greene?"

Rusty nodded. "The one and only."

"This place doesn't look like a back alley," Nick said, glancing around.

"It ain't always the surroundings that make it what it is," Rusty said. He pounded his fist on the door so hard I hoped he wouldn't bust right through. When his banging received no answer, he curved his hands around his eyes and peered in the window.

"Not home?" I said.

"Or not admitting it."

We were turning to leave when the lock snapped back and the door cracked open.

"Who is it?" a voice said.

Rusty looked back. "John?"

The door opened further, and along with the louder wave of music I got my first glimpse of the asshole Mandy had so named. I stopped short in surprise. Opposite of what I had expected from a hack—filth and lechery—Gentleman John looked like he fell off Masterpiece Theater and landed on the Ridge. Short, black hair combed off his forehead, a well-manicured mustache, and clothes that, while obviously not new, were clean and pressed. Diamond studs shone in his earlobes, but I saw no other evidence of body modification.

"Can I help you?" he asked.

"Come on, John," Rusty said. "Let us in."

The man smiled and waved his hand in a grand gesture of welcome. "Anything for you, my esteemed colleague."

Rusty made a growling sound low in his throat, but preceded Nick and me into the house.

John shook Nick's hand as he entered, and raised my hand to his lips, brushing it with a kiss. His eyes sparkled as he met my gaze. "Always a pleasure to have a beautiful woman in my home."

"Give it a rest, John," Rusty snapped.

I stiffened, surprised at Rusty's tone. Arriving here had changed his personality from collie to Doberman, and I wasn't sure I liked it.

Nick stared at my hand, lying in Gentleman John's, and I pulled away from John's grasp.

John raised his hands in a conciliatory gesture. "Should one not welcome new friends?"

Rusty glared at John, and John smiled. "Well, then, why don't we have a seat and talk about why you've come to visit me."

He led us into the front room, which consisted of worn Victorian-type furniture, gauzy curtains, and a free-standing marble chess set. The chess pieces were chipped, but the set itself was intact. John had us sit on a stiff, velvet-covered sofa, where we all perched on the edge.

"Can I offer you a drink?" he asked. "I have some refreshment close at hand." He made his way across the room to a bar area, where he pulled several wine glasses from a shelf.

"No," Rusty said, his voice leaving no room for argument.

Nick and I shook our heads.

"A pity," John said. "I received this new port for Christmas."

Port. He really was from PBS.

"And can you turn down that racket?" Rusty asked.

John poured himself a serving of the drink before adjusting the stereo one decibel lower and settling himself in the matching chair, crossing his right knee over his left. He waited, smiling at Rusty across the coffee table between us, apparently daring him to complain again about the music. His left hand was draped loosely over his thigh, his right hand held his drink, and he sat back in his chair, emitting an air of relaxation and calm.

I tried not to let my confusion show. This was the back alley hack they all hated so much? Where was the dirt? Where were the germs? I glanced around, wondering if his shop was part of the house.

Gentleman John followed my glance. "You're wondering where I do my work." He half-rose from his seat. "My studio is down the hall, if you'd like to see it."

"Later, John," Rusty said. "We ain't here to get lectured on how you abide by all the *laws*."

The venom in Rusty's voice startled me, and I snuck a peek at Nick, who was studying John with half-shut eyes.

"I guess I'll have to pass for now," I said. "But thanks."

"I'm sure you know why we're here," Rusty said.

Gentleman John lifted a shoulder, his face a picture of innocence. "Advice on the craft? A design for the young lady?" He winked at me, and Nick sucked in a quick breath.

"No, thank you," I said. "Rusty and Wolf take care of me."

He gave a small smile. "I'm sorry to hear that."

"Enough about her," Rusty said. "I want to know what you hear about Wolf and Mandy."

"*Her*?" John said, still looking at me. "How can we have enough of *her* when you haven't even introduced us properly?"

Rusty looked about ready to explode, so I jumped in. "Stella Crown. Friend of Rusty's. And of Wolf and Mandy. That's why we're here. To see if you know anything about what happened to them."

"Now why would *I* know anything?" He gazed at Rusty, his eyes wide. "I'm as shocked and saddened to learn of their misfortune as anyone, but what I know is only from the newspapers."

"Don't give me that crap," Rusty said. "You hated them and you know it. You're probably jumping for joy inside."

Greene shifted on his seat and pulled a newspaper from below the coffee table, tossing it onto the top. "My information source," he said. It was today's issue of Lansdale's *The Reporter*, with a front page photo of Wolf. The headline above him pleaded, "Has Anyone Seen This Man?"

"It's not my problem Wolf finally decided to murder his wife and depart with his mistress," Greene said.

What? I looked at Rusty, but he ignored me.

John continued. "It's not like Wolf and I were confidants or anything."

Rusty frowned. "Which is exactly why we're here."

"What? You think I had something to do with this…this tragedy?" Greene laughed. "You tell me how I did it, I'll be more than happy to take the credit if it will help. You know Mandy. Or knew her. She could've beat me into the ground in a heartbeat, as Wolf could've, as well."

I gawked at him.

He laughed again. "Don't look so shocked, Ms. Crown. I'm afraid I'm not a fighting man. Mandy was a strong woman, and she despised me. Of course she wasn't on my Christmas card list, either. She caused me more grief than anyone in my whole life. She and Wolf. But no matter about that. You tell me how I'd get her—*both* of them—out of their shop and anywhere else, and I'll turn myself in.

"As far as who *I* think could have done it?" He shrugged. "Like I said before, you should probably take a closer look at Wolf himself. He wouldn't be the first man to free himself of...shall we say...the ball and chain? And you might want to ask that little vixen who was after him. Wolf might've done the proper protesting, but even he couldn't hold out for long against *that*."

"You're talking shit," Rusty said. "Wolf wouldn't have left Mandy for anything."

Gentleman John swirled the drink in his glass, studying it. "Just saying what I heard, that's all. And where there's smoke..."

"Bullshit," Rusty said.

Gentleman John lifted a shoulder, half smiling.

Nick elbowed me in the side. I looked at him and followed his gaze, freezing at the look of rage on Rusty's face.

I cleared my throat. "Any chance I could see your studio now?"

He peered at me. "You're really interested?"

"Sure." If it would get Rusty out of the house before he strangled the man.

John set his glass on an end table, and stood. "Then please, follow me."

I got up, but turned back to Nick. "Why don't you guys wait for me outside? I'll only be a minute."

Rusty didn't seem to hear me, but Nick nodded.

"So what exactly did Wolf and Mandy do to you?" I asked John as we walked side-by-side down the hallway. The opera music followed us, piped through the speakers set in the ceiling.

"What *didn't* they do? Called the cops, tried to force me out of work. Bankrupted me, lost me customers. Of course I still have some loyal folks."

We walked through his kitchen to a closed door at the back, which seemed like an add-on to the rear of the house.

"It wouldn't be that the law had anything to come down on you for, would it?" I asked. "Tattooing underage kids? Piercing them?"

Gentleman John smiled and opened the door. "You think I *want* to get in trouble?"

I stepped into John's studio and once again tried to hide my surprise. At first glance it looked every bit as nice as Wolf Ink. Photo albums, flash on the walls, a dentist's chair. One door was marked as a bathroom for either gender, while another led directly outside, probably used as a business entrance so people didn't have to traipse through John's house. It was a bit strange, seeing the tattoo paraphernalia and having opera cranked on the stereo.

A few photos held a place of pride above his counter, and I stepped toward them.

"Your kids?" I asked.

He walked to my side. "My daughters. Twins. Graduated from high school last year and live in Philly now. Wanted to get to the big city, you know."

I glanced at his hand and didn't see a ring, so I assumed there wasn't a wife around.

"And the boy?" I asked.

"My nephew. More like a son, really. He's still in high school."

"Good-looking kid."

He nodded and turned back to the rest of the room.

"So who's the woman after Wolf?" I asked. "Anyone you know?"

He chuckled. "No. Just a rumor. But it does seem an unlikely rumor if it's not true. Everyone knows Wolf was fiercely loyal to his wife." A grin flashed across his features. "Could be he was too scared of her for infidelity. I would've been."

I didn't have anything to say to that, and began studying the studio.

John watched me for a moment before speaking again. "It's difficult to make a living without stepping across the line every once in a while. So you know, a mom brings in her twelve-year-old who wants a belly button ring? Who am I to say that mother's wrong? And why should I force a busy father to accompany his sixteen-year-old son to a routine sitting so I can see him sign the papers? It saves everyone a lot of time and stress to just look the other way every once in a while. You see what I mean?"

I nodded. Sure. I saw what he meant. Didn't mean I thought it was right. Or even smart. I mean, didn't Mandy say he'd been sued three times last year alone?

I also was beginning to see the small differences between the studios of Wolf Ink and Gentleman John's. A few rags sat on the counter—a no-no for a supposedly sanitary spot. Some dirty tools, a section of flash with a nasty vein, some still-greasy Vaseline cups. The vinyl floor was cracked and stained, and the walls were desperate for a new coat of paint.

But it sounded like it was John's attitude that really needed the work. A tattoo artist that defies the law in one area won't think twice about doing it in another.

I rocked on my heels. "I guess I'll get back to the guys. Should I go out here?" I indicated the business entrance.

"I haven't had a chance to shovel it yet. You'd be better off going out the front."

"Sure. Thanks."

At the front door he reached to open it, and I walked past him.

"So do you hate me now, too?" he asked. "Now that you know I bend the rules?"

I bit my lip and looked out at Rusty, whose face was turned away from the house. "I don't hate you, John. I have no reason to. But I can't say I'll be coming here to get work done."

"Sure. I understand." He closed the door.

Rusty's face was practically crimson when I reached the Explorer. Nick and I stood and watched him, clutching our arms to our coats to try to stay warm, as his face gradually relaxed and his color faded back to normal. His scalp had been frightening with the red underlying the continents.

He took a deep breath, a sob, and dropped his face into his hands. I laid a hand on his knee and left it there while he got himself under control. His shoulders heaved, and I had to look away when a tear trickled out from under his hand. Eventually his breathing returned to normal, and he lifted his head. Nick handed him a clean rag he'd found in my truck, and Rusty blotted his face with it.

Rusty took a huge breath and let it out. "Sorry."

I held up a hand. "Don't. He said some hurtful things."

"He's an asshole," Nick said.

My eyes swerved to his face, surprised at his words. Mandy's words. I just couldn't quite fit them with the actual guy yet. To me John seemed more like a pathetic worm.

"Hearing him talk about them like that..." Rusty's voice crumbled.

"I think you've had enough for today," I said. "Will Becky be home by now? And the girls?"

Nick glanced at his watch. "It's about two-thirty."

Rusty stared out his windshield. "They said they'd be home by supper."

I studied him. He wasn't in any shape to be driving, or spending time alone. "You're coming with us. Till Becky gets home."

"I don't—"

"For a little while, anyway."

He shuddered and allowed himself a glance toward Gentleman John's house. "Okay. Whatever. Just get me out of here."

I lifted my hand from his knee. "Keys?"

He gestured toward the dash, where the key ring lay against the speedometer.

"Drive my truck again?" I asked Nick.

He nodded. "I'll follow."

I shut Rusty's door and circled around to the driver's side, glad to get into the cab and escape the cold breeze. I glanced toward the house, but didn't see any movement. Gentleman John must've already gone back to his opera.

Chapter Twelve

When we pulled into the drive, Lucy and Tess were skipping up the sidewalk, bags in their hands. Tess' eyes went wide, and she gestured frantically for Lucy to open the door.

I stopped the Explorer at the end of the sidewalk while Nick drove past, toward the tractor barn. After parking he jogged back and met me at Rusty's passenger door.

"Guess we're not supposed to see the bags," Nick said, tilting his head toward the house.

"Guess not."

Rusty opened his door, bumping me out of the way.

"You okay?" I asked.

He nodded. His eyes were still red, but other than that he looked normal.

"Nice place," he said.

"Thanks. Come on in." I led Rusty and Nick up the sidewalk and opened the front door.

"Don't look! Don't look!" Tess shrieked.

I covered my eyes. "I'm not looking."

Lucy laughed. "Take that stuff upstairs so Stella doesn't run into something. You can't expect her to—" She stopped suddenly, and all sound ceased. I opened my eyes.

Rusty stood beside me, the recipient of startled stares from Lucy and Tess.

I cleared my throat. "Lucy, Tess, this is my friend Rusty Oldham."

Lucy got herself together and stepped forward, holding out her hand. "Lucy Lapp. Nice to meet you. I work for Stella."

Rusty shook her hand, an amused expression lighting his swollen eyes.

"And this is my daughter, Tess." Lucy turned toward Tess, gesturing her forward. Tess hesitated.

"I've got a daughter about your age," Rusty said. "Name's Rose. You're what? Eight? Nine?"

Tess nodded, her eyes wide. "Eight."

"Rusty's going to hang out here for a bit," I said. "His family's out shopping, and he wants some company."

Lucy caught my eye, realizing it was more than that. "How about some hot chocolate?" she asked.

I nodded. "Sounds great. Here, Rusty, how about you sit on the sofa?"

"Wait!" Tess cried.

Lucy laughed. "That's right. Give Tess a chance to hide her goodies. No peeking!"

I hid my eyes again while paper and plastic rustled, and the upstairs door finally shut.

"Okay," Lucy said. "You can open."

I dropped my hand and showed Rusty to the sofa, in front of a crackling fire. "Why don't you relax. I'll be right back with some cocoa. Nick will sit with you." I looked at Nick, and he nodded.

I hung my coat in the closet and followed Lucy to the kitchen. "Any messages for me? The detective call?"

She shook her head sadly. "Sorry. Oh, I guess you did have one message. Ma Granger called, wanted to make sure you were coming to the Christmas Eve service with us tonight."

I groaned. Usually I loved the service, but this year it would be pushing me.

"You'll come, won't you?" Lucy said. "It might be good for you."

I hung my head, stretching my neck. "I'll think about it."

She waited, and finally said, "Okay."

"What's going on outside?" I asked.

"Everything's fine. I haven't taken hay around this afternoon yet."

"I'll take care of it in a bit. Need any help with the cocoa?"

She reached into the cupboard and pulled out some mugs. "Fill the tea kettlewith water, would you? And put it on the stove."

I took the pot to the sink.

"So who's this guy?" Lucy asked, trying to sound casual.

"Rusty?"

"Um-hmm."

"Friend from way back. Did my cow skull."

"Ah."

"He's a great guy."

"I'm sure he is." Her voice was level.

I tried to hide a smile. "What's the problem here? I thought you were the queen of justice and fair treatment."

Her head jerked up, and her cheeks grew pink. "You have to admit, he is a bit..."

"Colorful?"

She smiled awkwardly. "That's a good word for him. I'm sorry. I hope I wasn't too obvious."

"He's used to it."

"That doesn't excuse it."

"Yeah, well. You weren't expecting a walking globe to come through the front door."

Her face shadowed. "Is he okay?"

"You mean in general?"

She laughed quietly. "No. If he's your friend I'm sure he's fine. I meant he looks like he's been crying."

"He has. He was good friends with Wolf and Mandy."

Was? Is?

"Oh. Well, you go on out and keep him company. I'll bring this in when it's ready."

I joined Rusty in the living room, where his feet rested on the coffee table. His head lay on the sofa's back, but he followed me with his eyes as I sat across from him.

"Where's Nick?" I asked.

He pointed his chin toward the front room. "Said he needed to call his family. I assured him I could handle sitting here by myself for two minutes."

"All right."

The door to the upstairs creaked, and Tess' right eye peered out at me. I smiled at her, but made no move to invite her in, afraid it would scare her away. Rusty either didn't notice, or pretended he didn't.

"I'm assuming you don't know anything about the woman Gentleman John mentioned," I said. "The one who supposedly was after Wolf."

Rusty shook his head wearily. "Can't be true."

"There could've been some lady who wanted him. Doesn't mean he'd have gone for it."

He considered this. "The woman would've been taking her life in her hands with Mandy around."

He was right. Anyone trying to steal Wolf had a suicide wish. But I should still mention it to Shisler. Speaking of which, I should call her.

"Be right back," I said. "Need to make a phone call."

He nodded. I went into the kitchen, where Lucy was dumping cocoa mix into the mugs and the teakettle was starting to rumble. I punched in Shisler's number, which I now knew by heart. As always, she answered immediately.

"Ms. Crown?"

I paused.

"Sorry," she said. "Caller ID. Do you have something for me?"

"I guess you don't have any news."

"Sorry. Did you have an interesting afternoon?"

"I saw John Greene."

"Ah… What did you think?"

"Confusing. Rusty hates him, and my friend Nick didn't like him either. I think he's crooked, but I don't have any real harsh feelings about him."

"Agreed, on both counts. But I have nothing on him for this."

"He have an alibi for the night Mandy was killed?"

"Claims to have been alone all night. Unfortunately, he has no friends—or none who will admit to it, anyway—to back him up. Not that they really could have, I guess, if he was alone."

"Not surprising. If anybody has reason to mess with Wolf and Mandy, it would be him. Claims they cost him his business. Although I've been told there were lots of others who had a hand in his problems, too."

"We're looking into it."

I hesitated.

"Anything else?" Shisler asked.

I forced out the words. "Greene claims there was a woman after Wolf. At least he repeated the rumor."

"After him, like hot for him?"

"Exactly."

"He say who this woman was?"

"He didn't know. And I'm not sure I believe it, anyway. I certainly don't believe Wolf did anything about it. Except maybe tell her to go away."

"Uh-huh."

"I mean it. From what I've seen, and from what others know, Wolf just wouldn't do it."

"We all like to think that about people we know."

"Detective—"

"Look, I hear what you're saying. But I'll have to look into it." She paused. "I'm surprised you even mentioned it, frankly."

"I want you to find Wolf."

"Me, too."

"So go find him." I hung up, feeling dirty. I didn't like casting doubt on my friend's loyalty to his wife.

"You all right?" Lucy asked. She stood in the middle of the kitchen, holding a tray filled with mugs.

"Not really," I said.

She studied my face, then looked toward the living room. "After you."

When we stepped through the doorway, we halted abruptly.

Tess sat beside Rusty on the sofa, a velvet coloring poster laid out on the coffee table. Their heads were bent together over the picture as they carefully filled in the white areas forming intricate butterflies. Lucy's eyebrows rose, and I gave her a smug smile. Lucy ignored me and continued into the room.

"Cocoa, anyone?" she asked.

I followed her in and took my seat across from Rusty. He glanced up and his eyes crinkled. "You've got quite the little artist, here."

Lucy ruffled Tess' hair. "You hear that, Tess? A meaningful compliment from an accomplished tattoo artist such as Rusty."

Tess smirked.

I was picking a mug from the tray when Nick came out from the front room.

"Everybody okay?" I asked. "Mad you're not home?"

He grinned. "Nah. Just glad I'm not on the road in this weather, and that I'm safe."

Safe. Was Wolf safe?

We sipped hot chocolate and enjoyed the fire while Rusty and Tess colored. I kept catching Lucy staring at Rusty's head, but Tess seemed to already have gotten past Rusty's appearance.

When we'd all emptied our mugs and Rusty had put the final touches on a butterfly, he sat back. "Guess I better get home before the womenfolk wonder what's happened to me."

Tess pouted. "Already?"

He laughed and squeezed her shoulder. "We've been coloring for almost an hour."

I blinked and looked at the clock. "Wow. I gotta get outside."

Rusty stood up and stretched. "Thanks for the company. And Tess, maybe you could come over and play with Rose sometime. Would you like that?"

She brightened. "Sure."

"Once Christmas is over. We'll call." He turned to Lucy. "Very nice to meet you. Thanks for the drink."

She stood up. "It's always good to meet Stella's friends."

"Even when they look like me?"

She smiled. "Even then."

Nick stood and shook Rusty's hand. "Thanks for the lessons on tattooing. I know more now than I ever thought I would."

"You decide you want one, you let me know."

"Will do."

I led Rusty to the door. "So how come you all hate Gentleman John so much? I know he bends some rules..."

Rusty bristled. "He doesn't just bend rules—"

I held up my hand. "Quieter, please."

He glanced toward the living room, and lowered his voice. "He *laughs* at rules. The first time he got sued we went to him. Told him how he brought down the whole community. Made us all look bad. He did a lot of bowing and scraping...then turned around and did it again. He doesn't care."

"But he acts—"

"I know. He's *sweet*. He's *polite*." Rusty shook his head. "He gets people *sick*. And it doesn't matter to him. Not one bit." He looked at me. "That's why we hate him."

I nodded. "Okay."

He turned the doorknob. "I appreciate your taking care of me. Thank you."

"Anytime. You seem okay to drive now."

"No problem."

"Keep in touch."

His face darkened briefly. "I'm sure we'll be talking. Thanks again."

I watched as he got his Explorer started and turned around. I went back to the living room, where Lucy was clearing mugs and Tess studied Rusty's butterfly.

Nick poked at the fire. "You folks do anything for Christmas Eve?"

I glanced at the clock. "There's a service at the church we could go to. It's a later time than usual church stuff. Nine o'clock."

"That sounds nice."

Okay. So maybe it would be good to have something to do. Better than sitting on my can waiting for the detective to call.

"I'm going to do some chores outside," I said. "Want to come along?"

He did.

Taking the hay around—in a new shower of snow—turned into checking water supplies, re-covering some pipes with rubberized heating tape and insulation, and checking on the pregnant cows. And all that led into the evening milking. With all three of us working—Lucy, Nick, and me—the process went quickly, and we were back in the house and eating supper in record time. By eight-thirty, Lucy and I had showered and changed, and Tess was dressed for church.

We were waiting in the living room when the front door opened and a large, red-haired man stepped into the foyer.

"Lenny!" Tess squealed. She ran toward the door and launched herself at Lucy's boyfriend, my biker buddy from years back. Lenny laughed and caught her, swinging her in a circle before setting her down and kissing Lucy. Lucy smiled up at him, almost disappearing under his huge arm, while Tess held onto his other hand and danced around, jiggling his arm so hard his beard shook.

"Hey, Len," I said.

"Stella. Glad I could finally make it over. Once the Level Three condition was lifted I had to dig Bart out of his place, seeing how I don't want him doing it himself, plus I gave a hand to the neighbors."

I thought of our friend Bart, who had been on the phone about Wolf and Mandy that day, and who until last month had been going to physical therapy after being attacked by a knife-wielding sleazeball in August. Since summer, Lenny had been running their business, the Biker Barn, a Harley-Davidson dealership, pretty much single-handedly. Only recently had Bart gone back to working full-time.

"We've been okay," I told Lenny. "Bart needs your help more than we do."

"Yeah." His face dropped. "I'm real sorry to hear about Mandy."

"Yeah."

"Wolf, too. Any leads?"

Tess looked up at Lenny in confusion, and he made a face, having forgotten she shouldn't be hearing about our tragedy.

"Sorry," he said to Lucy.

She patted his arm.

"Oh, Stella," he said in a lighter tone. "I hear you have some extra help." His eyes sparkled mischievously.

I glanced toward the downstairs bathroom. "He'll be out in a minute. He's cleaning up after working today."

Lenny frowned at the clock. "Gotta get a move-on, don't we, if we're going to make it to church on time."

"The service isn't till nine. We'll be fine."

He shook his head. "The snow's really coming down again, although not like the other day."

The bathroom door squeaked on its hinges, and Nick emerged, his hair damp from the shower. He wore a pair of khakis and a blue sweater that matched his eyes, and I had to work hard not to stare.

He smiled at Lenny and stepped forward with his hand out. "Nick Hathaway," he said.

Lenny grabbed his hand and shook it. "Lenny Spruce. Nice to meet you." He looked like he was going to say more, but Lucy gently elbowed him, and he grinned, instead.

"You ready to go?" I asked Nick.

"Yup."

"You know you don't have to go, if you don't want to."

"I want to go."

"You're sure?"

"I'm sure."

"Why don't we take my car?" Lucy said quickly. "If you don't mind squishing a bit."

"I don't know," I said. "Lenny doesn't fit too well in your Civic even if he's the only one in it."

Lenny grunted. "Fine. I'll sit in the trunk."

"You won't fit in there, either," Lucy said, handing him the keys. "You drive. I'll sit in the back with Stella and Tess."

I breathed a sigh of relief. Seeing Nick look so good got me back to feeling uncomfortable. At least in the car I wouldn't have to spend the whole ride avoiding close contact with him.

We pulled into the parking lot at Sellersville Mennonite Church in good time, and made our way through the falling snow to the foyer, where we shook the flakes off our hair and clothes. Nick and I squeezed our coats onto the full coat rack while Lucy hurried toward the fellowship hall to drop off a plate of her candy cane cookies. I took a deep breath, saying a small prayer for Wolf now that I was in the church, and hoping I could get through the evening.

"Thank goodness you're here." Zach Granger, my off-and-on fourteen-year-old farm helper, appeared at my side, grabbing my elbow. "Grandma's been asking every two seconds if you made it yet. You'd think the service would be canceled if you didn't come."

I sighed. Ma never lost an opportunity to get me to church, and she knew the special services were her best bet. The Christmas Eve one had always been my favorite, since it didn't start till nine, after milking was done. Little did she know how close I'd come to skipping it that night.

Zach stopped short at the sight of Nick, looking from his face to mine.

"Hi, Zach," Nick said. "Don't know if you remember me. I worked for Stella a few days this summer. Name's Nick."

"Sure. I remember." Zach's body was tight with tension. "You're back?"

Nick smiled. "Just visiting for a few days."

"So, Ma have seats saved for us?" I asked Zach.

"Uh, yeah. Come on." Zach walked toward the sanctuary, the five of us following, receiving small white candles from the usher as we entered. I only had to take one step inside to see why Zach was acting so bizarre.

Abe Granger was sitting next to Ma.

Oh, damn. I'd completely forgotten about calling him back to set up a time to see him, and now here he was, and Nick was with me. Never mind that Abe and I had decided several months ago to be "just friends," I still felt awkward as hell.

Nick stopped beside me, silent. He recognized Abe, I was sure, but had no way of knowing how I felt about him. As far as Nick knew, I could've still been struggling to figure out if Abe was the one for me. I took a deep breath.

"Stella," Lucy whispered behind me. "People are staring."

I forced my feet to move and by-passed Zach to slide in beside Ma. Nick sat next to me while Lucy, Lenny, and Tess scooted into the row behind us, with Zach and his family.

"Hi, Ma," I said quietly.

She patted my knee. "Glad you're here."

I hesitated, closing my eyes for a moment, then leaned forward and looked across her. "Hey, Abe."

He was already looking at me, and from a flick of his eyes, I knew he'd noticed Nick. He smiled, and my heart felt a bit lighter. Not much, but a little.

The sanctuary was beautiful and serene, lit only with candles—on the window sills, the piano, the railings, and, of course, the advent wreath. Only the thick white candle in the middle of the wreath remained to be lit. I couldn't help but think about where Wolf was that night. Most likely somewhere far, far from the soothing atmosphere of candles and the spirit of Christmas. Unless, of course, he was with Mandy.

The service was a quiet affair, with Isaiah's prophetic passages and the New Testament Christmas story interspersed with carols, sung mostly from memory. The unaccompanied singing wrapped around me in the worshipful atmosphere, and I almost forgot the events of the last few days, as well as who was sitting next to me, until we had to open the hymnal for a song and my finger touched Nick's. I quickly withdrew my hand, and he held the book open to "'Twas in the Moon of Wintertime" while I attempted to clear the frog from my throat.

We soon reached the part in the service for the lighting of the Christ candle, and I watched as Vera Longacre, the oldest member of the congregation, and her oldest great-grandchild, Liam, together held a flame to the white candle. The wick hissed as it lighted, and burned brightly. Vera and Liam each took a candle that lay on the table, lit it from the Christ candle, and, after Liam made sure his great-grandmother negotiated the stairs safely, went to opposite sides of the congregation. Liam was on our side, and stopped at the end of each row to light that person's candle. Nick was soon tipping his candle toward the flame, and once it lit, he turned to me. Meeting my eyes, he held out his candle. I touched the tip of my candle to his, and the flame sputtered and came to life. Ma's candle lit from mine, and soon the whole room was alive with the rows of light. The song leader began singing "Silent Night." We all joined in, exiting row by row, until everyone was making their way, candles extinguished, to the fellowship hall.

"What now?" Nick asked quietly.

"Cookies. Homemade ones, mostly. With hot chocolate and coffee."

"Great."

Lucy and Lenny walked in front of us toward the refreshment line, Tess in the middle, swinging on their hands and singing "Rudolph the Red-nosed Reindeer."

Nick grinned. "At least it's about Christmas."

I nodded. "I'm glad. The other day I heard her singing the 'Got a Peanut' song, the one where you end up pretending to puke."

"Hey, Stella."

Nick and I turned to find Abe in line behind us. Abe put out his arms and I hesitated, aware of what Nick must've been feeling. A flicker in Abe's eyes reminded me of our renewed status of friendship, and I stepped into him, hugging him back. It felt good.

When Abe released me, he turned to Nick, holding out his hand. "Good to see you again, Nick."

Nick shook Abe's hand, his face tentative. "You, too."

"Abe moved back to New York City in August," I said.

The tightness around Nick's eyes relaxed a bit. "Really?"

Abe watched Nick's face with interest. "I found I missed the urban life. This rural setting turned out not to be for me." What he wasn't saying was that he and I had found out we weren't for each other.

We'd made our way to the dessert table, and I eyed the array. Somehow I just wasn't hungry for the buffet of sugar and chocolate. I scooted ahead of Abe and Nick toward the end of the table, where I picked up a Styrofoam cup of hot water, and made myself some tea. After throwing away my tea bag, I turned to check out the room. Lucy and Tess were planted at one of the long tables talking animatedly with friends, including representatives of the extensive Granger clan. Lenny sat beside Lucy, his face a mixture of fear and defensiveness. I took the chair beside him.

"It's okay, Len," I said. "They only bite during a full moon."

He winced. "It's just I'm not used to being in a church. Haven't really been to one since I was a kid. And even then it wasn't much."

The chair beside me remained empty, and I looked around to see where Nick and Abe had landed. They stood toward the back of the room, leaning against the wall, their heads bent toward each other in conversation. I wasn't sure I liked that.

"So tell me about Wolf and Mandy," Lenny said.

I recounted for him what happened the day I went for my tattoo, and finished with our visit to Gentleman John.

"Don't know him," Lenny said. "That's probably best, if Rusty and Nick feel that strongly about him."

An image of another guy flashed through my mind. "You know a guy named Tank?" I asked Lenny. "Otherwise known as Matthew Snyder?"

He scrunched up his forehead. "Can't think of him. Bart might. Who is he?"

"A guy who was one of the last to see Wolf and Mandy, who's made a habit of preying on tattoo artists."

He frowned.

"Hi, Lenny. Stella." Peter Reinford, the pastor of Sellersville Mennonite, stood behind us, hands resting on our chairs.

"Hey, Pete," I said.

Lenny nodded.

"I'm very sorry to hear about your friend," Peter said. "Lucy told me about it."

I looked down at my tea. "Thanks."

"Have you heard anything more about the husband?"

I shook my head.

"If there's anything I can do, please let me know. Do they have a church? A minister I could contact?"

I shrugged. One of the many things I didn't know about the Moores.

"Hey," I said, looking up, "you know anything about a guy named Matthew Snyder? Goes by the name Tank? He's supposedly from a Mennonite family."

Peter frowned. "Can't think right off, but I could ask around. Who is he?"

"A guy who could very well have something to do with the Moores'…problems. I don't know anything else about him except he's been in jail until last year."

He nodded. "I'll see what I can do."

"Thanks."

"Well," Peter said, "it's nice to see you both here tonight. Ma drag you in?"

I smiled. "Not really. But it was a good guess."

Lenny hooked a thumb toward Lucy. "She's the one dragged me."

Pete slapped him on the back. "Glad to hear it." He moved on to the next group of people, and Lenny let out a big breath, rubbing his forehead.

"You ready to go?" Lucy asked, leaning across Lenny. He rested a hand on her back, and she smiled up at him. "I think Tess is about to hit the wall."

I held up my cup. "Let me finish this."

"Sure."

I drained my tea, glancing around to where Abe and Nick were talking. I sat for a moment, watching Nick as he laughed at something Abe was saying. It was disconcerting, but nice, to see him in this familiar place. Nick drank the last of his coffee, and as he turned toward the wastebasket, his eye caught mine. For a long moment we looked at each other, until I broke contact.

"Okay," I said to my tablemates. "Should we head out?"

I stood up and pushed my chair in, indicating to Nick with a tilt of my chin that we were leaving. He said one last thing to Abe, and they shook hands again. Abe waved to me, and while I wanted to talk with him some more, it just wasn't the right time.

"Stella!" Peter Reinford came trotting toward me. "I found something out about that man."

"Already?"

He smiled. "If you have the right resources, it doesn't take long." He turned and held a hand out toward an old man, sitting at the end of the far table. "Jonathan Long. Knows most people in the local Mennonite community. Been around a lot longer than most, too. Says you can go over to talk with him, if you want."

"Great. Thanks."

He nodded, his lips tight. "Hope it helps."

"Be right with you," I said to Lucy.

She smiled. "Take your time. We're fine."

Lenny didn't look so sure.

I made my way across the room toward Mr. Long, squeezing through the folding chairs and trying not to trample the little kids who ran from table to trash can. I finally got to the end of the table and stood in front of the old man.

"Mr. Long?"

He'd been following me the whole way with his eyes, and now he patted the chair next to him. I sat, taking in his thin hair, the folds of skin on his leathery face, and the bright blue eyes sparkling out from sunken sockets.

"Pastor Reinford informs me you can use my help," he said.

"Sure can. Anything you could tell me about Matthew Snyder's family or whereabouts is more than I know now."

He settled back in his chair, his hands relaxed, looped over the head of a cane. "Matthew Snyder's grandfather was my second cousin. Isaac Snyder. Grew up in Blooming Glen, never moved away. His son, Stan, moved to Dublin, not far, and had seven kids. Matthew was one of the middle ones. Third, I think."

He reached out a gnarly hand to fumble with his tea. I restrained myself from helping him, even though the cup shook with his effort. The tea made it to his mouth and back without incident, and I let out the breath I was holding.

"Somehow," Mr. Long continued, "Matthew went bad, started bullying kids already when he was in elementary school. Family about went out of their minds trying to set him straight."

"And now?"

"I'm getting there, I'm getting there." He took another sip of tea while I tried not to grind my teeth.

"His poor mother keeps me informed." He grinned slyly. "Well, I ask to be kept informed. And she let me know when he got out of jail last year. Those years about killed her, having him in prison, although I can't see how it's better now he's out and getting into trouble."

I glanced up to see Nick leaning against the doors to the foyer. I held up a finger to say I'd be there in a minute, and he nodded, turning and disappearing behind the double doors.

"Do you know where he is now?" I asked. "The cops can't seem to find him, and his family's not revealing his whereabouts."

Long's eyes crinkled. "Now where does a man go, if he's not home with his mother at Christmas?"

I understood. Another woman, replacing Mom. "Who is she? And why hasn't the family told the cops?"

"Name's Mary Detlor. As for the family not telling, I'd say it has a lot to do with Ms. Detlor herself. It's kind of the last straw for his folks, and they hate to admit she even exists. You'd understand if you saw her. She isn't any Sunday School teacher, that's for sure."

"And where do I see her?"

He reached again for his tea. "Now that, young lady, I'm afraid I don't know."

I squinted at him, not sure if he was being straight with me. He seemed to know everything *else*.

He held up his hand, hitting me in the knee with his cane. "Honest. I'd swear on the Bible if I weren't a Mennonite."

I laughed. "All right. I appreciate your help."

His face darkened. "Can't say for sure if it was Matthew or not who did this thing, but if it was, I don't care if he is family."

I thanked him and left. Nick met me in the foyer, where I shrugged into my coat.

"Got what you needed?" he asked.

"I think so."

He waited, leaning an arm against the coat rack. "So you and Abe..."

"We're good friends, just like always." I zipped up my coat, not looking at him.

He stood still, his ski jacket hanging by his side. "But you tried to be more."

I took a moment, pulling on my gloves. "We tried. It didn't work."

"May I ask why?"

I finally looked at him. "Because I know what feels right. And that didn't."

He studied my face, but when he opened his mouth to say something else, I pushed my way through the church's doors and walked quickly to Lucy's car.

Chapter Thirteen

"Still think Tess is up for a stop at Bart's?" Lenny asked.

Lucy looked down at her daughter, who smiled happily, if not energetically.

"Sure," Lucy said. "As long as it's a quick stop. We have things to do at home yet before bed."

Bart's light was on, since Lenny had warned him we'd be stopping by. He greeted us at the door, and I hugged him tentatively, wary of the chest wound he'd suffered that summer.

"Nick Hathaway," I said, gesturing to him. "Bart Watts."

Bart looked Nick up and down while shaking his hand. "I guess you look tough enough to handle her."

Nick laughed, and I gently slugged Bart's arm.

"Come on in," Bart said, ducking any more punches. His living room was free of Christmas decorations, except for a ceramic nativity set which covered the top of his coffee table amidst a spray of straw. The air smelled marvelously of lasagna and garlic bread, and Bart saw me breathing it in.

"Neighbor brought over supper," he said. "Thought I'd need my energy if I'd be getting to mass this evening."

"And did you get there?" Lenny asked.

"Sure. Still not too good with all the kneeling and standing, but I'm close."

"And how about that Latin?" Lenny asked. "I had to go the Menno way, but at least I understood what was going on."

"We don't do Latin anymore, you dumbass. It's all in English. Even you can understand that."

"Okay, okay," Lucy said. "It's Christmas Eve, remember? Love and laughter, and all that."

"What?" Bart and Lenny said innocently.

I snorted.

"Here," Tess said. She thrust a package toward Bart, and he placed a hand on his chest.

"For me?"

"Open it!" Tess jumped up and down, shaking the floor.

"Give him a chance, honey," Lucy said, smiling.

Bart made his way to a chair and eased himself down before tearing open the paper. "Oh, wow. Thanks." A set of the three wise men, hammered in metal, stood a foot tall each and gleamed in the lamplight. "Ten Thousand Villages?"

Lucy nodded. "They're from Guatemala."

I glanced at Nick. "Ten Thousand Villages is a Mennonite-run business. Gives fair working wages to artists in poor countries. Lucy likes to shop there."

He nodded. "I've heard of it."

"They're beautiful," Bart said. "Thank you."

"Now," Lenny said. "What can you tell us about Matthew Snyder?"

"Who?"

"Tank," I said. "Snyder's his real name."

"Oh, that asshole. Whoops, sorry, Lucy."

She smiled tightly.

"From what I know," Bart said, "Tank harassed tattoo artists, got put away back in 1996. That Detective Shisler says he's out now. Nobody told me."

"It was suggested tonight that I check out his girlfriend's place," I said. "You happen to know a woman named Mary Detlor?"

Bart's head snapped up. "Know her? Sure. Hardcore biker chick, pretty burned out. Not one of us. Met her at Lansdale Bike Night a couple years ago. Lives in Sellersville, if I remember right. She's hooked up with Tank?"

"That's what my source tells me."

"And your source?"

I smiled. "Old Mennonite guy."

"Figures."

"You know where she lives?"

"Nope. Give me a second, though." He pushed himself up and moved slowly into his kitchen, where he opened a drawer, ruffled through some papers, and pulled out the three-inch thick phone book. "Nope," he said. "Not in here." He grabbed his phone and started punching buttons. "Hey, it's Bart," he said into the receiver. "You know where Mary Detlor's living these days? Uh-huh. Which house? Oh, okay. Just wondering. Thanks, man."

He came back in and leaned on his chair, a pleased smile on his face. "Lives on Old Mill Road in Sellersville. You'll know her place by the beat-up Mustang parked on the street. Her truck and bike are in the garage."

"Wow," I said. "You work fast."

"Just have to know who to ask."

Like Peter Reinford. If you have the right resources…

I looked at Lucy. "Any chance we could stop at Detlor's place on the way home?"

She sighed, but nodded. "It's for Wolf and Mandy, right?"

"Yup. The cops have yet to run this guy down, and this seems as good a bet as any. I don't want to send the police out on Christmas Eve if it's a wild goose chase."

Lucy studied Tess, who was curled up on Bart's couch, her feet tucked under her. Lucy lifted a shoulder. "Eh, what's ten more minutes?" She squinted at me. "Shouldn't be longer than that, right?"

"I just want to see if he's there."

"All right."

"Sorry. Guess we should've brought two cars."

She waved that away. "There was no way to know. We'll be all right."

"Oh, Bart," I said. "Have you heard any rumors about Wolf having—" I glanced at Tess "—having interests other than Mandy?"

He frowned. "No way."

"Didn't think so. But Gentleman John said something today, and I at least needed to ask."

"Gentleman John's an assho... He's a liar."

"Okay. Well, Merry Christmas. Hate to beg favors and run, but—"

"Hey, Princess, it's good to see you at all. And I'll be hitting the hay soon anyway."

Lenny loomed over him. "Now don't you be shoveling that walk tomorrow. I'll be by when I can."

Bart rolled his eyes. "You'd think I was a baby."

Lucy laughed and kissed him on the cheek. "You know it's because he loves you."

"Oh, yuck," Lenny said.

"Besides," Bart said to Lenny, "you know my cousin's picking me up in the morning to spend Christmas with the relatives."

Lucy tugged Tess up from the couch and Tess turned to wrap her arms around Bart's neck. "Merry Christmas, Uncle Bart."

His face sure lit up at that.

Nick shook Bart's hand again, and we trooped out to the Civic, where Lenny had to brush the snow from the windshield.

"One more stop," I said. "Then we can go home."

Chapter Fourteen

"You sure this is the place?" Nick peered out the passenger window.

I tapped on the glass. "There's the Mustang Bart mentioned. And the garage." I pulled my gloves on. "Guess there's only one way to find out."

"You ain't going yourself," Lenny said.

"Come on, Len. What do you think's gonna happen?"

"Don't know. Don't care. Either me or Nick come with you, or you don't go."

Like he could stop me getting out my door and heading toward the house. But it was Christmas Eve. "Fine. You can flip for it."

I opened the door, shutting it quickly against the cold breeze, and started up the walk. A car door opened and closed behind me, but I didn't look back.

The doorbell at the top of three icy steps was a hazardous-looking contraption that might've electrocuted me if I'd touched it wrong. I banged on the door, instead, and Lenny stepped up beside me.

"Lost the coin toss, huh?" I said.

"Nah. Just told Nick I was coming. He didn't argue too much."

"That's because he knows I can handle a simple house call by myself."

Lenny grunted.

I banged on the door again, and finally heard some footsteps. I straightened my backbone, not sure what to expect from what Jonathan Long and Bart had told me about Mary Detlor. But it was Tank who opened the door, and I gasped at the sewn-up wound traveling from his forehead, through his eyebrow, and across the bridge of his nose. There must've been two dozen stitches.

"No charities," he said. "Get lost."

Lenny stepped forward to put his considerable bulk over the threshold. Tank squinted, and a shiver of unease ran up my spine at the sight of the two of them matching up.

"Come on, Len," I said. "There's nothing else for us here."

We had what we'd come for. We knew where Tank was. But I sure was curious about that cut on his face.

Lenny met Tank's eyes for a moment longer before stepping back. I was turning to go when someone called from inside.

"Who is it, Matty? Ain't you gonna ask 'em in?"

I just had time to register the slurred, sultry voice before the woman appeared at Tank's side. I tried not to gape at her, but Lenny's feelings were broadcast loud and clear on his face. Besides the woman's appearance—ratty to the point of slutty bag lady—the waves of alcohol radiating from her were almost enough to make me tipsy. A hideous tattoo of a devil molesting a naked woman covered most of her arm, which was bare to the strap of her filthy tank top, and tattooed black liner surrounded brown eyes that would've been beautiful had they not been bloodshot and watery.

"Hey, big guy," she said to Lenny.

Lenny cleared his throat, but was saved from replying by Tank pushing the woman back with his arm. "It's nobody for you, Mary."

She swayed against him and ducked under his arm, grinning slyly. "Nobody for you, either, 'less you like 'em big." She said this last while looking at me, and a touch of scorn marked her voice.

I wasn't that big, really, but I guessed she was at least three inches shorter than my five-nine, and God, was she scrawny. The brown mess of split ends on her head looked ready to topple her over if Tank hadn't held her upper arm.

"We're just looking for somebody's house," I said. "Sorry to bother you."

Tank looked at me. "Who are you, anyhow? You look familiar."

Shit. I didn't want him running before the cops could get there.

"Don't know why I'd look familiar," I said.

He studied me some more, but finally shook his head. Either he had a bad memory or he'd been sharing Mary's liquor. Or he'd been so mad at Wolf Ink he hadn't even noticed I was there.

"Come on, hon," Mary said to Lenny. "Why don't you come in, have some of the sweet Christmas pie I made just for tonight. I make a mean pie, don't I, Matty, baby? Bet I could win a blue ribbon if I entered a contest." She swiveled her shoulders, making me wonder if she was talking about an actual pie or something else altogether.

Lenny turned a bit green, but I guess it could've been the light shining through the doorway.

"We really have to get going," I said. "But thanks for the invitation."

She turned to me. "I didn't invite you."

How true.

Lenny and I picked our way down the steps, trying not to slip on the unsalted cement.

"Wait a minute," Tank said. "I know who you are. You got a tattoo at Wolf's place."

Crap.

I turned around, pasting a look of innocence on my face. "We were there at the same time?"

"Couple days ago," he said. "Monday."

"Sorry. I must've been zoned out."

His nose twitched. "Jackass Wolf wouldn't do me that day. I wanted to have it done for Christmas."

"He was all booked up?" I tried to sound sympathetic.

Tank snarled and shook his head. "I'll go back. He'll do me then for sure."

Sounded like a threat to me, but I was confused. Tank talked like Wolf wasn't missing. I considered whether or not I should say anything, but figured if he really hadn't killed Mandy he was too stupid to realize he'd be a suspect.

"You haven't heard?" I asked.

His eyes were blank. "Heard what?"

"Wolf's missing. And Mandy's dead."

He stared at me. "You shittin' me?"

"Nope."

"Well, goddamn. I guess somebody got to them before I could."

Lenny made a sound beside me, and I stepped forward, cutting off whatever approach he was going to make.

"You didn't know?" I asked, trying to keep the surprise from my voice.

He shrugged. "I been holed up here since Monday, with this and all." He pointed to his stitches. "Had a helluva headache. And I don't watch no TV that has news."

Lovely. I tried not to imagine what kind of shows he favored.

"So who done it?" he asked. "And where's Wolf?"

"I don't know."

He smiled nastily down at Mary, whose attention seemed to have left us and gone to some unfocused space in her front yard.

"Bet it has something to do with Wolf's other chick," Tank said.

I sucked in my breath. "What?"

"Like he was a saint. Oh, no, Wolf never does nothing wrong."

I took another step forward. "Who is she? What's her name?"

He made a face at that, like how was he to know? "Don't ask me. Just saw her one time with Wolf, at the Bay Pony Inn. Took Mary here out for her birthday, and wouldn't you know, there he was with this other broad, candlelight dinner and all."

I glanced at Mary, thinking there was no way she would ever fit in at a posh restaurant like that.

Tank followed my gaze. "She cleans up good when she ain't hammered."

I pulled my eyes from Mary. "This other woman. You never saw her before?"

"Why would I have? It's not like me and Wolf run together."

My frustration mounted. "You can't tell me anything about her?"

"Well, I didn't say that. Because yeah, there was one thing that stood out."

"And what was that?"

He touched his cheek. "She had a tattoo here. Of a butterfly."

The cold in the night air was suddenly warm compared to the ice in my chest.

"What?" Lenny said quietly. "You know her?"

I swallowed. "Let's go, Lenny. Now."

We turned to walk away, and Lenny grabbed my arm as I stumbled toward the car.

"You never did say what charity you were with," Tank called after us.

Lenny glanced at me, questions lighting up his face.

"Benevolence fund," I said over my shoulder. "For the cops."

I didn't have to turn around to know what Tank thought of that.

Chapter Fifteen

Nick's cell phone was the closest one at hand, but I couldn't see calling Shisler with Tess hanging onto every word. Even if she did appear to be in a stupor. Besides, I wasn't sure I was ready to share about Wolf's "other woman" with anyone but the detective. No matter what Tank had seen, I wanted to give Jewel Spurgeon, along with the butterfly on her cheek, a chance to tell me why she was on a candlelit date with Wolf.

Tess revived by the time we reached the farm, and beat us all into the house. When I stepped inside, she thrust a bulky Christmas stocking into my hands before turning to Nick and pushing one into his.

"For me?" Nick asked.

Lucy opened the closet to hang up her coat. "Can't have anyone without a stocking on Christmas Eve, can we?"

Nick's eyes shot to Tess. "But won't Santa wonder where the stockings are, if they're not hanging by the fireplace tonight?"

Tess giggled. "Santa's not *real.*" Her eyes went wide. "You knew that, didn't you?"

I looked at Nick. "I'm afraid you just burst his Christmas bubble, Tess."

"Not really," Nick said, ruffling Tess' hair. "I've known since I was at *least* twelve that Santa came in the guise of my mother."

I cleared my throat. "Before we dive into these wonderful stockings, can I make a phone call?"

Lucy glanced at me. "The detective?"

"I want to tell her where to find the lovely Mr. Snyder." And tell her the bombshell he'd dropped.

I gestured toward the fireplace. "Why don't the rest of you get a fire going?"

Lucy nodded. "I'll find some newspaper, if there's any left that hasn't been recycled."

I hesitated. "Can you see if anybody's dropped some off in the past few days? I wouldn't mind seeing them, since we don't get our own."

I remembered the paper at Gentleman John's Tattoos with its headline asking, "Has Anyone Seen This Man?"

She nodded with understanding. "I'll check."

I went to the kitchen phone, Lenny's eyes following me with curiosity, and punched in Shisler's number. She answered after the usual one ring.

"Stella?"

"It's me. I've got some news." I told her about Tank, and where I found him.

"Good work, Stella. Thank you. Anything else?"

I opened my mouth to tell her about Jewel. I was planning on telling her. I really was. But when it came down to it, my voice refused to work.

"Stella?" Shisler said.

"No," I said. "Nothing else."

"You sure?"

"Except Tank's got a huge gash on his face. Stitched up, but it looks awful."

"Hmm. We'll check him out. I'll send somebody right away to secure him. Again, good work."

I said good-bye and hung up before she could wish me a Merry Christmas. It was already a struggle on Christmas Eve.

I felt guilty as hell for not telling her about Jewel, but I wanted to talk to Jewel myself before blowing up trouble for her. I took a deep breath and went into the living room, where I found Lucy lighting the fire and the others sitting on the floor playing Uno.

Tess jumped up. "Are you ready?"

"Sure," I said. Somehow I managed a smile.

Lucy tossed a paper onto my lap. "This is the only one I could find about the Moores."

It was the same one I'd seen at Gentleman John's. I skimmed it, and it was really just a run-down of everything I already knew. Oh well. Lenny settled himself on a chair behind Lucy and rested his hands on her shoulders while she snuggled between his knees. I sat on the couch, at the opposite end as Nick. He looked a question at me, and I shook my head. I certainly didn't want to talk about my phone call or the visit to Mary Detlor's house.

"So why open stockings on Christmas Eve?" Nick asked Lucy, taking his eyes from me. "Why not Christmas Day?"

Lucy shrugged. "We've always done it this way. We raised Tess to believe that while Santa is a fun part of Christmas, he doesn't really come down our chimney and leave presents. Plus," she said with a slight grin, "it's another way to spread out the opening of gifts."

I watched her while she talked, and recognized the sadness flitting across her face. It had been two years, almost to the day, that her husband, Brad, had died. And no matter the wonderful man sitting with her tonight, she still missed the man who had been hers before. Seeing her grief reminded me of my own, something I'd been struggling with long before the situation with Wolf and Mandy. But I was determined to shove thoughts of Howie to the side, so as not to color the evening with my own sorrow. I knew Howie would have enjoyed Lucy and Tess, but since they came only because he was gone, he'd never known they existed.

We took our time, opening one gift at a time, deciding who went first by various tests: shoe size, birthdays, alphabetical order of middle names. Lucy and Tess had filled my stocking with all sorts of treats, from a new container of Bag Balm for my chapped hands, to a decadent bar of dark chocolate with almonds.

Nick's stocking, bought and filled within the past day—and probably what Lucy and Tess had been smuggling inside just that afternoon—held gum and candy, as well as a brand new pack of Dutch Blitz playing cards. His face had lost some of the tentativeness of earlier in the evening at church, and he smiled brightly. I wasn't sure I liked how good it felt to have him in my house.

I glanced around the room at its occupants and couldn't stop the warmth that seeped from my toes to my head. I missed Howie desperately, but knew also that I was lucky to be surrounded by these people. With a flash, I realized I even liked sharing my home. I'd always figured, ever since the August tornado took the garage and its accompanying apartment, that we'd rebuild it as it had been. That Lucy and Tess would move back out when it was ready. But now I wasn't so sure. I was finding it somehow comforting to come inside and find Tess at the computer, or Lucy in the kitchen whipping up something to eat.

I liked having someone to share the end of each day.

Tess shrieked as she opened a present from Lenny and discovered it was a new Hello Kitty diary. I could only imagine the pre-teen ramblings that would soon grace its pages, and laughed to myself. Nick caught my eye, making my laugh stick in my throat. I hadn't stuffed Nick's stocking with any presents. I wouldn't have known what to get him if I'd even attempted it. And while he had sneaked a couple of things into Tess' stack, mine had held nothing from him.

The floor was soon littered with scraps of wrapping paper and packaging, and I sat back into the sofa, my eyelids drooping. Tess' face, while lighted with happiness, also betrayed signs of weariness. It was almost eleven-thirty, after all. Tess climbed onto Lenny's lap, where she snuggled into the crook of his arm and twisted his beard around her fingers. When Lucy turned to watch them I again read sadness in her face, but also saw the newfound joy of Lenny, and what he represented.

Lucy laid a hand on Tess' leg. "Time for bed, sweetheart."

Tess wriggled deeper into Lenny's lap.

"Want me to carry you up?" Lenny asked.

She nodded into his neck.

"Okay, then, darlin'. Hang on."

Lucy stood while Lenny heaved himself out of the chair, Tess hanging around his neck.

"You okay?" Lucy asked him.

"You kidding? This little bitty thing?"

She smiled. It was true that Tess could easily wrap up in one of Lenny's shirts if the occasion warranted it. Lenny wasn't straining a muscle to hold her, and the stairs would hardly offer a challenge.

The three of them were soon gone upstairs, and Nick and I stared silently into the fire. We sat on the couch, the middle cushion separating us like a wall, and while my breathing stayed its normal speed, I heard every pulse in my veins.

A loud crack from the fireplace brought my heart to my throat, and I scooted off the couch and began picking up the paper scraps, tossing them into the fire. Nick joined me, and we were almost done when the door to the stairs opened and Lenny and Lucy stepped out, Lenny heading toward the front door and closet.

"She asleep already?" I asked Lucy.

She laughed quietly. "Practically. But then I about am, too." She met Lenny at the door, where he enveloped her in a hug. He let her go and took a step back into the room.

"Nice to meet you, Nick," he said. "Don't know if I'll see you tomorrow or not, but have a Merry Christmas."

Nick walked forward and clasped Lenny's outstretched hand. "Same to you. You've got a nice lady to share it with."

Lenny smiled at Lucy, who returned the expression full-force.

"That I do, Nick," Lenny said. "That I do." He kissed Lucy and opened the front door. "'Night, Stella."

"'Night. Careful on those roads."

"Always." He shut the door quietly behind him.

"Well," Lucy said. "That's it for me, too."

I picked up another handful of paper and flung it in the fire.

"Thanks for all the presents," Nick said. "And for having a stocking for me at all."

She stepped forward and planted a kiss on his cheek. "You're welcome. We're glad to have you here." She walked past me and opened the stairwell door. "Goodnight, Stella."

I met her eyes, and although I'm sure she read desperation in mine, she smiled warmly and disappeared up the stairs, shutting the door firmly behind her.

I continued throwing trash into the fire until there was none left to find. I stood and turned, only to discover Nick beside me.

"Stella," he said. He put his hands on the sides of my face, leaned in, and kissed me.

I planted my hands on his chest, ready to push him away, but stopped.

I was remembering a kiss four months before, in that very room. A kiss with Abe. A kiss that felt anything but how a kiss should feel.

This kiss was everything.

I slid my hands upward on Nick's chest, circling my arms around his neck, and returned the kiss with more energy than I thought I possessed at the moment. My breath came deeper from within me now, and as my heart raced I pulled myself closer to Nick, feeling his response in his arms and kiss.

But just when I decided I couldn't pull myself away, Nick stepped back. He reached up to grab my hands, and lowered them between us, resting them on his chest.

"What?" I said, more snappishly than I'd meant.

He smiled. "I'd say that felt right."

I raised my eyebrows. "But?"

"But it's late."

I stepped back from him, while he kept holding my hands. It *was* late. But I hadn't minded until he'd mentioned it.

He pulled gently, bringing me back toward him. "I'll see you in the morning." He kissed me again, more lightly this time, then let go of my hands and disappeared into the front room, where the couch awaited him.

I looked around, wondering what had happened and why I'd missed it. I closed the doors of the fireplace and went up to bed. Alone.

Chapter Sixteen

Christmas Day began with the smell of scrapple. Not a usual smell for that holiday, but a welcome one. After my alarm pulled me from a deep sleep and I'd put on jeans and beaten Lucy to the bathroom, I found Nick in the kitchen, frying up southeastern PA's version of breakfast meat. One of those things you eat but try not to think about too much, like hot dogs. But put a little apple butter on a slab of scrapple, and it's pretty close to early morning heaven.

"Couldn't sleep?" I asked Nick.

He turned away from the stove long enough to smile and warm me up from my stomach to the farther reaches of my body.

"Thought I'd start Christmas off with something good."

I thought of something that would start it off even better, but refrained from suggesting it, not sure how it would go over, or how I'd feel about it afterward.

"It smells great," I said. "Want help?"

"Just with eating it. Go ahead and grab a plate. I've got some ready."

I had just stuck my knife in the jar of apple butter when Lucy came in and spied the goods.

"Wow," she said. "And a Merry Christmas to you, too."

Nick laughed and pointed at the table with his spatula. "Have a seat."

Lucy gave me a look of delight and pulled out a chair. "You seen the news yet?"

My stomach jumped. "No. Why?"

She inhaled sharply. "Sorry. Didn't mean to scare you. I assumed the detective hadn't called, since I hadn't heard the phone, and wondered if there was anything on the news about Wolf. Or if the weather's better down in Virginia."

I put my knife down, my appetite gone, and went out to the living room, where the early news had nothing new to report. Didn't even mention Mandy's murder, let alone Wolf's status. You'd think a little kid being parentless on Christmas would've garnered more airtime. The one piece of relevant news was that the storm had moved on in Virginia. Roads were open, and Nick's family and fellow Virginians were free to slip and slide around the highways.

Lucy appeared at my elbow. "Sorry. Didn't mean to ruin breakfast."

I bent my neck side to side and felt it pop. "S'okay. Maybe it'll make me hungrier for lunch. You're cooking, right?"

"Yeah. Lenny will be over mid-morning to help with that. And to help open presents, of course."

"Of course."

Nick came out from the kitchen, apparently having heard our conversation. "I can help with the milking again, Lucy, if you want to get started in the kitchen."

Lucy looked at me.

"Fine," I said. "He's practically a pro by now. By this evening I'll let him do it himself."

Nick grimaced.

"What?" I said.

He stuck his hands in his back pockets. "I need to go home today."

I stared at him. After what happened last night, he was *leaving?*

He sighed. "I talked with Liz, my oldest sister, last night. Mom really needs us all there. You know, the first Christmas without Dad."

Lucy nodded. "You should go."

I glared at her, all the while knowing she was right. I looked down at my fingernails and concentrated on pushing back a dried cuticle. "When?"

"I was thinking after lunch. That way I could be home for the evening. If that's okay."

"Of course it's okay. I'm not going to keep you here if you want to leave."

"I meant is it okay if I stay for dinner."

"Oh." I was being a jerk, and I knew it. Of course his family would want him home. Just like I'd been glad when Lucy decided to stay with me for Christmas instead of heading off to Lancaster.

Lucy laid her hand on Nick's arm. "We'd love to have you stay for dinner. We have plenty of food."

He looked at me. "Stella?"

"Stay as long as you can. But I'm sure you're right. You belong there at least part of the day."

He smiled with relief, whether because I'd said it was all right or hadn't bitten his head off again, I wasn't sure.

We worked companionably in the barn, as we had the day before, and held off from repeating last night's events. We were part way through when the phone rang. I dropped my sponge in my bucket and jogged to my office. When I picked up the receiver, Lucy was already on the extension in the house, telling Detective Shisler I was in the barn.

"I'm here," I said.

"Oh," Lucy said. "Good." I heard the click as she hung up.

"You get Tank?" I asked Shisler.

"We did. He's supposedly 'helping us with our inquiries,' but won't say anything until his lawyer shows up. Try getting a lawyer here on Christmas morning—I have a feeling Mr. Snyder's going to be our guest for turkey and filling."

"Lovely for you."

"Tell me about it. Now I have a question. We've been trying to check up on his movements on Monday. What time would you say he left Wolf Ink?"

I considered this. "I don't know. Four-thirty, maybe? Quarter till five?"

"Would work. The only thing he'll tell us is that at six he was in the North Penn ER having those stitches sewn across his face. He claims he drove away from Wolf Ink—he says right after their disagreement—and slid his truck into a car parked along the road on the other side of town. Banged his face on his steering wheel and received a total of twenty-eight stitches."

"Thought it looked like a lot of X's. Do we know for sure he wrecked his face on his truck? Mandy or Wolf couldn't have done it?"

"We checked out his steering wheel, but he'd already cleaned it up. The front end of the truck is damaged, but there's no way of knowing when exactly that happened. And we have yet to find the other vehicle. It's possible the owner moved it from where Snyder claims he hit it, but nobody's filed a report."

"So he could've gotten cut in a fight? Like if he'd kidnapped Wolf and Wolf attacked him? It could even have happened in the truck, or earlier, before he hit Mandy. She wouldn't have hesitated to whack him one."

"We're certainly considering that. We're hoping to have a technician go over his truck for signs of Wolf, but seeing how today's a holiday it's hard to find anyone, and like I said, Snyder's already cleaned it out."

"Tank's big enough to overpower Mandy and then Wolf."

Shisler made a grunt of agreement.

"Much more likely than John Greene," I said. "Gentleman John's kind of a weenie."

She let out a laugh. "You're right about that. Unless, of course, he had a weapon. Then all bets are off."

Of course. And it wouldn't surprise me if Greene had some sort of pearl-handled pistol we didn't know about. That or a fancy sword.

"Tank acted like he didn't even know Wolf was missing," I said. "And certainly not that Mandy's dead. Not that he cared—he seemed glad to hear they'd had trouble."

"Yeah," Shisler said. "No matter what he did, he's still a jerk."

I wondered why he hadn't said anything about Wolf's "other woman." Probably just being as unhelpful as possible.

"What about Tank's girlfriend?" I asked. "Think she could've helped him?"

"What a sorry specimen," Shisler said. "Mary Detlor's had dealings with us but nothing ever violent. More alcohol and illegal substance issues."

Surprise, surprise.

"He won't say anything else?" Like Wolf having a girlfriend with a butterfly tattooed on her cheek? I held my breath.

"Not a word. He's shut up like an iced-over car door. Why?"

Why? "Just wondered." Pangs of guilt shot through my stomach.

A sound of something dropping in the parlor brought me back to the present.

"Anything else?" I asked. "I'd better get back to work."

"Not right now. I'll call if I have any more questions. Until then, we'll keep on Mr. Snyder." She hung up without acknowledging Christmas again, and I trudged back to the parlor, feeling even guiltier for holding back on her than I did the night before. I swallowed the lump in my throat and tried to concentrate on the cows.

"They get him?" Nick asked.

"Yup."

He let it go at that, seeming to realize I didn't want to talk. When we got back into the house around eight, after making sure everything was ready for the milk truck to empty our tank later that morning, Lenny was already there, and Tess was about to explode with impatience.

"They're here! They're here!" she screamed into the kitchen. "Time to open presents!"

Lucy called from the kitchen. "Hold your horses, honey! We're just about ready to put the turkey in the oven."

"Oh, turkey." Nick made salivating sounds, and Tess giggled and grabbed his hand.

"Come on. Let me show you which one's yours."

He threw me a glance, and I shrugged. I hadn't put anything under the tree for him. I let him be dragged off by the eager youngster, and went into the kitchen.

"Hey, Len," I said. "I guess I should say Merry Christmas but with all that's happened I can't really mean it."

"And a not-really-meant Merry Christmas to you, too." He slid the roaster into the oven and shut the door. "Any word on Tank?"

I told him about my conversation with Shisler.

"I guess it's good they have him," he said.

"I guess."

"And I suppose she didn't have any more news on Wolf's whereabouts?"

I shook my head. My night had been interrupted with dreams of where he might be, and none of the situations were good. I hated to think about Billy, wondering where his parents were this Christmas morning.

I leaned on the doorjamb. "Bart didn't hear anything, either?"

Lenny grabbed a dishrag to wipe some stray pieces of onion off his shirt. "Nope. Nobody knows anything. Lots of guessing, but nothing for sure."

Tess appeared in the door. "Are you guys coming or not?"

"We're coming, we're coming," Lucy said.

We trooped into the front room, where we'd set up the Christmas tree to get full use of the front windows. Any vehicle driving down the road in the dark got a great view of the white lights strung around our tree. Lucy was no skimper when it came to lights. We hardly even needed the lamps on in the room.

Tess had Nick situated on the floor, where he lay on his side, resting on his elbow. Lenny and Lucy took the sofa, which saved me from having to sit where Nick had been sleeping the last few nights. Nick smiled up at me and patted the floor in front of him. I hesitated, then crossed the room to sit by his feet, my knees pulled up in front of me. He scootched his legs so they were touching my back, and I sat up straighter.

"Okay, Santa," Lucy said. "Do your thing."

Tess clapped, then started passing out gifts one by one, until all of us had a couple of presents in front of us.

Lucy snuggled against Lenny and regarded her daughter. "Who goes first, sweetie?"

Tess tapped her finger against her chin, then began ordering who would open what, when. We had just gotten started, Lucy opening the *Fix-it-and-Forget-it* cookbook I'd gotten her with appreciation for her having become my personal chef, when the doorbell rang. Tess' face fell.

"Don't worry," I said. "I'll send them away."

A woman stood on the stoop with a boy, probably about eleven or twelve. With a start, I realized it was Billy Moore, and this must be his grandmother. What was her name? Eve something. Freed? Yes. Freed. Forgoing my promise to Tess, I opened the door. "Come in. Please."

The woman's eyes were rimmed with red, the half-circles underneath them dark and puffy. She gently nudged Billy, and he stepped into the house.

"Hi, Billy," I said.

He didn't answer, keeping his eyes toward the floor.

I looked at the woman. "I'm so sorry. For everything."

For leaving your daughter out in the cold to die.

She held out her hand, and I grasped it automatically. She patted my hand with her other one, then turned my wrist so she could see the half-done tattoo. Her eyes filled with tears, and she patted my hand again. "It's not your fault, sweetheart. No one blames you for anything."

Except me. *I* blamed me.

"Stella, are you coming?" Tess appeared in the doorway to the front room, Lucy at her heels. They both stopped short at the sight of Mrs. Freed and Billy.

Mrs. Freed took a breath. "I'm sorry. We should have called first. With everything that happened I almost forgot it's…it's Christmas."

"It's okay. Really. Lucy and Tess, this is—" God, what do I say? "This is Mrs. Freed. She needs to talk with me for a minute."

Lenny angled his way through the front room's door and came to the foyer. Mrs. Freed let go of my hand and accepted Lenny's.

"I'm so sorry," Lenny said.

She blinked. "You knew Mandy?"

"A little. She was an amazing woman." Lenny turned to Billy and bent down to the boy's level. "I'm sorry, buddy."

Billy shrugged with one shoulder, but still looked at the carpet.

"If it's a bad time—" Mrs. Freed began.

"It's fine." I nodded toward the sofa. "We can talk here, if you like."

She glanced at Billy, and I reconsidered. "We can go out to my office. Let me get my coat."

"Me, too?" Lenny asked.

Mrs. Freed looked up at him. "If you don't mind…I think I'd prefer just…Stella."

"Of course." He picked up her hand again, which had fallen to her side. "If I can do anything for you, please let me know."

"Tess," Lucy said. "How about you show Billy the computer? Maybe there's something he'd like to play."

Billy's head came up at that and Lucy gave Tess a gentle push.

"Sure," Tess said. "Come on, Billy."

Throwing Lucy a grateful glance, I grabbed my coat and led Mrs. Freed to the barn, through the winter wonderland of my yard. It really had turned out to be the white Christmas Bing used to croon about. We had other things to dream about this year.

Inside the parlor door Mrs. Freed stopped and gazed at the herd. Her face softened.

"You can touch one, if you want," I said.

Her face lit up, and she stepped toward Cinderella, who stood calmly chewing her cud. When Mrs. Freed put her hand on the cow's broad forehead the chewing stopped, and the cow watched her.

Mrs. Freed smiled. "She's so big. But her eyes are kind."

I patted Cinderella's sizable flank. "They're nice animals."

When Mrs. Freed pulled her hand back and stepped away, Cinderella resumed her chewing, and I led Mrs. Freed on through the short hallway to my office. I took the seat behind the desk, unzipped my coat, and gestured to the visitor's chair. Mrs. Freed lowered herself into it, at the same time pulling a tissue from her pocket and wiping her eyes. She didn't bother to take off her coat or even her gloves.

"How can I help you?" I asked.

She took a deep breath, looked out the window, then focused her eyes on me.

"You were the last one to see them."

"Yes, ma'am, I was."

"How was she? My Mandy?"

I folded my hands on top of my desk. "Herself. Lively. Funny. Happy."

She pinched her lips together. "I'm glad about that. I'd hate to think of her last day being a bad one."

I sat silently, not knowing what to say.

"Why I'm here," Mrs. Freed said, "is I'm so worried about Wolf. That he might be...:that he could be hurt."

Again, the desire to use the less threatening word. No one wanted to say *dead*.

"Do you have any idea where he might be?" I asked. "Anyone who might want him...hurt?"

She looked at her lap and twisted her hands together.

"Wolf and Mandy are...were...good people. Helpful people. But they also stood up for things. People's rights, including their own. They aren't pushovers."

I almost smiled. That last afternoon alone Mandy, especially, had pissed off—or talked about pissing off—several people: Tank, the mom who wanted her twelve-year-old pierced, and Gentleman John. Then there were the ones I'd heard of since that day, like Lance Thunderbolt and the gangbanger.

"What about their political activities?" I asked.

She blinked. "Artists for Freedom? They obviously had an agenda that was unattractive to certain people. But I can't imagine the senator or anyone in his contingent resorting to violence."

I shifted in my chair. "Jewel and Mickey Spurgeon told me Mandy had something on the senator. She was going to tell the group that night."

"Until the detective told me, I hadn't even known what meeting they were going to. They asked if I could keep Billy, but never got around to telling me where they'd be. You see, I had their cell phone number..." Her voice trailed off and I waited to make sure she was done talking.

"Do you know what Mandy found out about the senator?" I asked. "Something bad?"

Mrs. Freed frowned. "Mandy never mentioned anything to me. I always thought she hated the bill itself, but not necessarily the senator."

We were quiet for moment while I tried to match that image with the one the Spurgeons had given. An image of Mandy being furious with Trevor Farley.

"How's Billy holding up?" I asked.

Mrs. Freed swallowed. "It's hard. He seems so even-keeled, but of course it's all been way too much for him. He's only eleven."

"I heard about what happened last month. At the school."

"Oh, those awful boys."

"Do you know who they were?"

"Well, of course."

My pulse quickened. "No one else seems to. Except the police."

"Wolf and Mandy wanted it that way. It was so humiliating for poor Billy."

"Yeah. It's embarrassing to be beat up."

She lifted her gaze to me. "He wasn't beat up."

"What?" Hadn't Bart told me that? And Shisler?

"Those horrible boys...those boys held him down and scratched a tattoo into his arm."

"They did *what*?"

"Right on his shoulder. 'IM A FAG.'"

My breath caught. "Why would they do something like that? What did Billy do to them?"

She met my shocked eyes with her sad ones. "Not Billy. Wolf."

"*Wolf*?"

She stood and wandered toward the photos I had on the wall, crossing her arms over her stomach. "They came into the shop the week before and wanted Wolf to tattoo swastikas on them. He wouldn't do it. Won't do anything pertaining to racism or hatred. Wolf told them—well, Mandy probably told them—to get the hell out. They did, finally, but not without a fight."

Mrs. Freed obviously didn't realize the impact her words were having on me. Didn't she understand she had just pinpointed the most likely killers? A band of skinheads, not your typical southeastern Pennsylvania suburban kids, were as scary as a pack of Hell's Angels.

"So where are these boys now?" I tried to keep my voice level.

"Jail, mostly. Or the juvenile detention center. A couple of the younger ones are on probation, but the leaders are locked away. At least for now."

"Detective Shisler knows about this?"

"Sure. She helped put them in prison."

My mind raced, and I tried to rein it in. "Do you think they could have anything to do with Mandy's death?"

She winced, probably at my use of the "d" word. "I wouldn't know how. Like I said, the ringleaders are in jail."

I itched to call Detective Shisler. "Any other ideas?"

Mrs. Freed shook her head. "I know Mandy was strong. Too strong, sometimes. But for anyone to hate her this much..." Her voice broke, and she pulled another tissue from her pocket. "And now they wonder if Wolf could've done it. I know he never would've hurt my girl. *His* girl."

I concentrated on Carla's calendar on my wall, trying to keep my emotions in check by focusing on something neutral. I thought of the claims Gentleman John and Tank were making about Wolf and Jewel. If Mrs. Freed had any idea about that, she certainly wasn't saying, and she seemed to love Wolf like a son. And it would, of course, be way too tacky to ask her about it.

Mrs. Freed's voice softened, no longer quavering. "Please. Could you tell me about that last afternoon? Tell me what my Mandy did?"

So I told her. Told her the funny stories, the anger Mandy voiced at back alley hacks, the way she gave Wolf the finger with a smile. Mrs. Freed listened with rapt attention until I came to the end of my story.

"Thank you, Stella," she said, when I finished.

"I wish I had more to tell you."

"Me, too, honey. But this will have to do, won't it?" She stood. "Now, I'd better head back in and get Billy. It is Christmas, after all, and I'm the only family he has."

"What about Wolf's parents?"

She shook her head. "Been gone for a while now. Billy never knew them."

I zipped my coat and circled around the desk to join her. "Would you like to stay for dinner? We'd be happy to have you. I've been assured we have plenty of food."

"Oh, thank you. Thank you so much. But I think we'll go on home. In case Wolf calls, you know. This is the longest we've been gone since…since the other day."

"If you change your mind, the invitation's open all afternoon. All week, if you want."

She rested her hand on my arm, unconsciously covering the tattoo Wolf hadn't finished. "You're a darling."

I swallowed the lump in my throat. Would she be so generous if she realized—*truly realized*—that I'd let her daughter die?

"And you do know," she said, as if reading my thoughts, "Mandy did *not* die because of you."

It was almost enough to make me weep.

Chapter Seventeen

Detective Shisler sounded harried when I got her on the phone, and my guilt about holding out on her grew. But not enough to make me ready to sacrifice the Spurgeons just yet. Especially since Shisler had been holding out on me, too.

"What is it?" Shisler asked.

"You knew about the skinheads? What they did to Billy's shoulder?"

Silence on her end.

I raised my voice. "You there?"

"I'm here. But I'm surprised you know what happened."

"Eve Freed was just here. With Billy. Wanted to talk about Mandy."

"Ah. Poor Billy. Poor Mrs. Freed, too."

"And you don't think those Nazi freaks had anything to do with Mandy's death? After they fought for swastikas and defaced her son?"

"The main kids, the oldest and most problematic, are in juvie. They've been in custody for a month and couldn't have done it."

"What about other kids from the gang? They can't be nice if they're in a group like that."

"The only ones left are newbies. Young. I don't think they'd have the guts."

"But—"

"Plus, I checked them out. The only two not in prison are basically under house arrest by their own parents, who were horrified by their boys' actions. Not all kids with issues come from bad homes. They just get in the wrong crowd and their parents are more clueless than some."

"So they couldn't have been involved?"

"I really, really doubt it."

"Well, damn."

"Thought you had them?"

"Hoped I did. Then we might be able to find Wolf."

She sighed loudly. "I'm with you. I'd love to give that boy his daddy back for Christmas."

"Billy didn't look so good."

"I'd be surprised if he did."

I heard the rise and fall of voices in the living room, and knew I'd kept my family long enough.

My family.

I sat speechless as I allowed that thought to wash over me.

"Ms. Crown?"

I brought my mind back to the detective. "Sorry. You'll let me know?"

"I'll let you know."

I hung up and did my best to put on my happy face for my return to the living room. To my family.

Nick met my eyes as I came in, and I offered him a tight smile. Lucy and Lenny gave me the same study, but it wasn't the right time to be talking about Eve Freed's visit or the phone call with the detective.

"Okay, honeybun," Lenny said to Tess. "Looks like it's time to get rockin' again."

We all filed back into the front room and reclaimed our spots, Nick's leg again making my back warm.

Tess ordered Lenny to open the next present, not forgetting for an instant where we'd left off. He was delighted to receive from Tess a comb set, with trimmer, to keep his beard soft and tangle-free.

Tess kept the rest of the packages coming, and they revealed a casual conglomeration of goods: hand-made scarves, woolen socks, a poncho and a bracelet/necklace making kit for Tess, and a sweatshirt for me that said, "Home is where the Heart is." I took a short break to run outside when the milk truck came, but our driver, Doug—who was remarkably cheerful for having to work on Christmas Day, and thrilled with the loaf of bread Lucy had made him—had no need for me to get in his way. When I returned to the festivities in the house, present-opening went along just fine until the last package—the one Tess had gotten for Nick.

Nick sat up, pulling his legs from behind me and sitting close enough I could feel the warmth from his arm. He picked up the flat rectangular package and held it to his ear, shaking it.

"Don't!" Tess shrieked, giggling. "You'll break it!"

"No, he won't," Lucy said.

Tess rolled her eyes. "Oh, Moooom, I know."

Nick carefully pulled off the first piece of tape, and Tess scooted closer, her nose above his gift.

"Just rip it!" Tess chirped.

He smiled at her, put his finger under a flap, and yanked. The paper fell away from a picture frame, and I stared at it. Heat crept up my neck.

"Where did you get that?" I asked, trying to sound unconcerned.

Tess chewed on her lip. "I took it one day, with Mom's camera."

I glanced at Lucy, who smiled anxiously at me.

"I love it," Nick said. "It looks just like her."

It was a photo of me. Well, me and Queenie. We stood beside my truck, my hand on the open door. I was looking down at Queenie, smiling, while she crouched on her hind legs, ready to launch herself into the cab. It was surprisingly close-up, and I couldn't believe I was unaware it had been taken.

"When was this?" I asked.

Tess shrugged, grinning shyly. "A couple of months ago."

Nick held onto the sides of the frame. "It's a lovely present. Thank you, Tess. Now when I leave today, I won't have to try so hard to remember what she looks like. Stella, I mean. Queenie's easy to remember."

Everyone laughed at that, except for me. I guessed it was okay he had my picture. But I felt violated, even if the photo was the product of a little girl's creativity.

"Speaking of you leaving," Lucy said to Nick, "I should check on lunch, now that the presents are all done."

"Oh, lunch," Lenny rumbled.

Lucy pinched him gently. "And you need to come help, you big couch potato."

He sighed resignedly and pushed himself off the sofa. "Yes, ma'am."

"Like you really mind," Lucy said.

He smiled brightly and followed Lucy out of the room.

Tess pulled a new fluffy fleece hoodie over her head and lay on her stomach, cracking open the cover of the most recent "Amazing Days of Abby Hayes" book.

I was glad her attention was on her stash and not on Nick and me. Nick rubbed a finger across the picture he'd received and spoke quietly. "You mind very much?"

I lifted a shoulder. "What can I do? It's your present."

His expression was troubled.

"No," I said. "I don't mind very much. It just feels weird to see a picture I didn't know existed." I rolled my neck forward, stretching it from side to side.

"Neck sore?" Nick asked.

"Nah. Just tense."

Nick got up and sat on the sofa, tossing a pillow on the ground at his feet. "Come here. I'll rub your shoulders."

I eyed him warily, indicating Tess right there in the room.

He smiled wickedly. "All I'm offering is a shoulder rub."

I hesitated, then scooted onto the pillow. His fingers were strong, and while he did hit some sore spots, he also managed to relax some tension. I sat there, unwilling to move, until we were called to the table. Tess jumped up, disappearing quickly.

Nick patted my shoulders and stood, swinging a leg over my head to stand in front of me.

"Come on. Let's eat."

"Thanks for the rub," I said.

I grabbed the hand he offered, and he pulled me to my feet, holding me against his chest. "You're very welcome." It was a sort of stalemate, broken immediately by Tess' "Dinner!" from the next room.

Nick released me, and we walked together to the table, where we devoured our share of the turkey and trimmings. Lucy and Lenny had outdone themselves with homemade cranberry salad, oyster filling, crescent rolls, and chocolate pudding pie for dessert.

It was delicious, but it would've tasted a lot better if Wolf was at his house and Nick was planning on staying at mine.

Chapter Eighteen

It seemed that only minutes later Nick and I were standing in the foyer, his duffle bag at his feet. Lucy, Tess, and Lenny had said their good-byes, so now it was up to me to let Nick walk out the door.

"Thanks for letting me stay," Nick said. "And for sharing your Christmas."

I stuffed my hands in my pockets. "When will I see you again?"

He looked away. "When will you get down to Virginia?"

"Nick, it's the middle of winter. The farm..."

He closed his eyes. "Yeah. I know. The farm." He reached down and grabbed the handle of his bag before leaning forward to kiss me. I kissed him back, taking my hands from my pockets and resting them on his arms.

He pulled away and studied my face. "Stay in touch." He opened the door and stepped out into the cold.

"Nick," I said.

He turned.

I paused, the right words evading me. "Drive carefully."

He looked at the ground, biting his lips together. "Yeah. Sure. I will." He strode to the Ranger, which he'd already started and cleared of snow, then stepped into the cab, and shut the door. I heard the emergency brake let go, and Nick took one last look toward the house. I put up my hand, and he slowly drove out the lane.

When I could no longer see the truck I closed the door and leaned against it, questioning already whether Nick had really been in my house for the past few days. I wondered when—if—I'd ever see him again.

Pans clanged in the kitchen, breaking me out of my thoughts. I followed the sounds to find Lenny elbows deep in the sink, his back tense with the task of scrubbing the roasting pan.

Lucy glanced up from where she sat at the table, picking meat off the turkey carcass. "You okay?"

I wiggled my shoulders up and down, sitting across from her at the table. "Just how set are you about moving out this spring?"

She frowned. "Moving out?"

"To a garage apartment."

She pulled a piece of brown meat off a bone and ate it. "That's the plan, right? You rebuild the garage the way it was, and we live in the apartment?"

I leaned forward, my elbows on the table. "I was wondering if we might want to consider something different."

She paused. "Like what?"

"Like you stay here in the house with me."

The room went quiet. Lenny even stopped splashing and peered at me over his shoulder.

"What?" I said. "A woman can't change her mind?"

Lenny turned back to the dishes.

Lucy smiled. "You're serious?"

"You can think about it. You don't have to answer now."

"I don't have to think about it. The answer's yes."

Lenny peered over his other shoulder.

"You have a problem with that, Len?" I asked.

He quickly went back to scrubbing. "Nope. No problem."

"Good. I'm glad that's settled."

Lucy smiled some more and ate another bite of turkey. I was enjoying a good yawn when the phone rang.

"Guess I'll get it," I said. "Seeing how you guys are either wet or greasy."

"And it is your house," Lenny said.

I pushed back my chair. "Well, Lucy lives here, too." I picked up the receiver. "Royalcrest Farm."

"Stella? Merry Christmas."

I smiled involuntarily. "Abe. What's going on?"

"Ma and the women are cleaning up the dishes, while us guys are busy watching the kids and arguing over what game we're going to play. My vote is for Up and Down the River, but I'm being outvoted by Bull."

"The kids just want to say 'Bull' to the adults."

"Don't I know it. Hey, I was wondering if I could come over later this evening? Unless you've still got company."

There was a twinge behind my temple. "Nope. He's gone."

"I can't tell from your voice if that's a good or bad thing. You can fill me in when I come over. Would it be too late if I came after milking? I should probably stick around here for the afternoon."

"If you don't mind me conking out while we're talking."

He laughed. "Wouldn't be the first time. I'll see you then."

I hung up, and Lenny flung the dish towel onto the counter, having finished up the washing. Lucy still picked at the turkey, popping bites into her mouth. I grabbed the phone book and looked up the Spurgeons' number. I dialed it, but got their answering machine.

"Stella Crown," I said. "Rusty's friend. I wondered if I could come over sometime, ask you a couple questions. Give me a call when you get in." I left my number and hung up.

Lucy pretended not to hear my phone call, but Lenny stared at me with frank curiosity, which I ignored.

"I'm going on the computer for a bit," I said. "Unless Tess has hijacked it."

"About Wolf and Mandy?" Lenny asked.

"Yeah. I want to check out Artists for Freedom and that senate bill."

Lucy looked up. "You really think it could have something to do with it all?"

I thought of the skinheads. They would've been the top of my suspect list, if they hadn't been in jail. Since they were out of commission, I had to look at the lesser possibilities. Someone had committed these acts.

"You never know. Thanks again for lunch."

Lucy smiled. "I don't mind being the house chef."

I walked out to the living room, where the computer was free of game players. I took a seat and logged on. Lenny appeared at my shoulder.

"What?" I said. I really didn't want to avoid direct questions about what I was keeping from him. But he surprised me.

"Any chance you could watch Tess for an hour or so this evening while I give Lucy her Christmas present?"

I shrugged. "Sure. When did you have in mind?"

"I was thinking we could stay here till milking's done, then take off for a bit."

"Sounds fine. Abe's coming over, but that doesn't matter. He always likes to see Tess."

"Thanks." He went back to the kitchen.

I found AskJeeves.com and typed in the name of the senate bill, getting dozens of hits but only a few that pertained to my interests. I modified the search, putting quotes around "PA House Bill No. 752." Now I got only a dozen hits, most of them a well-distributed commentary by a guy at BAEzine, also known as BodyArt.com, an online magazine. Reading it was an education. He took the bill itself, broke it down, and explained the bill's weaknesses. There were a lot of them, most of which I'd already heard from Rusty and Mickey. I also found the bill itself, in all its unreadable prose. I printed it out, along with the BAE commentary, since I'd left the Spurgeons' copy at their house.

There were hits for a couple of articles mentioning Artists for Freedom and their work for the tattoo and body piercing community. Mostly the articles centered on Dennis Bergman, the lawyer/tattoo artist who headed up the lobby. There were photos of him, his shop, and his customers. But I found one last article from a small rally the lobby held in Harrisburg when the senate had last met. A raggedy bunch of protestors, and right out in front was a familiar face. Mandy's. My throat tightened at the shot of her waving a poster proclaiming, "Body Art is Beautiful." The photographer had caught her at her best, her eyes sparkling, her body tall and strong. I printed it out.

A search for Senator Trevor Farley found more hits than I could ever go through, but I skimmed the first few pages of sites. Lots to do with his campaign, his family, even his cat, for God's sake. I narrowed the search using his name with the bill number, and came up with a few articles.

"Finding anything?" Lucy peered over my shoulder.

"Some. I'm just now getting to the senator."

"Senator Farley? Isn't he the Democrat people were claiming acted more Republican? Or was it the other way around?"

I skimmed the first article. "I think he's a Democrat. Which makes it even more interesting that he'd go for a bill like this. There's gotta be somebody else pulling the strings."

"Or something about his life we don't know."

I went on to the next article, but only found more of his rhetoric. Nothing about his reasons for pushing such a bill.

I sat back. "Who would know this kind of stuff?"

"Have you asked Abe?"

"I doubt he'd be up on it."

"But he might know who is."

I thought about that. "Good idea. I'll ask him tonight."

"What about the other guy?" Lucy asked.

"What other guy?"

"The lawyer. The one who started Artists for Freedom."

"What about him?"

"Think he might be worth contacting?

I stared at her. "I don't know why I didn't think of that."

She patted my shoulder. "Because you're too close to it all, and you're burning yourself out thinking about it. Now come on, take a break."

"Let me look him up first."

She sighed and left while I checked out some specifics on Dennis Bergman. He posted his reasons for starting Artists for Freedom—everything you would expect, from the Bill of Rights to personal expression. I also came up with an e-mail address, which I immediately clicked. There was no way I'd find him by phone on Christmas, even if a number had been listed, but lots of people check their e-mail no matter where they are or what day it is. I hoped he was one of them. I wrote out a quick letter telling him of my interest, and sent it on its way.

A twinge shot from my shoulder up into my head, and I rolled my neck, realizing Nick's backrub had worn off. Lucy was right. I needed to take a break if I was going to be of any use to anybody.

So Lucy, Lenny, Tess, and I hung out in the living room, where we played games and snacked on party mix and Christmas cookies. Then Lenny and I each sneaked in a nap while Tess and Lucy watched "It's a Wonderful Life." I love Jimmy Stewart, but after seeing the movie every year since I was old enough to notice, I really didn't need to catch the ending.

After my nap I glanced at the clock to see it was almost five. Just about milking time. It struck me that Nick should be getting close to home. I wondered if he'd call when he got there, or if I'd be left assuming he'd made it. I had to figure his sisters would call if he didn't arrive.

I put on my milking attire, trying to convince myself things were now back to normal. And that that was a good thing.

Queenie had yet to be convinced, too, and when waiting by the parlor door didn't produce Nick, she dropped into her corner with a huff and sulked. I couldn't help being a bit annoyed with her for missing him and giving me the cold shoulder. It wasn't my fault, after all, that he'd gone back to Virginia.

I wished each cow a not-quite-heartfelt Merry Christmas, but most of them didn't respond. They endured the process with their usual patience, and soon Lucy and I were headed back into the warmth of the house.

"Anybody call?" I asked, stomping off my boots.

Lenny looked at me. "You could've heard the phone in the barn, right?"

"Well. Yeah."

He snorted. "Then I guess you know."

I sank onto the sofa. "I was hoping the detective might've found out something."

He looked at me. "And hoping someone else might call to say he got home?"

I pulled up my sleeve to check out my half-tattoo and avoid Lenny's smirk. "I'm sure he's there by now. And aren't you guys supposed to go somewhere?"

Lucy showered and changed, and Lenny helped her shrug into her coat.

"Take your time," I said. "We'll be fine." I glanced at Tess. "Tess looks pretty beat from our late Christmas Eve. She'll be snoozing pretty soon, I bet."

Lucy eyed her daughter. "I don't know. Maybe I should—"

"Oh, Mooom," Tess said. "I can go to bed by myself."

Lenny and I laughed, and Lucy grinned. "Okay, pumpkin. But in case I don't see you, it's been a very merry Christmas." She kissed her on the forehead, waved to me, and they left. I couldn't help but think of Billy, whose mother wouldn't be bidding him a Christmas goodnight.

"Want a leftover turkey sandwich?" I asked Tess. "I'm starved."

"Can I help make it?"

We were spreading the mayonnaise when there was a knock at the door.

"Abe?" Tess said excitedly.

"Probably."

"I'll get it."

I watched from the kitchen as she ran to the door and flung it open.

Abe grinned and reached down to hug her. "Merry Christmas."

"You, too!" she said. "Want a sandwich?"

He groaned and patted his stomach. "No room at the inn." He shut the door and smiled at me. "Supper?"

"Yup. Mind hanging out while we make it?"

He sat with us and talked while we finished the sandwiches and ate them with chips and hot tea. A perfect Christmas supper.

Soon after Tess' food had disappeared, her head began to loll onto her chest.

"Uh oh," Abe said, laughing.

"Come on, sweets," I said to Tess. "Time to hit the hay. Say goodnight to Abe."

Without even a token protest, she hugged him goodnight and headed toward her room. I followed her up the stairs to make sure she was awake enough to brush her teeth and get into her jammies. She shuffled to her room and snuggled under the covers.

"Sing me a song?" she asked.

I grimaced. "You sure you want to end your day that way?"

"Mmm-hmm." She closed her eyes.

I got through "Jingle Bells" without butchering it too much, then tiptoed out. If Tess wasn't asleep, she was close.

Back downstairs, Abe waited on the couch, shuffling through the papers I'd printed out that afternoon. I took a seat beside him and put my feet up on the coffee table.

"What's all this?" he asked.

"A bill that's trying to restrict tattoo artists and body piercers. Government wants to control them."

"How would they do that?"

"Make artists go to the extremes—doctor's signatures saying they're free of blood diseases, pleasing decor, dumb stuff that makes customers no safer than they were before."

"So why the bill?"

"That's what I'm trying to figure out. Trevor Farley has a bee in his over-sized bonnet, and I don't know what it is. Any ideas who to ask?"

He considered it. "Have you tried calling his office?"

"You think they'd tell me anything? No reasons have been printed anywhere, and you know the media—they'd snap up the info as soon as the words were uttered."

"You're right. And most likely his office is out till after New Year's, anyway. I'll see if I can come up with a name for you."

"Thanks. I'd appreciate it."

He studied me. "Why the intense interest? Because of your tattoos?"

I stared at him. "You don't know?"

"Don't know what?"

"A friend of mine was murdered the other day. The same day I went to get this." I thrust my wrist toward him.

He put a hand to his forehead. "I'm sorry. I just didn't put together the bill and her murder. This is her?" He held out the picture I'd printed out of Mandy at the protest.

I nodded.

"Pretty," he said. He put down the picture and looked at my wrist. "'How'? I guess it's supposed to say 'Howie'?"

"You guess right. My artist and his wife disappeared in the middle of it, and now he's missing and she's dead."

"I know. I saw it on the news. Plus, Nick told me about it at church. It's awful. I'm sorry I haven't been more sensitive about it. I didn't realize you knew them so well."

"I didn't really know them. I mean, not well enough, from everything I'm learning about them."

He squinted at me. "But for some reason you're feeling responsible."

I rubbed my forehead and closed my eyes. "When they went to the back room I fell asleep."

"And?"

"While I was napping, Wolf was abducted and Mandy was bashed over the head and left to die behind the shop."

He stared at me. "And you didn't hear any of it."

"Mandy had just turned on some music. I hadn't thought it was that loud, but I guess it masked whatever noises they made back there."

"What happened next?"

"I woke up twenty minutes later, looked around outside and in, couldn't find them, and let myself out. Mandy died lying ten feet from where I stood at the back door, and I didn't see her."

He was quiet for a few moments, then said, "You can't do this to yourself."

I pushed myself off the couch and strode to the window, where I looked out at the snow, brilliant under my dusk-to-dawn light. "Why not? I took a nap while Mandy was freezing to death. I could've saved her."

"You didn't kill her, Stella. Someone else knocked her out. Someone else left her there."

I closed my eyes. "But I—"

"*You didn't do it.* How were you to know she was out there?"

"*—I fell asleep.*"

Abe put the papers on the coffee table and turned toward me. "You were tired. You were lying in a comfortable chair. You had no reason to think something horrific was happening. Why would you?"

I leaned my forehead against the cool window. I had no answers. There *wasn't* any reason to expect it.

Abe got up from the couch and came to stand beside me, leaning his back against the wall. "Does feeling guilty about this stem back to feeling guilty about Howie?"

I stopped breathing. When I started again, it felt like someone had my chest in a vice grip.

"Because you know his death wasn't your fault, either," Abe said. "Someone else killed both of them, Stella. You didn't."

Headlights flashed up the lane, and I watched dully as Lenny's truck parked outside the door. He stepped around to the passenger door and opened it for Lucy, hugging her as he swung her down from the seat. I backed away from the window while they came up the sidewalk and opened the door.

"Abe!" Lucy said. She stepped forward, giving him a kiss on the cheek. "How lovely to see you." Her face glowed, and Abe smiled down at her.

"Abe," Lenny said, holding his hand out. Lenny was glowing, too, as he and Abe shook hands, and I squinted at him suspiciously.

"What are you two so happy about?" I said.

Lucy peeked up at Lenny, then thrust her left hand toward me. Her ring finger was circled by a band of gold, sporting a sparkly diamond.

I blinked.

"Wow," Abe said.

"What do you think?" Lenny asked.

I blinked again. "Is that what I think it is?"

"Yup. We're getting hitched next spring."

I cleared my throat. "I guess we really won't be needing that extra apartment."

Lucy's smile faltered.

"Congratulations," Abe said, glancing at me. "What a great Christmas present for both of you."

"Yes," I said quickly. "It's wonderful. I'm very happy for you both. You deserve it."

Lucy's smile came back full force. "I'm very happy, too."

"And I gotta agree," Lenny said. He gave Lucy another hug. "But it's getting late, and my fiancée needs to get to bed. She about fell asleep on the way home."

Lucy giggled, and I took a deep breath, closing my eyes. Lenny helped Lucy off with her coat, and Abe and I discreetly looked away while they said goodnight.

"Goodnight, Stella. Abe," Lenny said.

"'Night," I said.

Abe waved. "Goodnight."

Lucy watched out the window while Lenny lumbered down to the truck and pulled out of the drive. When she turned around, her eyes sparkled.

"Goodnight, you two. Oh, I can't wait to tell Tess!" With that, she practically skipped to the stairway and disappeared behind the door.

I stepped back and leaned against the window sill, holding my arms over my stomach.

Abe was silent.

I tilted my head back and looked at the ceiling. "People keep leaving me, Abe."

After a minute or so, he said, "Nick went home?"

I pushed away from the window and walked over to the sofa, sinking down onto it. "After dinner today. His mom and sisters wanted him home for Christmas."

"That's understandable." Abe came over and perched on the edge of the chair, catty-corner from me. "And?"

"And what?"

"How did you leave things?"

I thought back to the kiss the night before. Then to the way we'd said good-bye. "He wants me to go down to see him in Virginia."

"Good."

"Abe, it's *not* good. When am I going to do that? I can't leave Lucy here by herself in the middle of winter."

Abe sat back in his chair. After a few moments he said, "Missy and I are seeing each other again."

Several months earlier, Abe's then-girlfriend Missy had gone home to New York, leaving Abe in Pennsylvania because she thought he wanted to be with me. He thought so, too, at the time. So did I. We were all wrong.

"Is it serious?" I asked.

"I didn't get her a ring for Christmas, but I'd consider it for next year."

I chewed on my lip and watched the glowing embers, dying in the fireplace. "Well, that's nice."

"Yes. It is." He looked at me. "I guess I'm another person who's leaving you."

"No. You already left."

"Stella." He sat forward and grabbed my hands. "It's not about you. We all love you. Me, Lucy, Lenny. Howie. But life happens. If you don't want to be left alone, you're going to have to make some choices."

"I can't leave my farm and move to Virginia. And I can't expect Nick to leave his business to come up here."

Abe let go of my hands. "Well, then I guess you're stuck. And you just might end up alone."

I looked up at the sharp edge in his voice.

"Stella," he said, "look at you. It's Christmas. You have a great farmhand and little girl who love you. One of your best friends is spending his evening here talking to you, and you have a man who stayed as long as he could over the holidays before speeding home to be with his family for a few hours on Christmas. What more do you want?"

I was silent.

Abe stood up. "I gotta go. It's late and I'm headed back to New York tomorrow to have Christmas with Missy's family. She didn't come down to PA with me because her sister's due to have a baby any moment and she didn't want to risk being snowed in down here." He walked to the foyer, where he grabbed his coat from the closet.

I followed.

"I'm sorry," I said. "I'm just—"

He reached out and hugged me. "I know. It's been a rough few months, since summer."

I held my hands against my chest and buried my face in his familiar shoulder.

"Call me anytime," he said. "I'll be glad to listen."

I turned my face to the side so I could talk. "And to tell me exactly what you think."

He laughed. "You know it. No beating around the bush."

I sighed and relaxed against him.

"I do love you, Stella."

I reached around his waist. "I love you, too."

He kissed the top of my head. "Merry Christmas."

I stepped back and he let his arms fall.

"Have a safe trip home," I said.

He looked thoughtful. "Yes. New York *is* home." He moved as if to leave, then stopped. "And I'll think about who you could talk to about Senator Farley. I'll call if I come up with someone."

"Thanks. I appreciate it."

He went out the door and I closed it behind him, watching until he drove away. I glanced at the clock. It really was late. I took a moment to turn off the Christmas tree lights in the front room, avoiding looking at the sofa where Nick was no longer sleeping, then closed the doors to the fireplace. When all the lights were off except for the nightlight on the microwave, I headed up the stairs.

In my bedroom I undressed and pulled an extra-large Harley T-shirt over my head before tiptoeing down the hallway to brush my teeth. The toothbrush container held three brushes—my purple one, Lucy's yellow one, and Tess' Buzz Lightyear. By summer it would be back to one.

Less chance for catching colds, I told myself. *Less toothpaste and soap mess on the counter. No having to share the bathroom.*

I stumbled back down the hallway to my room and had just closed the door when I noticed something on my pillow.

A small jewelry box.

I sucked in my breath. *Oh God.*

I eased onto my bed, staring at the box, wondering if I should even open it. Nick wouldn't just drop off a ring and leave, would he? And he couldn't possibly think one kiss was enough support for a proposal. There was no way he was ready to leave Virginia and come live at the farm. And what if it *was* a ring? What would I do? What would I say?

I took a deep breath and reached for the box, running my finger over the velvety fabric. I swallowed. And opened it.

I was suddenly back in seventh grade, peering with envy at a pair of friends on the bus. Girls who had grown up together, best friends forever.

The heart in my box was better quality than what those junior high girls had been wearing, but it was the same idea. A heart split in half, a chain for each part.

I touched the gold of the heart, now locked together as one, then picked out the paper folded and tucked into the box. The note was hand-written.

> *Sometimes having only half of something is better than keeping the whole thing. And lots better than having nothing.*
>
> *Nick*

I put the note back in the case, and hid the box under my pillow.

And tried to sleep.

Chapter Nineteen

Lucy was humming and slicing a bagel when I got down for breakfast the next morning.

"Told Tess yet?" I asked.

She glanced up. "Haven't had a chance. She's still sleeping."

I brushed my hand through my hair. "That's right."

She frowned. "You okay?"

I opened the fridge and pulled out the orange juice. "Sure. Just didn't sleep that great."

Lucy's knife went through the last part of bagel and hit the cutting board with a whack. "Because of me and Lenny?"

"No." I took a big swallow of OJ. "I just couldn't stop my brain." I wasn't ready to tell her about the necklace still hiding under my pillow.

She stuck her bagel in the toaster and brushed by me to grab the cream cheese from the refrigerator. "You didn't seem too thrilled last night when we got back."

I rolled my neck. "I'm glad for you, Luce, you know I am. But I've gotten used to having you around."

She smiled. "I'm not going anywhere. I'll still work here."

"But you won't live here."

"Well, no."

I turned to open the cupboard.

"You remember," she said, "that four months ago you never wanted a housemate to begin with."

"Sure," I said. "I remember. It'll be fine."

She took a breath, like she was going to say something else, but her bagel popped and she plucked it out of the toaster.

I poured my cereal and ate it in front of the TV. Nothing new about Wolf. In fact, he wasn't even mentioned. I took my bowl back into the kitchen. "I'm headed out."

"Sure. Be there in a minute."

The temperature had plummeted to a frosty six degrees, and I bundled up to head outside. An unforgiving wind was also blowing, and when the first gust hit my face I wondered how frigid the wind chill factor was. I hoped with all my energy that wherever Wolf was, if he was alive, he was at least inside, where he wouldn't freeze to death. Like Mandy.

It was warm enough inside the barn, and Queenie met me with a little more enthusiasm than she had had the evening before.

"It's good you have a little nest in here, girl," I said. "You'd freeze your tail off outside." I'd offered different times during the cold weather to let her sleep in the house, but she seemed to feel that if the cows were penned up it was her duty to watch over them. Those sheepherding ancestors, I guess.

By eight o'clock I was milking Olive Oyl and Betty Boop, who had to be pumped separately because of being on antibiotics, and Lucy was checking on the heifers. I looked out the window at the tree branches waving and the snow sparkling with ice crystals. No way would I be doing any outside work that day, unless the auger was frozen or some such thing. I prayed it wasn't.

"Auger was frozen," Lucy said, stepping into the barn. "But I gave it a few good smacks and it came back to life."

"Thank God."

Lucy picked up a pitchfork to scrape a clod of manure from her boot. "So what are you gonna do today?"

I lifted a shoulder. "Not sure. You?"

"Thought I might call around a few places this morning. Check some dates. If that's okay."

I stared at her blankly.

"For this summer," she said. "My wedding."

"Oh. Right. Okay. At least you can do that inside, where it's warm."

She pursed her lips, her hands on her hips. "You sure it's all right?"

"That you're getting married?"

She rolled her eyes. "That I do some calling."

"Yeah. Yeah, that's fine. Go ahead. I'm about done here, anyway."

She looked at me. "You know that my marrying Lenny doesn't mean I'm walking out on you."

"Sure. I know." I reached down to feel Olive Oyl's softening udder.

"And it doesn't mean I don't love you."

I turned to check Betty Boop. "Yeah."

"You know," she said. "You might want to think about why you're so upset about me getting married."

I straightened up. "I'm not—"

"There's a man in Virginia right now who's waiting for your call. It would be good if you'd consider that. These cows are good for making a living, but they can't give you what Nick can."

My jaw flexed in preparation for saying something, but Lucy held up her hand. "Don't say anything. I'll shut up." She walked away, patting Queenie on the way out of the barn.

I went over to my collie, secure in her corner, and tried to force down my irritation at Lucy's little speech. "You're not leaving me, too, are you girl?" Her eyebrows shifted as she watched me, her nose on her paws. I knelt and rubbed her ears. "You just want Nick back, huh?" She snorted, blowing hay dust over my boots. "Keep me company?" I stood and walked toward my office, pausing at the door to the little hallway. Queenie stretched, shook herself, and trotted along behind me.

In my office I sat at my desk and pulled out the phone book while Queenie made herself at home in her usual spot. I checked the clock. Eight-thirty. Late enough to call Rusty and wake him up. I wanted to see if he could give me a line on somebody to talk to about Dennis Bergman, the guy heading up Artists for Freedom.

I picked up the phone, but Lucy was already on the line, so I turned on my computer and waited for it to boot up. Five minutes later I checked the phone again, but Lucy was still talking. To a photographer, it sounded like.

I labored for about an hour on paperwork, which I was doing myself again since Abe moved back to New York in the fall, and checked periodically to see if I could get on the phone. Lucy wasn't kidding when she said she had some calls to make. Finally, I got a dial tone. I immediately called Rusty's house, where I got Becky, his wife.

"He's still asleep," she said. "Big surprise." She laughed. "Can I have him call you?"

"Please."

"Don't know how long it will be. He's a sleepyhead."

"No problem."

"Is it about the Moores?" she asked.

"Well, yeah. I was wondering if he might know who I could talk to about Dennis Bergman."

"Who?"

"The guy in charge of Artists for Freedom."

"Oh, you don't want to talk to Rusty about him. You want to talk to Dreama."

"Dreama?"

"Our older daughter. She wrote a paper about Bergman for government class. Want me to get her? She's an early riser, unlike some other people."

I looked around my office. I was tired of paperwork. It was too cold to work outside. I was lucky to get three minutes on the phone, and Lucy was probably champing at the bit. "Okay if I just come over?"

"Sure. That would be fine. Dreama always likes an audience for her research. Need directions?"

She gave them to me, and I hung up. "Sorry, Queenie," I said. "I'd love to take you along, but it's too cold for you to wait in the truck, and I don't know if they let dogs in the house." She gave me a look that said she understood, and followed me back out to the parlor, where she sank down in her usual spot. "Take care of the girls," I said.

In the house Lucy was back on the phone, talking energetically about flowers and scribbling furiously on a tablet. Tess sat at the computer, Smoky on her lap, playing the Spy Fox computer game she had shown Nick only days before. Nick, who must've gotten home or I would've heard. At least I assumed so.

When Lucy hung up I told her where I was headed, and she glanced at the clock. "You planning on being back for lunch?"

"Can't imagine I'll be real long."

"All right. I'll make something good with our leftovers. See you then."

"Have fun calling," I said.

She grinned.

"Stella!" Tess came flying at me from the living room. "Did you hear? Did you hear? Lenny's going to be my new daddy!"

I caught her with a whoof of breath as she hit my stomach. "Yes, I heard. I guess you're happy about it?"

She looked up at me, her forehead wrinkling. "Shouldn't I be?"

I kicked myself for my careless words and glanced at Lucy, who glared at me with hooded eyes. "You should be, honey," I said to Tess. "You should be very, very happy."

I left before Lucy's expression turned even darker.

The roads were clear of everything but salt, and the snow along the shoulders was spattered with dirt and slush. Ugly. I took a detour through Lansdale, stopping briefly to peer in the front of Wolf Ink. It was dark and silent, and my throat clogged at the memories from the last time I'd been there. The apartment was also shut up tight, although the steps had been swept off. Perhaps by the police, who wouldn't want to break their necks climbing up and down.

Fifteen minutes later I pulled into a parking spot in front of Rusty's house, part of a development a few blocks from his shop.

A woman answered the door. "Stella?"

"That's me."

"Come on in. It's colder than Alaska out there."

I gratefully stepped into the warmth and stared at the woman, presumably Rusty's wife.

"I'm Becky," she said.

I opened my mouth, but no sound came out.

She laughed. "Not what you expected?"

"Sorry. I don't mean to be rude."

Becky Oldham was as old school as you could imagine. Hair permed and highlighted, make-up tastefully applied, small gold studs in her ears—only one earring in each lobe—a light blue twin-set over khaki pants. Fuzzy blue slippers—a perfect match to her sweater—encased her feet.

"Stare all you want," she said. "I'm used to it. If they're not gaping at Rusty, they're making faces at me, wondering what on earth I'm doing with him. Or him with me, for that matter."

"I have to admit I'm wondering the same thing."

She shrugged. "I guess when you love someone, you love all of him. Globe and all."

"But he didn't have that when you met him."

"Lord, no. All he had then was the woman on his arm, his swallow, and a few rings in his eyebrow. Those rings are gone now, for some reason. Guess he got tired of them."

"Only to be replaced by the large loop in his nose."

"All the better to lead him around with."

I smiled. "It's easy to see why he's with you."

She smiled back. "Yeah. Not all women are so tolerant."

"Not many at all."

"Anyway, come on in. We don't have to stand here in the hall." She led me into the living room and gestured at the furniture, a comfortable-looking couch and chair set, with floral designs on the fabric.

"Have a seat. I'll go find Dreama." She hesitated. "I'm very sorry about your friends. Rusty's broken up about it."

"Thanks."

"It sounds like they were wonderful people."

"Yes." I didn't like how she was using the past tense for both Mandy and Wolf, but knew it was something I might have to get used to in the very near future.

She left, and I chose the chair, studying the room from my seat. Classic colors, from the ivory walls to the ivory and tan carpet. A piano, some ornate lamps, and a glass-topped coffee table. A few more chairs sat along the walls, and a china cupboard displayed a set of dishes, along with a beautiful set of pottery.

I was just getting up to take a closer look at a framed painting I thought might be Rusty's work when a girl's face appeared in the doorway. Just the top half of her face. Her eyes peered around the corner, reminding me of Tess when Rusty had visited our house.

"Hi," I said. "Are you Dreama?"

She shook her head. "I'm Rose."

Ah. The one Rusty had told Tess about.

"Hi, Rose," I said. "You can come in if you want."

She did, her body appearing in increments as she slowly maneuvered her way around the doorjamb and onto the end of the sofa. She was a miniature of her mother, without the tinted hair and make-up. Her fuzzy pink sweater matched her slippers, and her jeans—a paler shade of pink—were the classic cut, with only a few sparkly sequins on the pockets.

"I'm nine," she said.

"That's great. I'm *twenty*-nine."

She brightened. "Really?"

I nodded.

"Are you here to talk to my sister?"

"Yes."

"She's seventeen."

"Great."

"What are you going to talk to her about?"

"Well, she knows some things about a man I'm...researching."

She nodded gravely. "That bad man."

"Bad? Dennis Bergman?"

Her forehead crinkled. "I don't know."

An older girl walked into the room and ruffled Rose's hair. "What are you telling her, sis?"

"Nothing."

I stood and shook Dreama's hand, unable to keep the smile off my face. Now *this* was what I expected at Rusty's house. Dreama's hair was dyed a startling shade of orange, which matched her lipstick and the sun tattooed on the side of her neck. Her black T-shirt hung over long and baggy jeans, the cuffs shredded from dragging on the ground. From what I could see she was barefoot, with rings around several toes. Her ears were lined with hoops, and when she talked I saw the flash of a stud in her tongue.

"I'm Stella," I said. "Rose was saying you're going to tell me about a bad man. I didn't think Dennis Bergman was bad."

She laughed and plunked down on the sofa. I sat, too. Rose still hung out on the end of the couch. "Bergman's not bad," she said. "But I started doing some research on Farley, the jerk. That's probably who she's talking about."

"Oh. Maybe you can tell me some about him, too."

"Sure. What I know." She had a thick folder in her hand, and she laid it on the coffee table. "This was all my research for my paper about Bergman. And this is the paper." She handed me a stapled stack of papers. "I printed out a copy for you."

"Thanks. I see you even wrote on your 'A' on the top."

She grinned. "Hey, you might as well know you're reading quality material. Anyway, what do you want to know?"

"Whatever you can tell me."

"All right." She settled back on the sofa. "Dennis Bergman is a tattoo artist, but also a lawyer. He does mostly title work, financial stuff, you know, and when he got wind of this bogus bill, he about blew his top. Got hold of everything he could to start fighting it. Wasn't hard to find others to jump in with him. Tattoo artists from all over the state, and body-piercers, too. Plus folks who just want to be able to modify their bodies how they want and not be arrested for it."

"Makes sense."

"Makes a lot of sense. Unlike the bill. You know about it?"

I nodded. "Your dad and Mickey Spurgeon explained it to me. Plus I found a good commentary on-line."

"The one from the Body Art e-zine?"

"Yup."

"That's a good one. So, you know the bill's a bunch of crap. Bergman set out to make people aware."

"So what's at stake for him is his tattoo business?"

"His way of life, mostly. I mean, he's a lawyer, he doesn't need to tattoo for a living."

Becky came into the room carrying a tray. "Thought you might want some refreshment while you talk."

The tray, which Becky set on the coffee table, held a teapot and cups, creamer, sugar, and some delicious-looking little biscuits.

"These are scones," Becky said. "I popped some in the oven when you said you were coming over. And this is homemade raspberry jam. Help yourself. Can I pour you a cup of tea?"

"Sure. Thanks." So much for Lucy's lunch of leftovers.

Becky filled a cup. "Sugar? Milk?"

I said no to both, but yes to the scones. They were amazing.

"Back to Bergman," I said, when I'd swallowed.

"Oh, yes," Becky said. "Don't let me stop you."

"It's a lifestyle thing," Dreama said. "If we let the government start to censor body art, where are they going to stop? It all comes down to your run-of-the-mill folks who don't want to have to see art on people's bodies. Why else would they ban facial tattoos? They're still allowing permanent make-up done by 'corrective cosmetic artists,' whatever they're supposed to be, but any individual expression would be prohibited. They just don't want to have to look at anyone who's not 'normal.'"

"So Bergman's really out to keep our country free—the way it's supposed to be."

"Sure." She paused. "The worst thing is this bill's not by people who admit they're censoring art, or who even know the business at all. It's really just because people are ill-informed and ignorant. You can't tell me if these people would see my dad's shop they'd believe it's unsanitary. It's like a hospital, it's so clean in there."

"It's ridiculous," Becky said, irritation seeping into her cultured voice. "The FDA is even getting involved in making ink. The government says otherwise Rusty could be sued if someone has a reaction to the colors he uses. Well, that's why people fill out the waiver before they get a tattoo. They're supposed to tell him about any allergies they have before he even starts work."

"Okay, Mom," Dreama said. "Calm down. The bill hasn't passed yet."

Becky smoothed invisible lines on her pants. "Sorry. It just gets to me."

"So tell me about Senator Farley," I said. "What's his deal?"

"No one knows for sure," Dreama said. "I've been looking into it for a follow-up project for government class. I even tried to set up an appointment to see him, but he claims to be busy until late January."

"Gotta love the accessibility of our senators," I said.

"I've found some stuff, and talked with a few people. But mostly it's just rumors."

"Like what?"

"Like some conservative bigwig is bankrolling it all. Like one of his kids got tattooed underage, or even that he's being blackmailed over something. It's hard to say."

"The backing is the interesting one to me. Isn't Farley a Democrat? Where is he getting political support for a bill like this?"

"He claims it's from both parties, but the only ones advertising are the ones on the far right."

I took another sip of tea and felt the warmth travel down to my stomach. It felt good. "And what about the blackmail? Or his kids? Anything to back that up?"

"Just this." She shuffled through her folder and pulled out a photocopied cover of a *National Enquirer* from a couple of years ago. The main picture was a blurry photo of a young teen, her exposed shoulder marred by a blotchy tattoo that was probably supposed to be a rose. Between the quality of the photo and the copying machine it was hard to tell. The headline screamed, "SHE WAS MUTILATED BY A FREAK!"

"Farley's daughter?" I asked.

"Yup. She was only fourteen, so it was completely illegal since her parents didn't know about it. And according to this article—but remember it *is* the *Enquirer*—she got so sick from infection she had to be hospitalized."

Becky sniffed. "Obviously she went to some back alley hack, and not a pro like Rusty."

I studied the picture. "Anybody know who the tattoo artist was?"

"No one knows *anything*," Dreama said. "This is the only thing I found *anywhere*. Farley kept it completely secret, if it really happened. Didn't want anyone knowing about it."

I thought about Wolf and Mandy, keeping Billy's attack to themselves. Not even their closest friends, Mick and Jewel, seemed to know about it.

Friends? Lovers? I hoped the Spurgeons called me back soon.

"Could that be enough motivation for the bill?" I asked. "That his fourteen-year-old got tattooed?"

"If it's true." Becky leaned over and re-filled my teacup. "I'm all for altering your looks artistically, but if Dreama had gone behind our backs and gotten some creep to do her when she was underage, I'd be going after him with both barrels."

"But to target the whole tattooing community?"

Becky smiled grimly. "You forget. Most people think they're *all* back alley hacks."

"Talking about me again?" Rusty stood in the doorway, yawning and parading color into the off-white room. This morning—late morning by now—I was treated to the whole view. He wore only a pair of paint-spattered sweat pants, leaving the city on his chest free and clear for all to enjoy.

"Daddy!" Rose squealed.

I jumped, having forgotten she was there, she'd been so quiet. Rose flung herself into Rusty's arms, and he laughed, almost dropping her in his groggy state.

"Just discussing your unethical counterparts, darling," Becky said.

The phone rang, and Dreama perked up. "Can I get that? I'm expecting Zane to call. I've told you everything I know."

"Sure," I said. "Thanks."

She jumped up and ran out, and Becky smiled. "Zane's such a sweet boy. If only he could see fit to take off the chain hooked between his ear and his nose, at least for church."

Rusty put Rose down gently. "Does my girl want to get me a big glass of orange juice to help me wake up?"

"Sure, Daddy." She hopped on one foot—just like Tess—out into what I assumed was the kitchen.

"Dreama helping you out?" Rusty asked me.

"Telling me about Bergman and Farley."

"You really think they have something to do with Mandy and Wolf?"

I ran my fingers through my hair. "I don't know. Mandy did say she had something on Farley. It wouldn't be the first time people have killed for politics."

Rusty blanched at my words, and I pushed myself off the couch, walking over to the painting I'd been looking at before. "Your work?"

"Yeah. Long time ago. You can tell."

Becky clucked her tongue. "Stop it, Rusty. It's beautiful." She looked at me. "He painted it for me when we got married."

I studied the piece, a swirling mix of color: clouds, lightening, water, and in the middle a couple entwined in each other's arms. Rusty had somehow encompassed all the passionate, sorrowful, joyful, freeing sensations of love. It was a masterpiece.

"It *is* beautiful," I said.

Rusty grunted. "Whatever. Thanks." He yawned again and rubbed a hand over his scalp. "Darn it, I was thinking there was something I wanted to ask you."

I waited while he closed his eyes, scrunching up his face.

"Can't think of it," he finally said. "Brain's not working yet." He turned to Becky. "I say anything to you?"

She shook her head, and he shrugged. "When I remember, I'll give you a call."

"Sure. But hey, before I go, I wanted to tell you that I found out more from when Billy got attacked at school."

Rusty's eyebrows shot up. "Yeah?"

"Who's Billy?" Becky asked.

"Wolf and Mandy's son," I said. "He's eleven."

"Oh, that poor boy. I've been feeling so sorry for him."

"Anyway..." Rusty said, waving his hand.

I sat down again. "He wasn't beat up. He was held down by a gang of skinheads, who scratched a tattoo onto his arm."

"*What*?"

"They were mad at Wolf because he refused to tattoo swastikas on them."

Rusty paled. "So they went after *Billy*?"

"That's terrible!" Becky said.

"Oh, my God." Rusty put his hands up to his face and pressed on his forehead. "Oh, my God."

"Honey, what is it?" Becky's eyes were wide.

He looked up. "Just the other day I turned away some kids. Wanted me to do some hate work. Swastikas, racial stuff. Told them I wouldn't do it. Took me a while to convince them."

Becky's hand flew to her mouth. "Our girls."

"It couldn't be the same group," I said. "The ones who got Billy are in jail. Except for two of the younger ones, and the detective assures me their parents have them on a real short leash."

Rose came back into the room, her feet slow and even so as not to spill Rusty's very full glass of OJ. When she reached him he took the drink, set it on the coffee table, and scooped her into his arms, holding her tight.

"Daddy!" she said, giggling.

But Rusty wasn't laughing.

Chapter Twenty

"Abe called," Lucy said.

I looked at the mound of notes at Lucy's elbow. She still sat at the kitchen table, phone in hand. I raised my eyebrows. "How in the world did he get through?"

"Left a message on voice mail, smarty-pants."

"Ah. So what did he say?"

She pointed at a piece of paper stuck to the fridge with an Indian Valley Library magnet. "Gave you a name of some lady who ran Senator Farley's election drive. Says he doesn't know her personally, but Missy—" She looked to see if I had any reaction to the name, which I didn't "—is good with this stuff, and after he called her last night and told her about it, she did all sorts of research and found this woman… Gloria Frizzoni. She's probably your best bet, he said, because she abandoned ship halfway through the campaign citing philosophical differences. Maybe she'll talk."

"Wow. Thanks." I eyed the phone in her hand. "Any chance I could call her?"

She smiled. "Sure. I need a break." She stood up and stretched.

"Don't tell me you've been sitting there the entire time I was gone."

"No. I got up once to use the bathroom."

Shaking my head, I reached for the phone. It ran and I jumped, snatching it out of Lucy's hand. "Royalcrest Farms."

"Stella? Mickey Spurgeon. You have news on Wolf?"

"No. No, I'm sorry."

He sighed. "But you wanted to talk to us?"

Not exactly. I wanted to talk to Jewel, but not with her husband in the room. "Yeah. Any chance I could come over sometime today?"

"You don't want to just talk now?"

"I'd prefer talking in person, if that's okay."

"Well, sure. How about after lunch? Jewel's at her mom's right now."

"Sounds good. Thanks." I hung up and took a deep breath. I hoped I could manage with them. I didn't really feel like getting slugged by a jealous husband.

I glanced at the message Lucy had scribbled and punched in the number Abe had left.

The phone rang three times before a woman picked it up and said hello. I explained who I was and that I was looking for information on why Farley was heading up the bill against tattoo artists and body piercers. "Any chance you could help me out?"

"Which side are you on?"

"Well, not Farley's."

"So you're all for people getting hacked up and disease-ridden for a few offensive pictures on their skin?"

I bit back my first reply and said, "Excuse me, but didn't you leave Farley's campaign because of philosophical differences? How could that be, if he's pushing this bill and you feel this way? I'd think you'd be all for it."

She made a sound of disgust. "You know, most of the time I can do my job no matter what the politician believes. When it comes down to it, every one of them is about having power and using it."

"So? How is Farley different?"

"He wanted to step off of his biggest platform because of his conscience. It would've ruined him, and I wasn't going to be able to stop it. So I left."

"His biggest platform being?"

"This bill, of course. About tattooing."

I was silent. Stumped. "He wanted to forget about it?"

"Yes. Somehow, after I left, he got back on the bandwagon. I guess somebody flexed enough he could feel it. But it wasn't me."

"Do you know why?"

"Why what?"

"Why he wanted to quit?"

"Said it had turned into something he never meant it to be. Whatever. I think it was his liberal friends giving him grief. He thought more of their advice than mine, but I guess they ended up losing in the end. Now, may I know why you're asking about this? If you're not on his side of the bill, I suppose you fit in with his liberal friends? You probably have a tattoo yourself. A nice rose on your chest. A ring in your belly-button."

"You know, Ms. Frizzoni, not all of us are stereotypes, no matter what you think."

"Well—"

"Thanks for your time." I hung up, fuming. And confused. If Farley was that wishy-washy about the bill, why couldn't a force like Artists for Freedom change his mind? And why had he started the bill to begin with?

I glanced over at the computer where Tess sat, Smoky on her lap. Spy Fox was diving into the water in some strange frog suit, and I didn't have it in me to interrupt. I found Lucy in the kitchen, where she was staring into the fridge.

"Luce? I'm going out to the barn to work on the computer. You going to be off the phone for a bit so I can go on-line?"

"Sure. Come on in soon for lunch, though."

"Will do."

Queenie met me in the parlor, impeding my progress by standing directly in front of me. I took a minute to rub her ears and back, then led her to my office, where she slumped by my feet at the desk. I reached down to lay a hand on her head while I went on-line. Was there something I'd missed about Farley? Some clue that he wasn't happy with the bill?

I looked everywhere I could, going back over the articles I'd read the day before, even reading the articles about his family more carefully. But I found nothing. Nothing that pointed anywhere but at his support for the bill and all it stood for. Maybe that's what Mandy had on him. She'd somehow found out he'd wavered. Someone in his campaign had leaked.

I sat back, pushing on my temples. If someone else would know about Farley and his thoughts on the bill, who would it be? Who might be privy to the same information as Mandy? The answer was quite obvious. Dennis Bergman. I found the Artists for Freedom web site and looked on the contact page. The same e-mail address I'd written to yesterday was listed, but no phone number. I shot off another note, reminding Bergman who I was and why I was interested, then searched around some more before finally finding a phone number for Bergman's tattoo shop. I called, got no response, and left a message. I hoped he wasn't off to some other part of the world, visiting family for Christmas.

Wanting to cover all bases, I clicked back to Farley's web site and sent him an e-mail, saying I had information that he had wanted to call off the tattoo bill, and I was interested in his relationship with Artists for Freedom. Could we talk about it? I expected he'd ignore the message, but I could at least hope his assistant would pass it on to him, if nothing else.

Queenie sat up, her ears pointing to the ceiling.

"What is it, girl?" I asked.

She got up and pranced to the door, her tongue lolling out of her mouth happily.

"Someone here?"

I glanced out the window to see Carla Beaumont's F350 with the Port-a-Vet closed tight on the top. So, my friend the vet who had talked to Nick and not told me had returned. I guessed her office had passed on my message, after all.

When she stepped down from the truck I rapped my knuckles on the office window so she'd know where to find me. She raised a hand and headed my way.

When the office door opened, Queenie presented Carla with a happy greeting of sniffs. Carla ruffled her fur and plopped down in my visitor chair. Queenie lay down on Carla's right foot.

"You called?" Carla said.

"Yeah. A few days ago."

"Sorry. I was with my folks. It was Christmas, you know."

"I know."

"So what's up?"

I stared at her, my eyes narrowing.

"What?" she said. "Did I grow another head?"

"You didn't tell me."

She wrinkled her nose. "Tell you what?"

"That Nick called you."

Her face flushed scarlet and she opened and closed her mouth a couple times. "No. No, I didn't. Should I have?"

"Should you have told me that a man I lusted after was asking about me? Gee, that's a hard one."

She was quiet for a moment, and from her expression I could tell she wasn't sure how to respond. Finally, she said, "I was trying to do what was best for you. You'd been through a lot, you know. Plus, Abe was here, and I thought you were working things out with him."

"That didn't mean I'd gotten over Nick."

"I didn't know you had to. He'd only been here a few days." She narrowed her eyes. "How do you know he called, anyway? I didn't tell anybody." She stopped, her mouth hanging open. "You've talked to him. He called you?"

I fought down a laugh. "Better than that. He was *here*."

"No way."

"Way. He stopped in on his way home from New York."

She goggled at me. "Tell me everything. Is he still hunkier than the Olympic swim team?"

"It was winter. I didn't see him in a Speedo."

"Too bad. So are you…together?"

I stopped laughing. "You tell me how that can happen, and I'll consider it."

"What do you mean how it can happen. It just happens."

"I move to Virginia? He moves up here? It's impossible."

She sighed and shook her head. "*You're* impossible. He obviously came here for a reason."

"Yeah. To mess me up."

She stood. "Give me a break. You have the most gorgeous man since Adonis coming after you and you can't figure things out? He was pretty darn nice, too, calling to check up on you this summer."

"He could've called *me*."

"And you would've told him what? 'Leave me alone, you stinking developer'?"

I stopped before saying anything else. Of course she was right. That's probably what I would've said.

"So instead of yelling at me for keeping it a secret," Carla said, "you should be thanking me for making sure you didn't blow it."

I let out a huff of breath and was glaring at her when the office door opened. Queenie lunged to her feet, trotting to Tess.

"Mom wants to know if you're ready for lunch, and if Carla wants to join us," Tess said.

Carla looked me in the eye. "Am I welcome?"

I thought about it. "I guess. Sure."

"Then one more question." She turned to Tess. "Did your mom cook something, or is this one of Stella's shove-whatever-you-can-find-down-your-throat days?"

Tess made a face. "What?"

I rolled my eyes. "Never mind."

"My mom made hot turkey sandwiches," Tess said. "With gravy."

Carla considered this. "Dessert?"

Tess lifted a shoulder.

"I'm sure there will be some," I said.

"Well, okay then," Carla said. "I'll stay."

Chapter Twenty-One

The roads were dry as I made my way toward North Wales, and they looked washed out, speckled with a coat of salt. The snow along the road was even dirtier than the day before, and it hadn't even begun to melt. Lovely.

It was nice having Carla with us at lunch. She hadn't been around for a while, other than to check the cows, and I'd forgotten how funny she was about good food. I was even close to forgiving her for the whole phone call with Nick incident. When we were done eating she went off to work while I went out to my truck.

I pulled up in front of the Spurgeons' house and fought a wave of depression. Only a day after Christmas, and the decorations spread over their house and lawn felt suffocating and dreary. The exact opposite effect they'd had only days before. The blow-up snowmen drooped with exhaustion, and I had to step to the side to avoid colliding with the sagging Grinch. The reindeer no longer moved, the colored lights no longer blinked, and the life-like cow in the nativity scene lay on its side. I refrained from checking out the sleigh and wreath on the roof.

Mickey and the rottweilers answered the door, and Mickey peered over my shoulder. "No Rusty today?"

"Uh, no. I really wanted to speak with Jewel, if I could."

He shrugged. "Sure. She's in here."

He led me through the front hallway to the kitchen, the dogs accompanying us, stumbling around Mickey's feet. Jewel was in the bright room, loading the dishwasher. The air smelled of turkey leftovers, just like my kitchen an hour before.

Jewel looked up and hesitated for a moment before placing a casserole dish on the dishwasher shelf and sliding it in. Her butterfly stood out brilliantly on her pale cheek, and I knew there was no way Tank had mistaken it.

"She wants to talk to you," Mickey said to his wife. "I'll be outside, if you need me."

We watched him head back toward the front door, where he opened the closet and began pulling out a coat and boots.

"Christmas decorations?" I asked Jewel.

She nodded. "They need to go."

Mickey closed the front door behind him, and Jewel gestured toward the table, where I pulled out a chair and sat diagonally across from her. I looked at her, not sure how to start. How do you ask a woman if she's been cheating on her husband with his best friend?

I took off my gloves and put them on the table, playing for time.

"What is it?" she asked. Her fingers picked at the tablecloth.

I cleared my throat. "I found Tank. Matthew Snyder. The guy who was at Wolf's place right before…"

She nodded. "Before. Did he…do it?"

I looked away, out the back window, at the snow covered, postage-stamp sized yard. "I don't think so. He didn't even seem to know about it. But I guess he could've been faking."

We were quiet for a bit.

"So why are you here?" she finally asked. "If you don't really have news?"

I shifted back toward her. "He told me something I have a hard time believing."

Her eyebrows rose.

"And before I tell the cops," I said, "I want to ask you about it."

"Me? What could he say that I could help with? I don't even know him."

I swallowed. "He says the cops should be checking out Wolf's other woman."

Color immediately rose in her cheeks. "What? Wolf didn't... Wolf wouldn't..."

"Tank says he saw her."

Jewel shut her mouth, her eyes flashing with anger. "Who is she? If it's true, I'll...I'll... Wolf would *never* do that. Not to Mandy."

"But Jewel, Tank says it was you."

She stopped talking, her eyes wide. "*Me*?" She gaped at me. "That's crazy. I would never... Besides, this Tank guy wouldn't know who I am."

"But he saw that." I pointed at her face, and she put a hand to her butterfly. "Tank took his girlfriend to the Bay Pony Inn, and Wolf was there. With you."

She looked at me blankly for a moment before her face relaxed, and she began to laugh. She laughed so hard tears ran down her face. It wasn't a fun laugh. I almost slapped her to snap her out of it, but before I could, she jumped up and ran to the front door.

"Mick," she hollered. "Mick, come here."

He came to the door and she pulled him into the kitchen, his boots tracking snow through the hall. "Someone told her Wolf and I were having an affair because they saw us at the Bay Pony Inn. She came here to ask me about it."

A series of emotions flitted across Mickey's face, until he ended up with amusement.

"What?" I said.

"Tell her," Mickey said.

"No, hon, you tell her."

He lifted a shoulder. "We get together every Friday night with Wolf and Mandy." He hesitated, probably realizing that tradition had now changed. "That Friday I came down with something. Cough, fever, you know. So of course I couldn't go. I didn't want Jewel to miss out, though, so she went without me. She got to the restaurant, and here Wolf was alone. Mandy was home with Billy, who probably had the same thing I had, and she didn't want Wolf to miss out. So there they were, Jewel and Wolf, at the Bay Pony Inn. Funny, really."

Hilarious.

"It was nice," Jewel said. "I hardly ever get to talk to Wolf. He usually talks to Mick, and I talk to Mandy, you know, about stuff." They looked at me, their faces half amused, half destroyed at the thought of their friends.

I felt like an idiot.

I stood up. "I'm sorry. I told you I didn't believe it. That's why I didn't tell the cops."

Mickey raised his eyebrows. "You were going to?"

"If it was true."

They watched as I slid my gloves back onto my hands.

"But it's not."

And now I could stop feeling so guilty about not telling Shisler.

"No, it's certainly not," Jewel said. She slipped her hand around Mickey's elbow.

"I'm sorry," I said again.

Mickey smiled. "Don't be. We're glad somebody's looking out for Wolf." He stopped smiling, and I was sure he was thinking the same thing I was.

Someone, somewhere, definitely wasn't looking out for Wolf. And we had to find him.

Chapter Twenty-Two

I had just hung my coat in my front closet when the doorbell rang. Detective Shisler stood on the front steps, her nose pink.

I sucked in my breath. "You found Wolf?"

She shook her head. "Wish I had. Can I come in for a minute?"

I stepped back. "Sure."

I closed the door behind her, and she rubbed her arms for warmth. "Goodness, it's cold."

"We've got a fire!" Tess announced from behind me, making me jump.

Shisler glanced into the living room. "So I see. I'd love to sit in front of it."

I took her coat and hat and hung them in the closet, then joined her on the sofa, where Tess was introducing the detective to Smoky.

After a minute, I leaned in. "Tess, Detective Shisler needs to talk with me about something for a little bit, okay?"

Tess lifted her shoulder. "Okay."

"Here," Shisler said, handing her Smoky. "I'm sure your cat would rather be with you than with me."

Tess' eyes took on a nurturing glaze, and she scooped up her kitten. "She thinks I'm her mother," she whispered to Shisler. "I'll wait till she's older to tell her I'm not."

"Good plan," Shisler said.

We watched as Tess squatted to pick up her new Abby Hayes book from the coffee table and disappeared into the front room.

"Cute," Shisler said.

"Yup."

She shifted on the sofa, turning toward me, and said, "You know, I'm glad Billy has his grandmother to be with, but it's just not good enough. The boy needs his father." She paused, her eyes betraying her frustration. "I've been over everything and can't get any kind of read on what happened. The snowstorm obliterated any evidence from the evening Mr. Moore disappeared and Mrs. Moore was murdered, and there are no signs anywhere that Mr. Moore ever planned on leaving. Nothing that might lend a clue as to where he went, or with whom."

"He didn't—"

"I know he didn't leave voluntarily. At least, I believe it. But every lead we get has either no solid footing or goes nowhere at all. I've got the DA breathing down my neck, and the lead Montgomery County detective watching my every move. It's a miracle I escaped him today."

"So are you here as a hideout? Or is there something you wanted? I've told you everything I know." As of a half hour ago. "Except that Senator Farley might not be so gung-ho on his tattoo bill as we'd all thought." I explained what Gloria Frizzoni had told me just that morning.

Shisler thought about that. "I'll check into it. See if my political connections can come up with anything. But no." Her lips twitched. "I didn't come here for a hideout. I wanted to see if you had anything else. Or had decided to tell me what you've been holding back." She looked at me knowingly, and my cheeks burned.

I looked her in the eye. "I'm sorry."

She nodded. "Just tell me now, please."

"It's old news."

"That's all right."

I told her the story, how Tank had told me about Jewel—backing up Gentleman John's unlikely story—and how I'd talked to her. And how it had ended up. "I'm sorry," I said again.

If I had to apologize one more time that day, I'd probably just go up to my room and not come down till tomorrow.

She pinched her lips together. "It turned out okay this time. But please, don't let there be a next time."

"Okay."

She sagged into the couch cushions. "It's not like I put a whole lot of faith in things people like Mr. Snyder and Mr. Greene say. Well, Mr. Snyder hadn't mentioned it, yet, for some reason. But I was hoping the other woman thing might actually be a road to explore."

"I wish I had more to tell you," I said. "Give you more to go on."

She waved her hand. "No, no. You're not responsible for giving me leads."

Just for leaving Mandy out in the snow and allowing Wolf to be kidnapped.

Shisler stood. "And anyway, you did give me one. That woman." She glanced at her notebook. "Frizzoni. I'll check out her allegations. I'd better get back to the station, anyway. The head honcho will wonder where I've gone off to. Heavens. I might be following up a lead without him."

I retrieved her coat from the closet and as she buttoned it up, she said, "I hope I have news for you soon."

"Yeah," I said. "Me, too."

After she shut the door I made sure Lucy was off the phone, went on-line, and checked my e-mail. Nothing. Not even an advertisement to enlarge my boobs or sell me misspelled drugs. I sent another e-mail to Senator Farley and yet another to Dennis Bergman. Dammit, if neither one was going to write me back, I would hound them till they did.

We were in the middle of milking when the phone rang. I hesitated to answer long enough that Lucy ran to the office and picked it up. It could be any number of people: Nick, Senator Farley, Detective Shisler, saying they found Wolf…

"Stella?" Lucy called from the hallway. "Dennis Bergman."

I stood up. "Really?"

"Really."

I went to the office and picked up the phone. "Hello?"

"Ms. Crown, this is Dennis Bergman. You sent me an e-mail, asking about Mandy Moore and Senator Farley."

"Yes. Thanks for calling."

"Could we get together to talk?"

I sank against the wall. I just wanted to ask the man a few questions. We didn't need an appointment. "Can't we just talk right now?"

"I'd appreciate a face-to-face meeting. We need to discuss some rather sensitive issues."

Well, then. "All right. Tonight?"

"Tomorrow. Breakfast?"

"Where are you?"

"Harrisburg."

"Then it'll have to be a late breakfast. I'm done milking around eight, and it'll take me two or so hours to get there."

"Let's make it ten o'clock. I'll meet you halfway. There's a restaurant in Morgantown called the Windmill Family Restaurant. Can you find it?"

"I'm sure I can. It's pretty near the turnpike?"

"Pretty near, but not right off the exit."

"I'll find it. See you then."

He hung up, and I stared at the phone, not sure what I'd finally said to gain his attention.

"What's up with the tattoo artist-lawyer?" Lucy asked when I returned to the parlor.

"He wants to meet tomorrow, to talk about the bill."

"That's good, right?"

"Right. But why do we have to meet? Why couldn't he just talk on the phone?" I walked back into the aisle, where I switched the milker from Mulan to Jasmine. Why would Dennis Bergman want to meet me? I hadn't made myself that much of a pain in the ass, unless you counted e-mails and one phone message at his shop. Maybe he really cared about Mandy. Wanted to help how he could. He was part of the tattoo community, after all.

"You going?" Lucy asked.

"Yeah. Meeting him at ten in Morgantown."

She raised an eyebrow. "Where?"

"The Windmill Family Restaurant."

She grinned. "Try not to spend too much on those Amish knick-knacks."

"Yeah, right."

She turned to walk toward the calf pen. "Should be interesting, at least, seeing what he has to say."

"Should be."

And perhaps I might even get a little closer to finding Wolf.

We finished up with the milking and headed inside, where Lucy had cooked up some turkey soup with the leftovers we hadn't yet eaten. Bread, fresh from the oven, had the house smelling like heaven, and I couldn't help but wonder what Mandy's heaven smelled like. Would it be the aroma of bread? Roses? Or perhaps something else, like the cleaning solutions in her beloved Wolf Ink?

Lucy and I were cleaning up the supper dishes, almost ready to eat the apple pie she had made that afternoon in-between her phone calls, when Tess cocked her head, perched her chin on her hands, and looked at me.

"Stella, how come you're so sad?"

I paused halfway between table and sink, my hands full of soup bowls. Lucy stilled, too, her knife poised above the pie.

"What makes you think I'm sad?" I asked.

She shrugged one small shoulder. "You're just… different."

I carefully rinsed the dishes, placed them in the dishwasher, and turned around to lean against the counter. I'd been sad the entire time I'd known Tess. Ever since Howie died. Obviously she realized something more was happening now, even though we'd tried to shelter her. So how did I explain the past week to Tess? Should I tell an eight-year-old that someone died? That someone else is missing?

"Is it because of us?" Tess asked, before I could speak. "Because Mom's marrying Lenny?"

Oh.

Tess' eyes sparkled with unshed tears, and I felt Lucy's gaze on the side of my face. I walked to the table and sat in the chair beside Tess.

"I'm happy for you," I said. "I'm happy for your mom, and for Lenny, too. It's the right thing for you. You're going to be a family."

That I'm not going to be a part of.

"So yes, I'm sad you won't be living with me anymore. But I'm not sad that your mom—and you—made this choice."

She sniffled and wiped her nose with her hand. Lucy leaned over and handed her a napkin, which Tess took, but didn't use. "So you're not mad at us?"

I placed my hand on her elbow. "I'm not mad at you."

She sniffled again and once more wiped her nose with her hand.

Lucy sighed.

"Okay, then," Tess said. "Can I have some pie?"

Crisis avoided, we dove into dessert, Tess taking over the conversation, talking mostly about Smoky, her new book, and how she couldn't wait to show her school friends her new fleece hoodie. Everything was going well until we were cleaning up the dessert plates. Something about the end of a course seemed to bring out Tess' zingers.

"Is Nick coming back?" she asked.

This time I continued on to the counter without, I hoped, a break in my stride. "Maybe," I said. "We'll have to see."

Lucy sucked in her lower lip, glancing at me. I hoped she wasn't about to start in with another lecture.

"I liked him," Tess said. "He was nice. You should marry him. Then you wouldn't be all by yourself after we move out."

I breathed in and out very carefully, not sure what to say in the face of love advice from a preadolescent.

"That's Stella's decision to make," Lucy said. "But I'm sure she appreciates your thoughts." She seared me with an intense stare.

"Sure," I said. "Uh, thanks, Tess."

"You're welcome. Thanks-for-dinner-Mom-can-I-be-excused?"

"You're welcome, and you may."

Tess flounced from her chair into the living room, oblivious to the issues she had flooded into the kitchen.

"Well," Lucy said.

I nodded. "All right."

We busied ourselves with clearing the kitchen of any remaining dinner clutter.

"I think I'll join Tess," Lucy said. "'Raymond' reruns are on tonight."

She left, and I took a deep breath. I hadn't been aware of shallow breathing, but apparently I'd been doing it. I walked to the sink and rested my hands on it, staring out the window.

The barn glowed red in the dusk-to-dawn light's circle of illumination, and the snow sparkled with ice crystals. Leaning slightly forward I could see the heifer barn, in all its new-built glory. Inside the two buildings, my herd slept or quietly stood, chewing their cuds. Queenie remained in the parlor, ever vigilant in her mission to protect the cows. Beyond the barnyard, in the darkness, lay fields—my fields—dormant now under the snow, awaiting spring and yet another round of tilling, planting, and harvest. Land which had belonged to my parents, and my grandparents before them. Land Howie—my mentor, friend, and partner—had died to protect.

Now everything was mine.

And mine alone.

Chapter Twenty-Three

The phone woke me before my alarm was set to go off. I scrabbled around on the nightstand in the dark, finally getting a hand on the receiver.

"Whuh?" I said.

"He's gone!" a woman cried. "He's gone! What should I do?"

"Wolf?" I said fuzzily.

"Rusty! He's not here!"

I pushed myself up on my elbow, trying to clear the fog from my brain.

"Rusty? Where did he go?"

Becky—for that's who it was—sighed loudly, obviously frustrated with my lack of understanding. "I'm saying I don't know!"

"He left last night?"

"Yes." A sob escaped her. "He was on the phone, then came rushing into the room, said he was going out for a bit, that he might be late. He never goes anywhere I have to worry about, so I didn't. I woke up twenty minutes ago, and he's not here."

Sleep, again. If only we didn't have to sleep, maybe nothing bad would happen.

"The girls?" I asked.

"They're fine. I checked on them right away. They're still asleep."

I sat up, leaning my back on the headboard, and rubbed my eyes. "Do you know who the phone call was from last night?"

"No. But Rusty must've called them. I didn't hear the phone ring."

"Have you called anyone else this morning?"

"Just you. Since he's been in this thing with you, trying to find Wolf..."

"And are you using the phone he used?"

"What? Oh. Oh, no. I could've hit redial." She sobbed again.

"It's okay, Becky. There are other ways." I hoped. "Now, where might he be? Any ideas?"

"I can't think of anything. He doesn't go to bars. He's not answering at the shop. He wouldn't be hiding from anything."

"Okay." I swung my legs over the side of the bed. "Are you going to call the cops?"

"The cops? No. He'd hate that."

"He'd hate it more if he was in trouble and you didn't contact them. Tell them about Wolf and Mandy, and how Rusty's involved. I'll call the detective here. I'll also get in touch with some other people, see if they know anything."

"Oh, thank you. I don't know what I'd do if—"

"He'll be fine. We'll find him. Maybe he had a car accident and is waiting for the tow truck. Maybe he had to stay overnight somewhere and didn't want to wake you."

"Sure."

Sure. Then why was my heart suddenly pounding? "I'll be in touch." I punched the flash button and dialed Shisler's number. Thank goodness it was now burned onto my brain.

Shisler had been sleeping, too.

"Stella Crown here," I said. "We've got a situation." I explained Becky's frantic phone call.

I heard Shisler rustling around, probably sitting up. "This is Rusty Oldham, the tattoo artist you've been asking around with?"

"That's him."

"You think something happened?"

"His wife thinks so."

"You don't think he got drunk somewhere? Or he's with another woman?"

"You wouldn't even ask if you knew him. He's not either place. It obviously has to do with that phone call he made last night. Can you find out who it was to?"

"I'm not sure—"

"Becky will give you whatever permission you need. She wants him back. So do I."

I heard more rustling and the murmur of voices, then the sounds of movement.

"I'm going to the other room so my husband can sleep," Shisler said. "Now, let's go over this again. He made a phone call last night, then ran out, saying he'd be late."

"And never came home."

She was silent. "Okay. Has she called the police in North Wales?"

"I told her to."

"I'll call them, as well, get them in the picture. Although they know about our case. Everybody in the area does. I'll tell them how Rusty is involved."

"The phone call?"

"We'll do what we can."

"What can I do?"

She sighed. "Try to think where he could've gone. And pray."

I hung up and leaned my head against my headboard for a moment before stumbling out of bed and down the stairs, where I could find my phone book. The light on my phone was blinking, saying I had two voice mail messages. I wondered why I hadn't heard the rings. I picked up the receiver, punched in my code, and listened to Rusty's voice.

"Stella, I remembered what I was going to ask you. Give me a call when you get this, and I'll fill you in. I think I know someone we should talk to, and I don't know why we didn't do it before. I'll go ahead and set up the appointment and let you know tomorrow. Have a good night." The message had been left at nine-thirty-eight PM.

The second one was at nine-fifty-two. "My God, Stella. I think I know. I think I know where Wolf is. I need… Oh, shit." And he hung up.

"Stella?" Lucy stood in the kitchen doorway, her face wrinkled from sleep and concern. "What's wrong?"

I looked at her, my chest tight.

"Rusty's missing. He never got home last night."

Her eyes widened with alarm. "What happened?"

"I don't know. But he left a couple of voice mails here that I just now picked up."

Her forehead crinkled. "Why didn't we hear the phone?"

"They were after I went to bed. Nine-thirty-eight and nine-fifty-something. Were you still up?"

Her face drained of color. "I was on the phone, talking to my mom. I didn't think about checking voice mail when I was done. I just went to bed." She put a hand to her mouth.

I closed my eyes and took a deep breath, not sure what to say.

"I'm so sorry, Stella." Lucy's voice shook.

I looked at her. "It's not your fault. You didn't do anything to Rusty."

"But—"

"But he said he knew where Wolf was. Dammit, why didn't he tell me?"

Lucy's voice was soft. "What are you going to do?"

I picked up the phone. "Tell Shisler."

"Do whatever you need to. I'll take care of milking and get ready for the milk truck."

Shisler's number was busy, but I kept punching redial until she answered. I didn't even wait for her to speak. "Rusty left me a message saying he knew where Wolf was."

Shisler inhaled sharply. "Where?"

"He didn't tell me. He hung up. He sounded wild."

"And you have no idea?"

"Just what we've talked about before."

"Okay. Thanks." She hung up.

I glanced at the wall clock. Four-thirty AM. Not a time one welcomed phone calls, but folks would have to understand. I grabbed the phone book and found the number for Mickey and Jewel Spurgeon. Mickey answered immediately, his voice hushed.

"Mickey? Stella Crown."

"What? What is it?"

"Rusty's not there, is he?"

"Rusty? Why would he be?"

"Because he's not at home, and Becky doesn't know where he is."

"What?" His voice rose.

"He didn't call you last night, did he?"

"No. No. Oh God. Not Rusty, too."

"Any idea where he might be?"

"What? No. No idea. Oh, God. I gotta tell Jewel." He hung up, apparently dropping the receiver right back onto its cradle, from the sound it made. I hung up on my end, feeling guilty and sad. I thought about calling Bart or Lenny, but neither of them knew Rusty, and all I would accomplish would be to roust them out of bed.

I grabbed the phone book again and looked under restaurants. Giovanni's, of course, was not yet open, and I didn't know Giovanni's last name. I left a message on the restaurant's answering machine, turned on for call-ahead orders, and hoped the big Italian would get the message. I hung up and stared blankly at the phone book.

"Were there any calls he was supposed to make for you?" Lucy asked. "About Wolf and Mandy?"

"No. No, I don't think so. Not that I can remember." I sat at the kitchen table and rested my face in my hands. He did say he thought of someone we should talk to. Who was it? Not Gentleman John. We talked to him already. Tank? He hadn't been along when we'd stopped at Mary Detlor's on Christmas Eve.

What if Tank had Rusty? What if he really was taking revenge on all the artists who refused to offer him leniency? Was that enough of a reason for kidnapping and murder? I guessed if one was cracked enough.

"Here." Lucy set a glass of orange juice in front of me. "Drink this before you pass out or something."

"Thanks." I downed it and looked in the phone book for Mary Detlor. I called her house but got no answer. I checked the listings for a Matthew Snyder. There were a few of them, but no way to know which was Tank. Oh well. I started dialing, angering a few sleepy folks, until my "Tank?" got the right response. He wasn't any happier than the other people I'd wakened. I hung up without saying anything and crossed my fingers he didn't have caller ID.

"Found him?" Lucy asked around a bite of toast.

"I did. So I'll go check out his place, in case Rusty's there."

"Think you'd better call Shisler and tell her?"

Oh. "Guess I should." I dialed her number again and got a busy signal.

Grabbing the phone book, I looked up John Greene. There wasn't a listing under that name, but there was one for Gentleman John's Tattoos. I dialed the number, but got only an answering machine with an automatic voice telling me to leave a message. I hung up.

"Want some toast?" Lucy asked.

I shook my head. My stomach was already rebelling against the orange juice.

"If you're going to check out Tank's place," Lucy said, "you might want to put on some pants."

I looked down, surprised to see I was still in my underwear. Good thing I had a housemate. At least for a few more months.

I went upstairs, put on the necessary items of clothing, and came back to the phone, where I tried Shisler again, getting through this time.

"Matthew Snyder?" Shisler said. "I'm already sending someone by his place to check it out. But it's good to know he's home and not at Mary Detlor's. I'll let them know."

"And Gentleman John?"

"We'll go by there, too. See if he'll talk to us."

My brain was scrambling for ideas. "What else can I do?"

"Let me know if you think of anything else."

"Keep me informed?" I asked.

"As much as I can." She hung up and I stared at the receiver.

"What's your plan?" Lucy asked.

"Not sure. I'll call Becky again, let her know what's happening."

"You still going to see Bergman later?"

Something twinged behind my eye. In all the excitement I'd forgotten about my meeting with the lawyer-tattoo artist.

"I'll go as long as I can't do anything else about Rusty." I considered the meeting. "Who knows? Maybe Bergman has information about Rusty and that's why he wants to meet me."

"What time did Rusty leave last night? Before or after Bergman's phone call?"

"Long after. Bergman called close to seven-thirty, and Rusty's voice mails were a couple hours later." Probably not connected.

I called Becky and told her what had happened so far. "Did you call the cops in North Wales?" I asked her.

"Yes. They're coming over."

"Good. The detective from here is calling them, too. Is there anything else I can do for you?"

She sobbed. "Just find my husband. Find my Rusty."

I told her I'd do my best. What I didn't say was that I was already batting zero.

One body modification artist dead. Two missing.

Chapter Twenty-Four

Lucy had the cows clipped into their stalls by the time I made it to the barn. She glanced up when I entered the parlor. "I'll take care of this if you want to keep looking for Rusty."

I knelt to rub Queenie's ears and nose. "I don't know what else to do."

"How about that tattoo guy you went to see with Rusty and Nick? What was his name? Gentleman John?"

I grimaced. "Yeah. Shisler's sending people to check him out. I'm not sure what they can do at any of these places, though. Tank's house, Gentleman John's. It's not like they can go barging in without a warrant."

"Look for tracks in the snow? Ask neighbors?"

"I guess." I stood up, breathing deeply in and out. "Should I get the feed?"

Working with the cows is usually a calming process, leaving my mind free to wander or organize thoughts and details. That morning autopilot wasn't working. I'd missed my target on three feed bowls, tripped over a pipe, and slipped in manure, dumping our bucket of soapy water, before Lucy had finally had enough.

"Inside," she said. "Or to your office. You're not helping here."

She was right. I was a mess. I went inside, took a shower, and forced down some Rice Krispies. It still wasn't even seven. Way too early to head toward the meeting with Bergman. But I knew someone who was awake.

A cop answered the door at Rusty's house. "Help you?"

"I'm a friend of Rusty's. Can I see Becky? Mrs. Oldham?"

He glanced behind him, then gestured me into the foyer. "I'll make sure it's okay."

"Stella?" Dreama stood in the hall, her face white beneath her shocking orange hair.

"Know her?" the cop asked Dreama, pointing his thumb at me.

Dreama nodded, and I took that as an invitation to enter.

"You holding up all right?" I asked when I reached her.

She didn't respond.

"Where's your mom? Hey. Dreama. Your mom?"

She blinked and tilted her chin toward the living room. The off-white room. "In there. With the cops. Rose is with her."

Her eyes rolled and I grabbed her elbow, squeezing. "Hang in there, Dreama. Come on, let's get you sitting down."

I led her into the kitchen and perched her on a stool, her elbows on the counter. I stood beside her until I was sure she wasn't going to fall off, then stepped to the refrigerator. I found a can of Pepsi and opened it, setting it in front of her. "Drink."

She looked at it blankly, but obeyed, taking a sip.

"You happen to know who your dad called last night?" I asked.

She stared at the microwave over the stove, her hand tight around the Pepsi can, but shook her head slightly.

"Gentleman John?" I said. "A guy named Tank? Dennis Bergman?"

"Bergman?" She jerked her head back and looked at me. "Why would Dad be talking to him?"

"About Wolf and Mandy? I don't know. I'm brainstorming."

She licked her lips. "Bergman wouldn't have anything to do with this. With Dad. He's a good guy."

"You're sure?"

"Yeah. Farley's the bad one."

And now I wasn't sure about that.

"What would you say if I told you Farley almost pulled out of the tattoo bill?"

Dreama turned toward me. "What? I haven't read anything about that."

"But it might be why he didn't want to meet with you. Did you tell him who your dad is?"

"I didn't talk to him."

"Well, whoever you talked to, did you tell them about your dad?"

She thought. "Not at first. I didn't think they'd let me talk to Farley if they knew. I, uh, might've sort of mentioned it when they told me I wouldn't be able to see the senator."

"So they were aware of your connections with tattoo artists."

"Yeah." Her eyes widened. "You don't think it's because of me that Dad's gone?"

Oh lord. "No. I don't think that at all."

Her eyes filled with tears. "What if it's because I called?"

"It's not." I laid my hand on her arm, which was shaking so hard it threatened to spill her soda. "You didn't do anything wrong, and this—" I gestured toward the living room "—is not your fault." God, I hoped I was right.

The cop who had opened the front door peeked into the kitchen. "Everything okay in here?"

I looked at Dreama. Thought about why the cop was there. No. Everything was definitely not okay.

"I want Mom," Dreama said softly.

I took my hand off her arm and stood. "Sure."

I walked with her to the living room, where Becky sat with a man in plainclothes and a female uniformed officer. Rose was curled on Becky's lap, and when Dreama went to her, she huddled under Becky's arm, looking like she wanted to join Rose against her mother's bosom.

When Becky saw me, her face lit for a moment, then darkened again when she realized I had no news. The cops looked up at me, glancing immediately at my cow skull.

"Stella Crown," I said. "Friend of Rusty's."

"He did that, I'm betting," the detective said, pointing at my neck. He stood. "Detective Folsom. Just trying to get the details straight from Mrs. Oldham. She said you were the first person she called this morning. I also got a call from Detective Shisler in Lansdale, who put me in the picture. Okay if I ask you a few questions?"

"Sure."

"Let's go in the other room, give Mrs. Oldham and her girls some space." We walked together back into the kitchen, where Folsom perched on a stool and took a Pocket PC from his suit coat. The uniform stayed in the living room, so I stood on the other side of the counter, across from the detective.

"Shisler told me what's going on in Lansdale. Usually we wouldn't jump on a missing adult like this, but it sounds like it could be connected to your homicide. Would you mind walking me through the past week?"

I sighed. "I take it Shisler hasn't had any luck yet, at the places they're visiting?"

He shook his head. "You gotta remember she's got no warrants to go inside any of these places."

"So he could be in any one of them."

He shrugged. "Could be. Now, your story?"

So I told it. Again. From that first horrible day when I left Mandy to die up until that morning, when I'd gotten Becky's phone call.

"And since then?" Folsom asked.

I leaned my elbows on the counter and looked at my hands.

"Called some friends of Rusty's—the Spurgeons—who immediately freaked out. I'm surprised they're not here. Tried Giovanni's Deli and Tank's house. I didn't talk with Tank, but at least figured out he was home and told Detective Shisler."

"Nothing since?"

I shrugged. "Nothing to do. I don't know where he is, and nobody's answering their phones." I looked up. "Speaking of phones, have they found out yet who Rusty called last night?"

"No. The process may be sped up in this situation, but it still won't be fast. I believe they do have the necessary paperwork to show the phone company."

I banged the counter with my clasped hands.

"I know," Folsom said. "It's a bitch. And now, what's your plan?"

"My plan?" I figured he wanted to make sure I wasn't going to go shooting off, messing up their work. "I have a meeting that was scheduled last night, that could shed some light on things."

"With?"

"Dennis Bergman." I explained who he was and why I was meeting him.

"Maybe I should come along," Folsom said.

I shook my head. "Not if you want to hear anything. Besides being a tattoo artist, he's also a lawyer."

Folsom made a face. "Not about to talk in front of me."

"I'll call Shisler with any news I get."

He sighed. "All right. I guess that's it for now. When are you meeting Bergman?"

"In an hour and a half. I'll head out soon." I spread my fingers on the counter and studied them. "Find Rusty."

Folsom stood, pushing some buttons on his PC. "I'll do my best. I promise you that."

I stayed for another fifteen minutes, trying to comfort the family, but was just in the way of the cops. I finally said my good-byes, realizing that the best way I could help was to keep finding out what I could. The next thing on the schedule was the meeting with Dennis Bergman. Dreama was convinced he was on our side. I'd find out soon enough.

Chapter Twenty-Five

I guess the day was clear, with the sun glaring off the snow, but I remember it that way because I know I needed my sunglasses. My mind was so full of information and anxiety I couldn't take in any unnecessary detail. I was lucky I made it to Morgantown in one piece.

A family place, highlighted by its namesake turning slowly above it, the Windmill Family Restaurant smelled like sausage and home fries. When I stepped in the door my stomach rumbled, despite the fact I wasn't hungry. I stood inside for a moment, eyes adjusting from the outside light, and looked around the room.

At the far end, his back to the wall, sat Dennis Bergman, looking just like his photos on the web. I started toward him, then stopped. There was someone sitting with him. A man. The man turned to look at me.

It wasn't Wolf.

It wasn't Rusty.

It was Trevor Farley.

I stood in place so long a waitress nudged my arm. "Sorry, hon," she said. "But I need to get through."

I stepped to the side and she eased around me, laden with a heavy tray of eggs, scrapple, and baked oatmeal. Bergman and Farley watched as I slowly came to my senses and moved toward them. I stood beside their table.

"Have a seat," Bergman said.

I stayed standing. "What the hell is this?"

"Please," Bergman said. "Sit." He leaned over and pushed out a chair.

I sat. A waitress came over immediately, holding a pitcher.

"Coffee?" she asked.

I shook my head. "Glass of milk would be nice."

"Sure." She warmed up the cups of the two men. "Ready to order?"

Bergman looked at me.

"Go ahead," I said.

"Stack of blueberry pancakes, side of sausage," Bergman said. "And a slice of shoo-fly pie."

Farley declined to order, as did I. The waitress picked up the menus and left.

"I gather you recognize him," Bergman said, his eyes flicking toward Farley.

I looked at the senator. It was obviously Farley, but not quite the man I was used to seeing on TV and in the papers. This man lacked the sheen, the self-confidence, and the energy. Even his salt-and-pepper hair looked dull.

"Sure," I said. "I know him. What I don't understand is what he's doing here, with you. Aren't you guys sworn enemies?"

Bergman smiled slightly.

Farley looked down at his coffee.

"You study the news articles enough," Bergman said, "as well as my arguments, you'll see I never attack the senator. Just the tattoo bill."

I thought back to my research. He was right. I couldn't remember one instance of Bergman running down the senator himself.

"And you'll notice," the senator said quietly, "the same on my end. I've never once said anything negative about Mr. Bergman."

I sat back and closed my eyes briefly. "Okay. But I don't get it."

Bergman's mouth twitched. "Most people don't. Why do you think we're meeting here, and not closer to the capitol?"

I glanced around the restaurant, where no one paid us any mind. They didn't have a clue who was sitting there. Together. As far as the other diners knew, Bergman and Farley were just a couple of guys, having breakfast.

"So what's going on?" I asked. "Do you know where Wolf is? Or Rusty?"

"Rusty?" Bergman asked. "Rusty Oldham?"

"Yes," I said. "He's missing."

Bergman's mouth formed an O, and he breathed in deeply.

"Who's Rusty Oldham?" Farley asked.

I tapped the cow skull on my neck. "Tattoo artist. He's been working with me, trying to find Wolf Moore."

Farley's face paled even further, until I was afraid he was going to keel over into my lap. I know politicians are actors, but from these guys' reactions, I realized they had no idea about Rusty's disappearance. My heart dropped.

"When?" Farley croaked.

"Last night. He made a phone call, then took off, telling his wife he'd be late. He never came home."

Farley ran his hand over his face and focused on something outside the window. Bergman lifted his coffee cup as if to take a sip, but set it down before drinking anything.

"Here you are." The waitress cheerfully plunked Bergman's plate in front of him. "Anything else I can get anybody?" When we offered no response, she drifted away. Bergman looked at his plate. From the expression on his face, he was no longer hungry.

"You think it's to do with Mandy and Wolf?" Farley asked.

I looked at him. "You tell me. Two tattoo artists disappear and a body piercer is murdered, all within a week. Seems to me they have to be related."

Farley's shoulders sagged and he looked up, meeting Bergman's eyes. "Is it because of us?"

Bergman jerked his head no. "How could it be?"

Farley's eyes sparked, if only for a moment. "It's a definite possibility, and you know it." His eyes darted toward me. "She knows it. It's why she wrote to my office. And why she contacted you."

Bergman shifted in his seat. "But I still don't see—"

"Mandy had something on you," I said to Farley. "She was going to tell Artists for Freedom the night she died."

The men shared another look.

"Did she know you tried to back out of the bill?" I asked Farley.

His head snapped back. After a moment he said, "How do you know that?"

I stared at him. "Was it? Did she die because you changed your allegiance?"

He rested his face in his hands, silent.

"Okay," I said. "If you won't tell me that, at least tell me why you started the bill to begin with."

He remained quiet.

I glanced at Bergman, who watched Farley. I tried another tactic. "I know about your daughter's tattoo." If the *Enquirer* article was true. "She got a crummy tattoo from a hack and ended up in the hospital. Is that what sparked your anti-tattoo agenda?"

Farley sighed deeply, his eyes closed, then lifted his face toward the ceiling. When he brought it back down, he focused on the table's sugar container. "It was the final straw. I'd considered it for years, but it wasn't until Diana ended up in the hospital that I put it into action. And for a while it was good." He stopped.

"But then?" I said.

"But then other people cut in. I wanted the bill to be about safety. About regulating health standards. I never meant it to become a way for the government to censor body art."

Bergman leaned toward me. "We all know there are folks claiming to be tattoo artists who have no business marking up people's skin."

I nodded. "Sure."

"But after I drafted the bill," Farley said, "people kept tacking on more and more regulations—room specifications, FDA-approved ink, the notarized doctor's statement… I couldn't get them to understand that the legitimate tattoo artists, the professionals, want the scratchers out as much as everybody else. It became a full-out war on alternative art. I couldn't stop the ball from rolling. I'd begun it, but it was clearly, and quickly, out of my hands."

"So you tried to step back."

He nodded. "Told my campaign manager I couldn't support a platform I didn't believe in."

"Gloria Frizzoni."

He glanced at me. "You talked to her?"

"She's how I knew you wavered."

He made a face, unsurprised. "Horrible woman. Don't know why I ever hired her."

"Because she's good at what she does," Bergman said. "You couldn't help it she was a freaking nutcase."

"Yeah, sure." Farley's voice was thin with weariness.

"But you came back on board," I said.

"I did."

I waited.

Farley continued. "I thought I had enough other good things to do in office. An education reform bill, some work on drug rehabilitation. Healthcare issues. I decided the tattoo bill might just have to go on, no matter how I felt."

"And sacrifice the livelihoods of artists all over the state."

He flinched. "It's awful, I know."

I looked from him to Bergman. Bergman met my gaze steadily.

"And your part in all of this?" I asked.

He nodded toward Farley. "The senator and I got talking early on, at an informal debate. We continued our conversation long after the crowds had gone home. We found our ideas to be much alike."

"And joined forces?"

"In a sense. We couldn't declare it, but we've shared information."

I stared at him. "So *you're* the spy in Artists for Freedom?"

He smiled twistedly. "Kind of strange to put it that way, seeing how I'm in charge of it all."

"You betrayed your people. Your colleagues."

His face darkened. "I was after what was best for us all. I never compromised our anti-bill campaign."

I wasn't so sure. I sat quietly for a moment, trying to digest everything I'd heard.

"So if Mandy had confronted you about this?" I finally asked Farley. "If she had gotten to the meeting and Bergman let her go with it, telling the group about your waffling?"

He smiled, but without humor. "In a way I would've welcomed it. Maybe Artists for Freedom could've exposed the bill for what it was. Exposed me for what I am."

I studied Farley. "And just what are you? Why write the bill in the first place? You said your daughter's tattoo was the final straw. What came before?"

He took a deep breath, held it, and let it out. Then he reached up to loosen his tie.

"Senator..." I said.

He shook his head.

Once the tie was undone, he undid the top few buttons of his shirt and reached up to pull back the shoulder, along with the white T-shirt underneath. He turned his back toward me, and I looked at his exposed shoulder blade. An ugly tattoo of a devil, about the size of my fist, defaced his skin. It was a crude design, the colors faded and non-distinct. The lines were rough, the details, what there were, ill-defined.

"Wow," I said. "That's one ugly tattoo. I can see why you want to put non-pros out of business."

"I was in college," Farley said, turning back around. He buttoned his shirt, but let his tie hang loose. "My buddies and I went to Atlantic City, back in, oh lord, the seventies. Found a guy on the boardwalk who agreed to do us all cheap."

I winced.

"Yeah," he said. "It was a bad decision. I found out way too late that not only am I stuck with this hideously ugly tattoo, I'm also stuck with something worse."

I looked at him.

"Because of this ugly tattoo," Farley said, "I now have hepatitis C."

Chapter Twenty-Six

Bergman let me use his cell phone to call home before I left. There were no messages. Rusty was still missing.

Outside the diner I watched as Bergman and Farley, undeclared partners, got into Bergman's car. Bergman held up a hand as they pulled away, but Farley's eyes were focused somewhere else. To think that up until an hour ago I'd been thinking of him as the bad guy. Now I saw that in a lot of ways he was yet another victim in an often unjust system.

I got in my truck and drove home, not much more aware of my surroundings than on the way to the restaurant. Lucy and Tess were gone when I arrived at the farm, with a note tacked to the fridge saying they'd gone to lunch with Lenny but they'd be back soon. Ignoring the small pang of feeling left out, I picked up the phone and dialed Detective Shisler's number. It took her a few rings to answer this time.

"Anything going on?" I asked.

"Lots, but nothing productive."

"So no Rusty?"

"I'm sorry."

"And no luck with any of the guys you checked out? Gentleman John? Tank?"

"Nothing. But then, we didn't get a look in their houses. Both were pretty annoyed to be wakened, although you'd already done that with Mr. Snyder, and neither were conducive to letting us search their premises. Couldn't blame them, really."

"You can't just go in? You do have reason to believe one of them might have him."

"Unless we have good reason to go busting in, hard evidence, we can't. It's all about rights, Stella."

"What about Rusty's right to live? And Wolf's?"

"I know, I know. We're doing our best. You have to believe that."

I did. But I also believed it wasn't good enough.

"What about the phone call? Have you found out yet who Rusty called?"

"Oh, yes. He actually made two interesting calls. The last call was to John Greene. But before that he talked to Lance Thunderbolt."

"*Lance Thunderbolt*?" The wussy tattoo artist who'd taken Wolf to court. "But he was out of town when Mandy was killed."

"Right."

Unless his family really was covering for him.

"So what did he and Rusty talk about?"

"Making an appointment to get together."

Why was Rusty wanting to see him? That must've been the idea Rusty had had the night before, because we hadn't talked with Thunderbolt at all.

"And did they set a time?" I asked.

"Apparently not."

"Why not?"

"Thunderbolt didn't know. Said Rusty hung up on him in the middle of the call."

"Have you been out to see him, or did you just talk to him on the phone?"

"We saw him at his shop in Pennsburg. He obviously doesn't like cops, and we couldn't get him to sway on his and Rusty's conversation. Said he couldn't remember anything more."

"Did you believe him?"

"I had no choice."

I needed to talk to Thunderbolt.

"And Gentleman John? If he was the last one to talk to Rusty, it makes sense John would know where Rusty went."

"Mr. Greene says he never talked with Mr. Oldham. Says Rusty left a message telling him they needed to talk about Thunderbolt. He doesn't have the message anymore, but the phone records back it up, since the call lasted less than half a minute."

I thought about it. "If Rusty found out something about Thunderbolt, he might call Gentleman John to check it out, if the guys knew each other."

"Maybe. But Greene's not saying, and neither is Thunderbolt."

"Maybe I'd have better luck."

"Maybe. But we don't know what went on with Thunderbolt and Rusty. If there was a problem, I don't want you walking into it."

"Sure."

Shisler was quiet. "You won't do anything stupid?"

"Of course not."

Shisler promised to keep in touch, asked the same of me, and hung up.

I looked at the clock. It was now past noon, and I prayed Thunderbolt hadn't gone out for lunch. I found his number and dialed.

He answered, sounding disgruntled. "Cops were already here," he said. "Can't you guys leave me alone?"

"I'm not a cop," I said. "I'm Rusty's friend. And Wolf's."

"Well, goody for you. I'm not."

"Look, Thunderbolt, all I want to know about is your phone call with Rusty."

"What about it?"

"He hung up on you?"

"Yeah. Said he wanted to make an appointment, but never did."

"Why?"

He was quiet. "Look, I'm in the middle of a tattoo. The cops already got me behind schedule, 'cause I had a before-hours appointment they messed up. If you want to talk, you're going to have to call back. Say in an hour or two." He hung up.

I stared at the phone and thought that Mandy's name for Gentleman John would fit this jerk, too. But I was damned if I was going to sit around waiting to call him. I put my coat back on, trotted out to my truck, and took off for Pennsburg.

Thunderbolt's shop sat on a side street with only one lane plowed open. I circled around the block until I found a place to park. I wasn't sure it was a legal spot, but if they wanted to ticket me, they could go ahead.

By the time I got to the parlor, my cheeks were numb and my eyes watered from the brisk wind that had started up. I pushed open the door and stepped inside, where I halted in surprise. Besides being warm, the parlor was also clean and well-lit. Flash decorated the walls, and while Thunderbolt's art lacked the fire and detail of Wolf's or Rusty's, it was at least semi-interesting and well-organized.

A small waiting area held a leather couch, with a colorful mat covering the floor. A bookshelf with photo albums sat beside the couch, along with a few tattooing magazines on a small table. Behind the waiting area in an open work area Thunderbolt—for it had to be him—was bent over a woman who lay on her stomach on a padded table. Lance was tattooing a Native American design on her lower back, made up of reds and greens, and from what I could tell, it looked okay. Her upper back was covered with a sheet, and her legs with a warm blanket.

Thunderbolt glanced up. "Be with you in a minute."

I stood there, watching and studying the tattoo artist. He was a tall, fit-looking man, his long black hair lying in a braid down his back, his skin unseasonably dark. A tanning booth or self-tanner, I figured. Trying to look deserving of the ancestry he claimed.

There weren't any other closed doors in the place, except for one proclaiming itself a bathroom.

"Okay if I use that?" I asked, pointing at the door.

He looked up. "Sure. Be my guest."

I walked toward the bathroom, taking a moment to peer into a back room which had no door shutting it off. Chairs, a little kitchen area, and an autoclave. No kidnapped tattoo artists.

Getting to the bathroom, I opened the door and stepped inside. It was exactly what it claimed to be, with no room to hide anything, let alone a person. I studied the insides of the medicine cabinet for a minute—ibuprofen, hand cleaner, and Band-Aids—before flushing the toilet, in case he was listening for it. I headed back out to the main room.

Thunderbolt leaned close to the woman's back, working on a small detail, so I stood in the waiting area and thumbed through what looked like the newest photo album. Lots of roses, barbed wires, and crosses. Competent work, but nothing real imaginative. I stopped when I found a photo of a teen-ager with a swastika on his neck. I glanced up at Thunderbolt, disgusted he'd stoop to doing hate work. When I looked back at the photo, I paused again. The kid looked familiar. Dark hair, dark brown eyes…

"Take a rest for a little bit," Thunderbolt said to the woman. "I'll be right back."

He walked over to me, his assessment taking in the tattoo on my neck. "What can I do for you?" he asked, pulling off his latex gloves.

"Stella Crown. We talked on the phone a little while ago."

His face hardened. "I told you to call me back later."

"I know. But Rusty and Wolf are missing, and I can't wait any longer."

He rested his hands on his hips and looked around the room, his nostrils flaring. "Fine. You can talk to me while I work." He went back to the woman and sat in his chair, pulling on another set of gloves and picking up the machine. I hoped he wouldn't take his irritation out on the poor customer.

"Rusty called you last night?" I asked.

He grunted affirmation.

I continued. "He was going to make an appointment to come see you today. Talk to you about your problems with Wolf."

His head jerked up and the woman on the table flinched. "*Problems*? You call stealing flash a *problem*? I call it a felony."

I resisted telling him his work wasn't worth stealing. "Okay," I said. "Whatever you want to call it. You stopped legal proceedings a while ago. October?"

He looked down at the woman, but didn't seem to be really seeing her. She, however, was entirely too aware of him and what he held in his clenched fingers. She met my eyes with her wide, fearful ones, and I raised my eyebrows, thinking she was crazy for staying anywhere near that needle.

"October?" Thunderbolt said. "That sounds right. Finally realized the wheels of justice weren't going to turn for me. I was spending a fortune for recognition that wasn't ever going to come."

I tried not to let my feelings show on my face. "And have you spoken to Wolf since then?"

He looked down at the machine, as if wondering what it was doing in his hand. "Not that I can remember. If I did, it wasn't about him stealing flash."

"So you haven't been threatening him?"

"*Threatening* him?"

"He's missing, and Mandy's dead."

He spun around. "Look, lady, the most I threatened him with was suing his ass. Not hurting him or his old lady."

So Rusty had remembered that right.

"What were you telling Rusty last night that made him hang up on you?"

He shifted in his chair, like he was going to start tattooing the woman again. "Nothing, really. I can't remember."

I stepped forward into the tattooing area. "Don't even try that bullshit with me. You know good and well what you were talking about."

Thunderbolt froze, the needle almost touching the woman's back. "I'm telling you—I. Don't. Remember. It wasn't a big deal."

I moved closer and leaned over Thunderbolt, my face inches from his. "You gave that line to the cops because it's the sort of thing you do. It's not going to work with me." I stood there, unmoving, until the woman on the table rolled out from under Thunderbolt's hand.

"I'm outta here," she said.

"Wait," said Thunderbolt. "I'll finish it."

"Not till you're done talking. Tell the woman what she wants to know, or I'm getting somebody else to tattoo me."

Thunderbolt stared at her for a few moments, then lowered his face to his hand and rubbed his eyes. "Fine. Take a seat in the waiting area, and I'll be with you in a couple minutes."

She wrapped the sheet loosely around herself and stalked over to the couch, where she chose a magazine and rolled onto her stomach to read.

"So?" I crossed my arms over my chest.

He leaned back in his chair and rolled it away. "Rusty and I were talking about Wolf and Mandy."

Big surprise.

"What about them?"

"Rusty thought I might know where Wolf was, and who killed Mandy. Or at least have some ideas."

"Did you?"

"Sure. I mentioned that political group they're involved in, whatever it's called."

"Artists for Freedom."

"Yeah. That. Plus, I heard there were some guys they'd pissed off. Well, Mandy had done most of that, I guess."

"Names?"

He shook his head. "Just stories that came down the grapevine. Gangbangers, drunks. Dopeheads." He stopped.

"That's it?" Not enough to cause Rusty to go storming off, not telling Becky where he was going.

Thunderbolt stood up and walked around his chair toward a shelf, where he fiddled with instruments as he spoke. "He asked me about some guy named Tank, who I haven't had the pleasure of meeting yet."

"Not really a pleasure, believe me."

"Yeah, well, and he asked me about Gentleman John."

"What about him?"

"Rusty seemed to think he had a lot of motive, with Wolf and Mandy going after his business. But a lot of people wanted to see John go down. I don't know why it would be just the Moores he had a problem with."

"You know him pretty well?"

"I guess. We went to a convention together a little while ago. Since his wife left him we bunk together sometimes, save money on hotels."

I remembered John's ringless fingers. "When did John's wife take off?"

"A while ago. Last year sometime, in the middle of all his lawsuits. We actually saw her at a convention this summer, since she took up with another artist. Pretty uncomfortable."

"Yeah, I guess." I thought about John's wife. "Did John blame Wolf and Mandy for his wife leaving him?"

"Oh, I don't know. He mentioned them, but he talked about lots of other people, too. He blames the entire community."

Gee, he wouldn't want to blame *himself* for bad business practices.

Thunderbolt continued. "His daughters left him, too, you know."

I remembered their pictures, two ordinary, teen-age girls. "He said they graduated, and that's why they moved out. They wanted to be in Philly."

He snorted. "They'd barely thrown their grad hats in the air before they were outta there. The penny-pinching and lawsuits had gotten to them, too, just like with their mom."

"And this is what you were talking about when Rusty hung up?" I asked.

He made a face. "I guess. I really didn't think about it any more."

I raised my hands to press on my temples, and Thunderbolt flinched. "I mean it. It didn't seem like a big deal."

"Rusty didn't say anything more about coming over here?"

"No."

I studied Thunderbolt's eyes for a hint of deception, but all I saw was irritation.

"Now can I get back to my customer?" he asked.

I sighed. "I guess." It's not like he was going to admit to me that he'd kidnapped Rusty and was hiding him out back.

I guessed I should check out back.

On my way to the front door I watched as the woman slid her feet to the floor and returned to the tattooing area. I glanced at the photo album I'd been paging through, and walked over to check out the picture of the teen-ager again. My breath caught. I remembered where I'd seen the kid before. On the wall in Gentleman John's studio, right next to the twins. It was John's nephew.

I held up the album. "Thunderbolt. You remember doing this kid's swastika?"

He saw the photo and his nostrils flared. "What about him?"

"You know who he is?"

He shrugged. "Nobody special. Just some kid who was having a hard time finding somebody to tattoo him."

"Yeah. Some people have standards."

His jaw bunched. "Money gets tight sometimes."

"Whatever. What was his story?"

"I don't know. It was a few weeks ago."

"Come on, Thunderbolt. Think."

He sat back, letting out a huff of air. "Well, he said he and his friends had been looking for a place, but then most of them got busted for something. He still wanted to get it done. Solidarity, you know."

My skin prickled. Eve Freed had told me about a group of skinheads who were trying to get hate tattoos. They'd been arrested after attacking Billy.

It seemed Gentleman John's nephew was one of them.

Chapter Twenty-Seven

The run back to my truck was a slippery one, and while I did my best to dodge the icy patches, I slipped several times, once hard enough I swore when my knees hit the ground. When I finally reached the truck I fumbled my keys out of my pocket, dropping them into the slush by the curb. Continuing to curse under my breath I picked them up, jammed them into the lock, and swung myself into the seat.

There had to be a connection. Gentleman John's nephew helped to attack Wolf and Mandy's son, and now Mandy was dead and Wolf was missing. Was there more to the skinhead group—or Gentleman John—than Shisler realized?

I glanced at the photo of John's nephew I'd ripped from Thunderbolt's album. Did this kid somehow mastermind the whole thing? Or was it his uncle? And *why*?

I hit my steering wheel. What wasn't I seeing?

Think.

I spun out of my parking place and drove too fast through town, hitting Route Six-sixty-three to head back home.

Gentleman John's nephew, a lovely skinhead, was part of a group who attacked Billy because Wolf wouldn't do their tattoos. But by the time Mandy was murdered and Wolf was missing, most of the kids were in jail. No way could one kid pull this off. Unless there were more kids. Or a kid and his uncle.

But…

My heartbeat slammed in my throat. *Why was Gentleman John's nephew going to somebody else for his tattoo?* Why not just have John do it? He didn't have any scruples. He would've tattooed the whole gang of them.

But they didn't ask him.

When it came right down to it, to trusting someone to give him a tattoo, the boy didn't go to his own uncle. He went to one of his uncle's worst enemies. Wolf and Mandy helped clamp down on Gentleman John's business, causing his wife and daughters to leave him, and now even his nephew. It might've been one loss too many.

I skidded around the corner onto Allentown Road, driving recklessly toward Lansdale, where I could only hope Shisler would be waiting. I wished desperately I had Nick's cell phone.

I'd seen Gentleman John's place. His house and his studio. Wolf wasn't there.

Too many minutes later I pulled into the parking lot at the Lansdale Police Department, stopping in what was probably an illegal spot. I slammed the truck into park and ran inside. The receptionist's head shot up with a spark of fear in her eyes.

"I need Detective Shisler," I said. "It's urgent."

The woman wasted no time in picking up her receiver and punching a button on the phone. Before I knew it, Shisler was banging through the door.

"What?" she said.

I held out the picture. "You know this kid?"

She looked at it. "Sure. That's Darren Wilcox—one of the skinheads who attacked Billy Moore. He's on probation. Why do you have that?"

"It's Gentleman John's nephew," I said. "He got a tattoo at Lance Thunderbolt's."

She chewed on her lip. "Tell me why that's important."

I took a deep breath to calm myself. "Wolf and Mandy helped destroy John's entire family. His wife left him, his daughters, and now even his nephew."

"And you think—"

"John's gotta have Wolf and Rusty. He's got them both. I'm sure of it."

Visions of John's closed door in his parlor swam before my eyes. I'd believed him when he told me it led to a bathroom. What if it didn't? What if Wolf had been behind the door? Gentleman John's opera music would've drowned out any noises coming from that back room. Assuming Wolf was still alive to make any.

"Okay," Shisler said. "Say he's got Wolf. He has Rusty, too?"

"Rusty hates John. I'm guessing Rusty went to confront him after talking to Thunderbolt, and now he's a captive, too."

I remembered the voice mail Rusty had left and tried to push down my anger—at Rusty for going without me, at Lucy for being on the phone, at myself for missing all the connections.

"But what did Thunderbolt say to Rusty?"

"I think he mentioned rooming with John at conventions because they're both single now. John blames the tattoo community for his family leaving him, and Rusty probably wanted to talk to John about it. I don't think he knew the nephew connection."

"But this is all guessing?" Shisler asked.

"Goddammit! What more do you want?"

She remained calm. "Something physical, linking Greene with Wolf or Rusty. Or Mandy."

"I don't—"

"But I trust your instincts. You know these people. I'll call over to Perkasie right away to dispatch some cops. They know the story up to what you told me. If Wolf or Rusty are at Gentleman John's Tattoos, they'll get them out."

"And you?"

"I'll get busy with warrants."

"Warrants? Wolf and Rusty could be hurt in there!" Or dead.

"I realize that, Ms. Crown, and the Perkasie police will take care of them. I'll be there as soon as I can, too. But I've got to cover the paperwork on this end. Now, is there anything else I need to know?"

"I can't think of anything."

"Okay. Now why don't you have a seat here, while I get the ball rolling."

She left me in the waiting area, the receptionist staring at me with wide eyes.

I thought of Shisler's command. *Wait there?* I didn't think so.

I raced out the door and jumped into my truck.

I careened through Lansdale, pounding the steering wheel when I got caught up in traffic. Not an unusual occurrence in the area—just one I didn't normally encounter during a life and death situation. I unconsciously blew through one stop sign, much to the annoyance of other drivers, who leaned on their horns. I'm sure they did other things, too, but I wasn't even aware of the intersection until I'd already passed it. I was lucky I hadn't gotten myself killed, along with the others at the crossroads.

About twenty minutes later I drove up the road toward Gentleman John's Tattoos. A couple hundred yards before the house I was stopped by a police officer who'd parked his cruiser across the road. I jumped out of my truck, startling the cop into reaching toward his gun.

"Whoa," I said, holding up my hands. "I'm the one who called this in."

He pursed his lips. "Still can't let you go back there, ma'am."

I stepped to the side, trying to see around him. "What's going on now?"

"Ma'am, I can't—"

"Are they in the house?"

"We just got here. I don't think—"

"I need to go back there, Officer—" I looked at his badge. "Grady."

"You can't—"

I pushed past him, surprising him, and ran as fast as I could up the slippery road.

"Hey!" Grady yelled after me, obviously annoyed, but I assumed—hoped—he wouldn't shoot me.

I kept running, stumbling and slipping on the ice, until I came up to several other cop cars and an ambulance, with clusters of officers perched behind them. At my approach several of them turned, and with a glance behind me at Officer Grady, grabbed me and pulled me down to the ground, behind a car. Grady dropped down beside me, his eyes sparking. He reached behind him for his cuffs and clipped one over my wrist.

"I'm just—" I started, but was stopped by the sound of wood splintering.

We halted mid-wrestle and a couple of the cops peered over their car hood.

"They're in," one said.

"In the house?" I asked.

"Shut up," Grady said, and clipped the second handcuff over my other wrist.

"What is going on over there?" A harsh whisper came from another car.

"Suspect apprehended trying to get onto the scene, Detective," Grady said.

From my position on the ground I could see the feet and legs of a man duck-walking toward us. I tried to glance up, but couldn't turn my head far enough. The man stopped a couple of feet from my head, then said, "Stella?"

I twisted a bit more and was rewarded with the glimpse of a familiar face as the man leaned into my view. I tried to speak, got a mouthful of dirty snow, and spat it out.

"Let her go, guys," Detective Willard said.

Grady let out a blast of outrage. "But—"

"I said, let her go."

With obvious reluctance, Grady lifted his knee off my back. Willard helped me to a sitting position, keeping us both behind the car. "I thought when I helped you straighten out your problems this summer I'd seen the last of you." He unlocked the cuffs and I brought my wrists around to the front of me, where I rubbed them.

"Why are you here?" I asked. "Did Shisler call you, too?"

He shook his head. "Perkasie did. Figured we were close enough we could help out. Being Christmas-time and all they were a little short-handed. But what are you doing here?"

I glared at Grady. "Like I *tried* to tell other people, I'm the one who called this in. I think Greene has my friends in there."

Noises from the house stopped us again, and we watched as two officers exited, a red-faced but dignified John Greene between them. I sucked in my breath. Did that mean—?

A plain-clothed detective stepped onto the porch, his face pale. "Paramedics. Now."

Several EMTs, waiting by the ambulance, rushed onto the porch, brushing past the detective. I shot up, and Willard latched a hand onto my elbow.

"Hang on. Stay here." He stood and walked toward the detective on the porch.

Grady pouted beside me. "You're lucky you know somebody."

The other two cops looked me up and down, probably thinking the same thing.

I strained to see into the house, wondering how bad it was. Were Wolf and Rusty both there? Were they alive? Since the detective asked for the paramedics, it must mean they're not dead, right?

"You!" The voice floated from several feet away. Gentleman John stared at me, his eyes glassy. Whether they were full of tears or just empty, I wasn't sure.

"You brought them here?" he asked, indicating the cops.

I shook my head. "No, John. I didn't bring them here. You did."

"But I thought you didn't hate me."

My mouth dropped open, but the sadness of the situation kept me silent.

The cops pulled John toward the cruiser, and he turned his head away, following obediently.

I focused again on the porch, where Willard spoke with the Perkasie detective. After an eternity, Willard gestured me forward. He and the other detective met me on the ground in front of the house.

"This is Stella Crown," Willard said. "She knows these guys. Called it in." He turned to me. "Detective Burnham, from Perkasie."

"Are they alive?" I asked. "Are they both in there?"

Burnham looked at the ground, then met my eyes. "There are two men in there. One with lots of hair, lots of tattoos—"

"That's Wolf. And the other? He has a globe on his head? A ring in his nose?"

Willard blinked, but Burnham nodded. "He's there."

"They're alive?"

He nodded again, and my knees threatened to collapse. Willard grabbed my arm, and I closed my eyes, trying to gain my balance.

"Where were they?" I asked. "I saw his studio the other day and there was no sign of Wolf."

"There's a door in his studio, leads to a bathroom?"

"Yeah, I saw it."

"Well, there's a door on the other side of the bathroom, goes into a bedroom. We found them both in there."

"Coming through!"

Willard led me to the side as the paramedics carried a stretcher gently down the stairs. I pulled my arm from Willard as the stretcher went past, and I caught a glimpse of Rusty. His neck was locked into a brace, and I couldn't see much of his face, hidden by an oxygen mask, except to note that his eyes were closed. They had some sort of IV in his arm, and one of the medics held the bottle high in the air.

I started to ask questions, but the EMTs pushed past me, on a mission toward the ambulance. More footsteps sounded on the porch, and I swung my head to see another stretcher being brought out of the house. Wolf's beard stuck up over the sheet, escaping his oxygen mask, and a sob caught in my chest. He, too, had a neck brace and IV, but as the paramedics carried him past, I saw his eyes were open, and blinking.

"Wolf!" I called. I rushed to his side, bumping an EMT. "Wolf!"

The visible part of Wolf's face was blotchy red, and heat radiated from him. The sheet slipped to the side and I could see the top of an angry, swollen shoulder. His eyes, obviously unfocused, finally landed on me, and recognition lit in them.

"Wolf," I said. "You're going to be all right."

"Billy…" he said, his voice muffled behind the mask. "Did you…did you find Billy?"

"Billy?" I stared at him. "Billy's fine. He's with Eve."

Wolf's eyes closed and he let out a sigh before his eyes snapped open. "He's not with Mandy? Why isn't he with Mandy?"

My eyes filled but no words came, my chest tight, my throat closed. Wolf studied my face, and when he read there the words I couldn't say, he tilted his head back on the stretcher, closed his eyes, and wailed. The sound shocked the scene into silence—the paramedics, the cops, even the faraway sounds of traffic—Wolf's keening cry hovering over us like the chill call of a coyote hunting for the mate he has lost.

Chapter Twenty-Eight

Wolf's cry soon turned to sobs, and the paramedics shoved me out of the way to resume their journey to the ambulance, where they slid Wolf in next to Rusty and slammed the door. I stood transfixed, my head pounding, as I watched them drive away.

"You okay?" Detective Shisler appeared at my elbow, surprising me out of my trance.

"No. You just get here?"

She nodded. "Detective Willard says he knows you."

"Yeah."

"I'd heard about the troubles you had. Just didn't connect it all before now."

I lifted a shoulder. "Doesn't matter."

We watched as cops and other law enforcement personnel entered Gentleman John's Tattoos. I didn't like to imagine what was in there that I hadn't seen, and had no desire to find out for sure. Whatever it was, it would be nasty.

"Did they tell you what's wrong with Rusty?" I asked. "He was unconscious when they took him out."

She pinched her lips together. "They don't know. I suppose once he gets to the hospital they'll be able to figure it out."

"Which hospital?"

"Grand View's the closest. I assume they'll take him there." She looked up as Willard joined us. "You know where they're taking them? Which ER?"

"Grand View."

"I'm going," I said. "I want to be there when Rusty wakes up. By the way, has anybody called Becky?"

"His wife?" Shisler asked. "I doubt it, since he was just found five minutes ago." She took out her phone. "Know her number?"

"No. What about that North Wales detective who was looking for him?"

"Folsom?" Willard asked.

"Yeah. Him."

"He's on his way here," Shisler said. "I'll call him to confirm Rusty's been found, and he can relay the message to Mrs. Oldham."

"And what about Eve Freed? Billy?"

Shisler nodded. "I'll stop by their house in a few minutes. I wanted to see Wolf and find out what I could before telling them."

Wanted to make sure he was alive.

"I'm outta here," I said.

"Going to the hospital, you said?" Willard asked.

"Yeah."

"Need a ride?"

"Truck's down the road."

He put his hands in his pockets. "I'll walk you."

I turned to go.

"Stella?" Shisler held her hand over the receiver of her phone. "Thanks for all your help. We wouldn't have found them—at least not yet—without you."

I nodded. She was right.

"I'll probably see you at the hospital before too long," she said. "I'll need to talk with Wolf."

To tell him that I left Mandy lying in the snow to die.

"Come on, Stella," Willard said softly. "Let's get out of the way of these folks."

I followed him away from the noise and the cop cars, from the people who were trying to find out what had happened in that quaint-looking log cabin. The road was a lot easier to walk on this time, seeing how I wasn't being pursued by a cop. I did move quickly, though, since I wanted to get to the hospital, and Willard caught my arm once when I slipped on some black ice.

"How are things at your place?" Willard asked.

"Lucy's getting married."

"To Lenny?"

"Yup."

He was quiet for a bit. "This new?"

"Very. He gave her the ring on Christmas Day."

"I see."

I glanced sideways at him, but he was looking ahead.

"Your truck?" he asked, jutting his chin toward the F150.

"That's it."

He walked me to the driver's side, then leaned on the door as I scooted in. "You okay?"

"I'll be better once I know Rusty and Wolf will be all right."

"Sure. But I meant in general. You're all right?"

I gripped my steering wheel and tilted my fists back and forth. Was I? Was I "all right"? "In general. I guess."

"Well, if you need anything, you call me."

I looked up at him. "I hope I don't need help from the police ever again."

He smiled gently. "I hope that, too. I meant you could call me as a friend."

"Oh. Okay. Thanks."

"Sure. You be careful driving, okay?" He shut the door on any response I might have made and stepped away from the truck.

I backed up to a spot where I could turn around, and headed down the road. In my rear view mirror I could see Willard, watching me go.

The ER was full, as ERs usually are, and I scoured the crowd for familiar faces. No Becky yet. No Billy or Eve. The only person I recognized was Detective Folsom, who must've gone directly to the hospital once he got Shisler's call. I made my way over to him.

"Any news?" I asked. "On either of them?"

His head turned my direction, and he put away the Pocket PC he'd been working on. "Not yet. Still waiting to hear from the doc."

"Becky on her way?"

He nodded. "Dreama and Rose, too. One of my guys is bringing 'em. Didn't want the missus driving."

"Good call."

A phone rang, and Folsom reached into his pocket. He looked at the number. "Excuse me." He stepped away to a corner, talking into the little contraption.

I looked around me at all the people I didn't know, some of them distraught, some simply bored with the wait they were enduring. A seat close by opened up, and I sank onto it, perching on the edge. During the past half year, I'd been in the same emergency room twice before. Once when Bart had been attacked. Once when Howie had died. I prayed these two men would have the same fortune as Bart.

A while later the outer door swung open and Becky swept in, the girls jogging along behind her, clinging to her coat. She searched wildly around the room, and I stood and waved. She forged her way toward me. "Where is he? Is he all right? What's happened to him?" Her eyes were red, and her fingers clutched my arm.

"I only saw him for a couple seconds when they brought him out of the house. He looked…asleep. I haven't seen him here yet, or been told anything." I stepped away and gestured toward my chair. "Here, Becky, sit."

"I couldn't sit." She did, though, for a second, but popped up again and crossed her arms, her fingers tapping her elbows.

Rose and Dreama stuck close beside her, Rose's arms wrapped around her mother's elbow. Detective Folsom left his corner, where he'd been punching more things into his little computer, and joined us.

"Mrs. Oldham."

She whipped toward him. "Is he all right? Have they told you?"

"I haven't heard anything yet. The nurse said the doctor would be out as soon as possible."

Becky stifled a sob and put a hand to her mouth. Rose sniffled, and Dreama bent over to hug her.

"I don't suppose Ms. Crown here told you," Folsom said, "but it was because of her we found your husband. She made the connections so it was possible for us to get him out of the situation."

Becky's mouth opened as she turned toward me. "Stella?"

I lifted a shoulder. "I'm glad—"

Becky flung herself at me and threw her arms around my shoulders, squeezing the air out of me. I tried to lift my arms to hug her back, but she had them pinned to my sides, and all I could manage was a little pat on her hips.

"Thank you, thank you," she said into my hair. "I knew the first time I saw you that you were a good friend for my Rusty."

"I'm glad I could help," I said.

"Um, Mrs. Oldham," Folsom said. "The doctor—"

As quickly as Becky had grabbed me, she let go, and I almost lost my balance as she leapt toward the man in blue scrubs. The girls stayed glued to her side, and I stepped forward so I could hear.

The doctor was smiling. "I'm happy to say Mr. Oldham is coming around," he said. "And asking for his girls."

Becky sobbed louder this time.

"It seems," the doctor continued, "that he was sedated heavily, but nothing else appears to be wrong with him."

"Oh, thank God, thank God," Becky said.

"He woke up pretty quickly," the doctor said, "but we're still running some tests. A CAT scan of his head and neck, and EKG, chest x-ray, labs. We want to figure out exactly what he was given and make sure nothing else happened to him."

"When can we see him?"

He glanced at Rose, most likely considering her age, then tilted his head. "You can see him right now for just a few minutes. As soon as the tests are done we'll move him to a regular room, where we'll keep him overnight. You can sit with him then for a little longer. I do have to warn you that he's not quite himself yet."

"I don't care what he's like," Becky said. "I just want to see him."

"Doc?" Folsom said. "Can I talk with Mr. Oldham tonight?"

The doctor nodded. "Give us a chance to get him in his new room. As soon as he's settled, assuming he's still awake, you can talk to him."

"Great. Thanks."

The doctor gestured toward the back and led Becky, Dreama, and Rose through the double doors. I hesitated, wanting to go, but knowing I wasn't needed at the family reunion. Or wanted. Becky hadn't even looked back to see if I was coming.

"That phone call I got?" Folsom said to me.

"Yeah?"

"Detective Shisler. She's on the way with your other friend's family. His mother-in-law?"

"And son. Billy."

"Right." He shook his head. "Wouldn't want to be in your guy's shoes. Poor man. Losing his wife like that."

I closed my eyes and took a deep breath through my nose. When I opened them, Folsom was back on the phone, and I was left to my own thoughts again.

Mandy, lying in the snow. Wolf, his body hot with fever.

I held up my wrist and rubbed the inscription there. *How.* How could I ever let them disappear while I lay in the chair, oblivious?

"These your folks?" Folsom angled his head toward the door, where Eve and Billy had entered, Shisler at their side. Eve and Billy stood as if shell-shocked, doe-eyed in the bright lights. Shisler gently took Eve's arm and led her into the room. She caught my eye and nudged her charges my way.

"No word yet," I said when they arrived.

"But he was alive?" Eve's voice held hope that hadn't been there on Christmas Day.

"I talked to him."

She took a shuddering sigh and reached down to squeeze Billy's shoulder. Rather than hope, or even joy, the boy's face betrayed only exhaustion and despair. Appropriate in someone who'd so tragically lost his mother. I knew Billy would soon be glad to see his father. His emotions just hadn't had a chance to catch up yet.

A family cleared off a sofa, and Shisler claimed it for Eve and Billy.

Folsom hung around the edges, waiting for his chance to talk with Rusty, and Shisler stood at the end of the couch, punching a number into her cell phone. I stuck around, too, not sure what to do with myself. A hand clutched my sleeve, and I turned to Eve.

"I hear it's thanks to you the police were able to find Wolf," she said.

I cleared my throat. "I was able to talk to some people the cops couldn't reach. It helped to link things."

"Thank you," Eve said. "Thank you for saving my Wolf."

A while later a woman in the same kind of outfit as the earlier doctor stepped out of the doors and cast her eye about the room. Shisler perked up and walked toward her. They exchanged a few words, and the doctor came to the sofa.

"Mrs. Freed?"

Eve, who had been watching Shisler's conversation with the doctor, stood up.

This doctor didn't smile. "Mr. Moore is very ill." She glanced at Billy, but the boy was still seated on the couch, his attention focused on something none of us could see. I drifted his direction and blocked the doctor from him, just in case he came back to the present. The doctor nodded her thanks.

"Mr. Moore has something called cellulitis—infection of his skin and underlying soft tissues. His tattoos have been defaced, and it looks like someone has taken a needle, a knife—I'm not sure at this point what all exactly was used—but he has suffered many injuries to his skin. Because of this, he has incurred infection so severe it's starting to affect his body functions. We have him on our strongest intravenous antibiotics, and we've called in the hospital's infectious disease team to monitor him and give recommendations. Besides those things, he's had a chest x-ray and we've drawn blood and urine cultures to send to the lab. We're just not sure what we're dealing with."

Eve sucked in her breath, but made no comment.

"I believe," the doctor said, "that Mr. Moore will be able to overcome it, but that depends a lot on the condition of his health before he became sick."

"He was very healthy," Eve said. "In good shape. Didn't smoke. Not on any medications."

"That's good," the doctor said. "That's very good." She glanced around me toward Billy, then looked back at Eve. "I'm sorry you can't see him just now, but he's sleeping, with help of a sedative, and we're doing what we can to cleanse his injuries. He's also in a private room, since we're not sure if he's infectious or not. We'll let you know as soon as he's awake and can see visitors."

"Thank you, doctor," Eve said. "Thank you very much."

The doctor nodded and disappeared back through the double doors. Eve turned to sit and crush Billy in a hug, her face crumpling. Billy's face remained as it had been. Blank as a barn wall.

A commotion erupted at the front door, and Folsom and I spun around to see Mickey Spurgeon shoving his way into the room, Jewel swimming along in his wake. I raised my hand and Mickey changed his course, startling several waiting room occupants out of their stupors. Many eyes followed the pair as they crossed the room, not entirely because of the force of entry. Mickey's mustache was flying, and his facial jewelry sparkled under the harsh fluorescent lights.

"Where is he?" he demanded, inches from my face.

I jerked my thumb toward the double doors. "Back there."

He made a move in that direction, but Shisler stepped in his path.

"I'm sorry," she said. "No one's allowed through."

Mickey reared back. "Who the fuck are you?"

"Mickey," I said, "this is the detective who helped find Wolf."

He glanced back at me, and Jewel placed a hand on his chest. "Come on, sweetie," she said. "Settle down."

"Settle down? What do you mean settle down? My best friend is lying at death's feet and I'm supposed to *settle down*?"

I held out a hand toward Mickey, but Shisler stepped forward. "Mr....?"

"Spurgeon," Jewel said.

"Mr. Spurgeon. Mr. Moore's family is sitting here, waiting until they're allowed to see him. They are just as anxious, but are trying to be patient."

Mickey whipped around to see Eve and Billy staring at him, almost fearfully.

Mickey's stubborn expression faltered. "I'm sorry. I'm sorry. I'm just so..." He collapsed onto the cushion beside Billy and dropped his face in his hands. Jewel placed a hand on her husband's shoulder.

Shisler looked at me, her eyebrows raised, and breathed out a soft whistle. I certainly understood how Mickey was feeling, but after seeing his outburst I was especially glad we'd suffered no problems from the misunderstanding with Jewel the day before.

I stepped toward Shisler and said quietly, "So where's Gentleman John?"

"At the police station. I wish I could get my hands on him, but the Montgomery County guys are already there, taking over."

I breathed through my nose. "I just can't understand how he got Wolf and Mandy both outside and was able to kill Mandy. Like he told me, she alone was more than a match for him. Unless his nephew helped. What was his name?"

"Darren Wilcox." Shisler shook her head. "He couldn't have been there. His mother has been keeping him under lock and key since he snuck out to get that tattoo from Thunderbolt. Whatever Greene did, he did on his own." She shrugged. "I have to think he had a weapon. Something to keep the Moores from kickin him out." Her phone rang, and she answered it, fading away toward a more or less unoccupied corner of the room. I tried to hear her conversation, but with all the people around, along with the television in the corner, her words were lost.

I turned back to the couch, where Eve still hugged Billy and Jewel was trying to comfort Mick. I considered going over to them, but realized I would be redundant. They all had someone already. The memory of Wolf's wail outside Gentleman John's Tattoos entered my mind, and I tried to force it away. The depth of his pain at Mandy's loss was bottomless, almost too much to comprehend. Did I have anyone who would mourn like that if I were to die?

Shisler snapped her phone shut and looked at me with haunted eyes across the room. I walked to her.

"He didn't have a weapon," she said.

"Then how—"

"He told a lie."

I stared at her. "A lie?"

"When Mandy went to the back room he was already inside. Probably got in while Tank was making his ruckus out front. Mandy saw Greene and immediately told him to get lost. He says he smiled at her and told her if she wanted her son back she'd let him stay. He figured they were even—she and Wolf took his nephew, he took their son. That's when she dropped the tray. He told her to call Wolf into the back without bringing his customer—you—with him, and when Wolf got there, Greene explained that he had Billy, and if they wanted him alive, they'd come with him without making a fuss." Shisler stopped and looked at me.

I had been sitting right there, in the parlor, and they couldn't ask me for help.

Shisler continued. "When they went outside, he told Wolf to get in the back seat of his car. As soon as Wolf was in, Greene slammed the door on him, and Mandy attacked him. Pulled his hair, went for his eyes. He got in a lucky shove that sent her sliding on the ice. She fell backward and hit her head on the corner of the Dumpster. Wolf couldn't get out of the car, because Greene had activated the child locks on the back doors. Greene dragged Mandy behind the Dumpster, whacked her head on the ice for good measure, then ran back to the car, where Wolf was climbing over the front seat. John told Wolf that if he didn't behave, he'd do the same thing to him. Or to Billy. I guess Wolf decided to go after his boy."

"He probably thought I'd come looking for Mandy." I squeezed my eyes shut, fighting dizziness, and put a hand on the wall for support.

Shisler made a noise in her throat. "We don't know that. Anyway, the rest is pretty self-explanatory."

"Yeah. Gentleman John's nuts."

"Right. Once he got Wolf to his place he jabbed him with a sedative, tied him up in the back room, and went to work on him."

My mind swam. If only I had been suspicious enough to look in John's bathroom.

"Greene says he realized too late that Mandy would be a witness and the cops would come after him," Shisler said, "but by the time he thought about it, she was already dead, and it had hit the news. He got lucky."

Lucky.

"I'm not sure he meant to actually kill anybody," Shisler said. "They're still talking to him, but it sounds like he was just hell-bent on revenge. He hadn't planned out how he was going to end it all. Just how he was going to start it."

I leaned my back against the wall and looked toward the couch, where Wolf's family waited for him. Billy's eyes were vacant, while Eve's face shined with tears. Gentleman John had gotten lucky when Mandy died. Her family got only heartache.

"And Rusty just walked into it?" I asked Shisler.

"Apparently. He called Greene saying he wanted to talk, and Greene invited him over. I don't think Greene had a plan for him, either. He probably was sedating him, waiting until he was 'done' with Wolf before starting on Rusty. So Rusty should be glad—he came out relatively intact."

The double doors swung open and Rusty's "girls" walked through, a lightness surrounding them that I hadn't seen earlier.

I stepped toward them. "He's good?"

Becky smiled. "He's great. Not quite himself, but enough I know it's him."

"Yeah," I said. "It's hard to mistake him."

She laughed, and several people turned toward the unusual ER sound.

"We're waiting now for him to get moved. The doctor says we can sit with him for a while yet this evening."

"That's great. I'm really glad." I glanced at the girls. Rose was occupied with tying her shoe, so I asked Becky, "Did he say anything?"

Her smile wavered. "About what happened?"

"Right."

"He said he'd suddenly realized you'd both completely forgotten about Thunderbolt."

"But he had an alibi for the night…for Monday."

"I know. But Rusty thought maybe he'd know something. He thought the two of you should go talk to him. And then Thunderbolt started telling him about Gentleman John's wife leaving him, and Rusty wanted to talk to John about it. So he called him, and John invited him over." Her voice wavered.

I closed my eyes briefly, then opened them to find Becky staring at me, studying my face.

"I'm sorry I didn't get his voice mail, Becky," I said. "I'm sorry I wasn't with him."

Becky looked around the waiting room, biting her lips. Finally, she put a hand on my arm. "It's okay, Stella. He's going to be all right."

I looked away. "I'm glad."

Rose plucked at her mother's arm. "Can we go now, Mom?"

Becky patted her hand. "Sure." She turned to me. "I have to fill out all that nasty paperwork while Rusty's getting moved. You know how it is."

"Sure."

But Becky's voice sounded tense now. She was angry. Angry that I'd gotten Rusty into this mess and couldn't keep him from getting hurt. I knew it was irrational. She was the one at home, the one Rusty should've confided in and told where he was going. But I also knew Becky had been more terrified in the last several hours than anyone ever should be. I hoped she'd forgive me, eventually.

I hoped I'd forgive myself.

She and the girls left me, and I stood alone in the middle of a room full of people. Shisler was on the phone. Folsom punched keys on his Pocket PC, his back to me. Eve, Billy, and the Spurgeons nestled together on the couch.

I studied the ceiling tiles for a few moments.

Then I turned and walked outside, into the cold.

Chapter Twenty-Nine

I sat in my truck in the tractor barn. I'd turned off the engine, but hadn't yet moved. The cold seeped around my feet and niggled its way under my gloves to stiffen my fingers.

Wolf and Rusty were alive. They were with their families. Or what was left of them. They didn't need me. After all, what help had I been, when it came down to it? Sure, I put things together to find them, but if I'd been more observant to begin with, neither of them would've ended up where they'd been.

My door creaked as it opened, and my toes shot needles through my feet when I stepped onto the ground. I guess I'd been sitting in the cold longer than I'd thought. The lights in the living room shone through the frosty window panes as I slid my feet up the walk, and Lenny's truck sat by the side yard.

When I opened the door, Lucy rushed from the kitchen, her face a mask of concern. "Did you find him? Is he okay?"

I dropped my gloves to the floor and blew on my fingers. "Found them both. Rusty's just fine. Wolf should be okay, eventually."

"What happened? Where were they? Who had them?"

"Let her get her coat off, hon." Lenny lay his hands on Lucy's shoulders and rubbed her upper arms.

"You're right," she said. "I'm sorry, I just… You need some supper?"

I sniffed the air. "Pizza?"

"Homemade. With ham and pineapple."

"My favorite!" Tess appeared in the kitchen doorway, tomato sauce on her chin.

"That's right," I said. "It is your favorite."

I hung my coat in the closet, took off my boots, and looked at the three of them. "Why don't you guys go ahead and finish. I'm really not hungry."

"You're sure?" Lucy's eyebrows came together in a frown.

"I'm sure."

"Well, all right. You come when you're ready. There's plenty."

"Unless Lenny eats it all!" Tess said.

"Me?" Lenny said, going after her with wiggling fingers. "What about you?"

Tess shrieked and disappeared back into the kitchen, Lenny thumping along behind.

"You okay?" Lucy asked.

I lifted a shoulder. "Go on and eat."

She wasn't convinced she should let me off so easy, I knew, but she went back into the kitchen. After standing in the foyer for a few minutes, not knowing what else to do, I joined them. Lenny and Lucy both glanced up at me as I entered, but neither commented. I went and stood by the window while they ate.

They behaved like I wasn't there, although I knew Lenny and Lucy were dying from curiosity. But we weren't going to speak about Wolf and Rusty's escape from death with Tess in the room.

After a few minutes Tess said, "Dessert?" with a hopeful uplift of her voice.

"In a few minutes," Lucy said. "Why don't you go make sure Smoky has food in her bowl."

"She does."

"And water?"

"Yup."

"How about you just go play with her?"

Tess eyed her mother suspiciously. "Are we having dessert or not?"

"In a little bit."

Tess reluctantly left the room, and Lenny and Lucy turned toward me.

I told them of the day's events.

"So this Gentleman John guy was mutilating Wolf to get back at him?" Lucy asked.

"Basically, yes."

"Sicko."

Lenny fingered one of his tattoos, a skull with a clerical collar, and pursed his lips. "Nasty stuff."

"Very," I agreed.

"And that poor man," Lucy said. "Wolf. Losing his wife like that. And poor little Billy."

There was nothing left to say to that.

"You okay?" Lucy asked me again.

I studied her, her eyes bright with caring, her back leaning against the arm Lenny had placed on her chair. They looked so right together.

"I will be. Now you'd better give your daughter dessert before she rebels."

She gave a soft laugh and called Tess back to the kitchen.

I went upstairs.

The little box from Nick was still under my pillow, where I had left it. I sat on my bed, opened the case, and smoothed the note on my thigh.

Sometimes having only half of something is better than keeping the whole thing.

I looked at the golden heart that could be split in two. I did have the whole thing, the complete necklace. Just like I still had my own heart. Maybe it wasn't exactly intact, but I hadn't given half of it to anyone, either. I looked at the note again and read Nick's final scribbles.

And lots better than having nothing.

Which is what I had. Nothing of Nick's but this shiny golden heart. At least nothing I was claiming.

Rusty had Becky and the girls.

Wolf still had Billy.

Lucy had Lenny and Tess.

Gentleman John had no one, and look where it had gotten him.

I rubbed my thumb over the heart, then took it between my fingers and snapped it apart. The chains slid free of each other easily, and I looped one around my neck, my fingers shaking as I hooked the end ring into the clasp. I tucked it under my T-shirt, against my skin. The other half of the heart I slipped back into the case.

I found my duffel bag in my closet, dusty and smelling slightly of mildew. I pulled some jeans, shirts, and underwear from my drawers and shoved them into the bag, along with my toothbrush.

The little jewelry box I tucked into my pocket.

Lucy watched me silently when I entered the kitchen.

Lenny and Tess seemed to be having a contest for who could eat the biggest piece of cake.

"Think you can keep things running for a couple days?" I asked Lucy.

She blinked. "Well, sure."

"I need..." I let out a big breath of air. "I'll try not to be gone long."

She licked her lips. "If you're going where I hope you are, you take your time."

"Where are you going?" Tess asked.

I looked out the window above my sink, where I could see the barn lit by the dusk-to-dawn light. Again, I saw the beauty of my home. The snow. The fields. The buildings. But for the first time, I knew—*really knew*—that they weren't enough.

I gave Tess what I was sure was a crooked smile. "Somewhere I should've gone before."

Lucy's expression softened, and Lenny's fork paused mid-air.

"But—" Tess said.

"Shush," Lucy said. "I'll explain it in a minute."

"I'll see you," I said. "Thanks." And I walked out of the kitchen, and out of my house.

I stopped off in the barn to let Queenie know where I'd be. I think she understood.

My breath hovered in front of my face as I sat in my truck, waiting for it to warm up. I pulled the jewelry case from my pocket and set it on the dashboard, where I would see it during the trip. To remind me where I was going, and keep me awake when the hour got late.

The two-story house on the hill was dark when I pulled into the drive. I turned off the truck and sat for a moment, double-checking the address to make sure I'd found the right place. I was sure I had.

I pushed the doorbell and tucked my arms around myself while I waited, biting my lip. Footsteps soon sounded inside, and the porch light flicked on. The door opened, and then he was standing there, his face a mixture of sleep and confusion.

"Hi, Nick," I said.

His confusion turned to pleasure, and when he opened his arms, I walked into them without hesitation.

It felt right.

To receive a free catalog of Poisoned Pen Press titles, please contact us in one of the following ways:

Phone: 1-800-421-3976
Facsimile: 1-480-949-1707
Email: info@poisonedpenpress.com
Website: www.poisonedpenpress.com

Poisoned Pen Press
6962 E. First Ave. Ste. 103
Scottsdale, AZ 85251